Vina Jackson is the pseudonym for two established writers working together for the first time. One a successful author, the other a published writer who is also a city professional working in the Square Mile.

Get to know more about Vina Jackson on Facebook or follow her on Twitter @VinaJackson1.

D0684211

Eighty Days
Amber

Vina Jackson

An Orion paperback

First published in Great Britain in 2012
by Orion Books Ltd,
Orion House, 5 Upper St Martin's Lane,
London WC2H 9EA

An Hachette UK company

3 5 7 9 10 8 6 4

A CIP catalogue record for this book
is available from the British Library.

ISBN (Paperback) 978 1 4091 2905 9
ISBN (Ebook) 978 1 4091 2904 2

Typeset at The Spartan Press Ltd,
Lymington, Hants

Printed in Great Britain by Clays Ltd, St Ives plc

The Orion Publishing Group's policy is to use papers that
are natural, renewable and recyclable products and
made from wood grown in sustainable forests. The logging
and manufacturing processes are expected to conform to
the environmental regulations of the country of origin.

www.orionbooks.co.uk

Eighty Days
Amber

I

Dancing with the Bad Boys

I'd always been attracted to bad boys.

And, as I grew older, they became bad men.

It was six months after I'd left Chey and I found myself in New Orleans. December was coming to an end and my mind was whirling like a dervish as I tried to imagine what resolutions I could possibly make when the clock struck twelve on New Year's Eve. One minute I was bereft of ideas and the following moment I had a fast-moving jumble of thoughts and emotions flitting like birds through my head, yet I was unable to catch any of them in flight. I couldn't focus, couldn't concentrate.

I was bored. Life had become a repetitive succession of dance, eat, drink, sleep, sometimes fuck, travel, dance again, eat, drink, sleep, and so on.

I missed Chey.

I missed the bad men and the bad boys.

Even though it was winter, heat still lingered in the air, humid, fragrant. Ticking the hours off walking through the narrow but beautiful streets of the French Quarter, my bare arms were caressed by the soft breeze rising from the nearby Mississippi. It felt unreal, as though I had become a feature in someone else's dream. Less than a week ago, I'd spent Christmas with Madame Denoux and we'd eaten on the terrace of her house on the other side of the lake, with some of her family friends. One of the men present, a far-flung cousin of hers, had driven me back to the city, his car gliding over the low bridge that spanned the immense Pontchartrain, and it felt as if we were driving on water and I could almost skim the wet surface of the lake with my fingers if I extended my arm just that little bit further through the car's open window. Like a mirage, with the horizon of lights from the Vieux Carré in the distance, flickering on and off, and the seasonal lights draped in celebration across the houses on the shore. I ended up sleeping with him and he was a disappointing lay. A clumsy and ungenerous lover. I didn't stay for breakfast at his apartment on Magazine. I walked back the half-mile to Canal, through the deserted Financial District with a hunger in my belly. And it wasn't for food.

New Orleans was such a strange place. So unlike Donetsk where I was born and where every building was straight lines and eminently functional, and the only horizon we had was a broken line of factory chimneys belching dark smoke through night and day.

Madame Denoux's club had been closed for five days over Christmas, but tonight reality would return and I would be dancing again.

As I walked into the dressing room I attempted to remember Christmas and New Year in the Ukraine, but none of the memories stood out; it was all an unremarkable blur. There were three other women there already, in various stages of undress, adjusting their make-up in the large mirrors, fiddling with their outfits, tightening straps, spraying perfume across their bodies, dabbing powders, juggling cheap jewellery. I'd arrived from California, and prior to that New York, and they'd always resented my presence and my big city experience, the fact that Madame Denoux had preferred me to them as her star attraction. They thought I was beautiful and aloof, which was a bad combination when it came to making friends. But then I was beautiful – people had been saying so since I was barely a few years old and I'd taken it for granted. I'd always lived life by my own standards with no need for female friends. I had little in common with them. They knew it, I knew it.

I turned my back on the women and undressed, feeling their eyes on me, like daggers. They were all watching, their attention focused on the cleft of my arse, the slight bump of my tailbone when I bent over to loosen the straps of my sandals. Let them. I was used to being watched. A lot.

There was a buzz and through the loudspeakers in the dressing-room wall we heard the music: Duke Ellington's 'Minnie the Moocher'. It was Pinnie's signal to step on stage. She was short, curvy, mixed race and beautiful. She had dark, lustrous hair falling halfway down her back, which she liked to drape around her body while she danced, titillating the customers with it as it partly concealed her brown-tipped breasts in a curtain of tease. Her other unique selling point was the fact that her pubic hair was totally unkempt, luxuriant, spreading far and wide, wild like a jungle creature's. She also had a brown mole right at the centre of her forehead and, rather than hide it away or divert from its presence, she drew attention to this unusual feature by cutting her hair at the front in a fringe, straight and geometrical as if drawn by a knife. She was the only dancer who was polite to me, and attempted the occasional conversation between sets, while the others steadfastly ignored me. As I did them.

It would be at least another hour until it was time for my own set. I came last.

I pulled the book I was reading from my wicker basket and settled into my chair, temporarily blanking out my immediate surroundings. Reading novels had recently become my biggest addiction. This one was about a travelling circus. It was baroque and colourful. I had never been a great fan of realism. I'd had too much of that in the books we were assigned back at school in the Ukraine and, later, St Petersburg – worthy but endless tomes about the travails of humanity which I had never connected with.

I looked up as I heard music fade to the end of a song – Van Morrison's 'Into the Mystic' – and Sofia stormed back into the dressing room, swearing under her breath because of a minor costume malfunction during her set. The look she gave me as she sat at her own table and began cleaning her stage make-up away was pure evil, as if I was the one to blame for the trivial incident, because the dress I wore for my own act was so simple and didn't bother with Velcro snaps, belts, quick-release devices, buttons or zips.

I had five whole minutes before the stage was mine and I closed my eyes. Getting into the zone. There was nothing sexy about stripping. Just a job; but when I managed to ignore the environment, banish it to another dimension altogether, I could float through my whole set as if transported on invisible wings. For the past year, I'd been using Debussy's 'La Mer' as my soundtrack, and I knew every wave of that imaginary sea, every sensuous curve of the melody. It had been Chey's favourite piece of music. He had always liked the ocean. The first time I had danced to it, it had been for him. In private.

The dancing, the undressing, the exposure, it became like

a secret ceremony in which I was both the sacrificial lamb and the high priestess handling the fatal blade, a fantasy in which I retreated, another world I inhabited for the duration.

I switched off.

As I always did.

I heard my cue from miles away as Madame Denoux placed my tape in the machine and the initial breath of silence filled the loudspeakers. I tiptoed silently to the almost inaudible hum and made my way to the stage in total darkness and settled into my position.

I switched on.

Then they gasped.

Each night the response was the same and I knew that a short distance away, hidden by the backstage curtain, Madam Denoux would be smiling.

First, just the most infinitesimal movements. As if I was gathering my energy, retreating to that place inside where there was nothing but stillness and an ever-humming core, an invisible power waiting to be collected, sent into every part of my body and then used. I was the puppet master, moving my own strings.

For the first minute, mimicking the feel of the breeze brushing over the surface of the waves, the almost invisible droplets of water and mist that hung in the air on a day that promised a storm, the constant pull of the tide, just a soft movement of my arm here, a flick of my wrist there, a sway of my hips in time with the gentle rise of the music, the sweet, sad sound of the piccolo joining the gentle thrum of the harp and the percussion beat, like the softest rain beginning to fall, the first signs of the storm gathering.

Then the second movement began, the darker notes of

the clarinet and the oboe, a muted drum the first sign of thunder brewing, energy coiling in the water and in me, the waves growing and my movements becoming correspondingly fiercer, quicker, more athletic.

Now I owned the almost invisible audience, and the beat. I could relax, look around, think. I knew every step; every sway to the rhythm was tattooed beneath my skin. It matched the beat of my heart and the pumping of my blood and carried me, unthinking, to the end of my set, not as though I was being tumbled through the waves, pushed here and there by the ceaseless dialogue between the wind and the sea, but as though I was the rider of the storm, the conductor of the orchestra, responsible for the rise and fall of the ocean.

Sometimes it was not so romantic. Just a matter of training. Chey had said that about almost everything.

It was always a matter of training, or plain old blood, sweat and tears. But it appeared to be instinctive from the outside, I knew. I could see it in the way that the silent onlookers stared at me, their faces agog, as though they were revellers come to see the strange woman or the illusionist in the book that I was reading, oblivious to all of the other cogs in the machine, each step from the entrance, through to the ticket hall, to the particular smells and tastes of each refreshment, the quality of the air, the attire of the hostess, Madame Denoux's elaborate but always tasteful costumes, her white mask, the peculiar way that she held herself, a practised and perfected languor that made her seem like a mystic when she was just an ordinary woman like the rest of us, albeit one who made her living from selling the bodies of other women.

Tonight was not as busy as I had expected. It was the

night before New Year's Eve, and New Orleans had already become a party town. The air was ripe with expectation, heavy with the promise of an ending colliding with a beginning, and all the residents of the city were out to watch one year flee and another born. It was the one time when everyone on the streets became equal, the crooks, the tourists, the whores and the shoe-shine kids, all united in the feeling that their lives were slipping away into the night, fading with the passing of the year like the firecrackers that flowered over the Vieux Carré, lighting the sky for a brief bright moment and then disappearing again, leaving little behind besides a flash of beauty, the memory of a good time and, in most cases, a hangover.

I wondered what I would leave behind. Being a dancer wasn't like being a musician. No one would record my contribution to this night and play it back. I'd be forgotten, each step hung in time for a fraction of a second, reflected in the faces of those who watched, perhaps burned into their memories if they liked it enough, but never to be repeated in quite the same way.

There were two here tonight who caught my attention. One of only a handful of couples. Different from the rest. The other women with their husbands or lovers looked bored, they'd seen it all before and more, or they looked discomfited, jealous, fearful of what their man might want them to do at home after they had seen me on stage, self-conscious of the way that their bodies moved when they undressed, the way their breasts hung, affected by the inevitable weight of time and gravity, the softness of their thighs.

But the redhead with the black dress had eyes like fire, full of heat. Her body was taut and her arm outstretched, gripping her man's thigh like a vice as she followed every studied movement of my limbs. And he wasn't watching me, he was watching her watching me, his gaze fixed, focused, like a lion that has just spotted a gazelle alone on an open plain. He had thick dark hair, broad shoulders, a compact, neat torso and a confident air about him, self-assured but not cocky. Like Chey.

I pirouetted a little to face them, though still appearing to be unaware of my audience. That was always Madame Denoux' advice, though few of the girls followed it. Dance like no one's watching. The audience, they want to feel like voyeurs, like they're intruding on a private moment, as though they're taking something intimate and forbidden from the dancer. Otherwise, you're just a girl taking her clothes off for money, nothing special.

There was something about her, the girl that watched with her handsome man. She reminded me of me. The way she appreciated my body. The way she devoured the theatricality of it all. She was seeing herself on the stage, wondering what it would be like to have all of these people watching her instead of me. And Madame Denoux hadn't missed it. I'd seen her circling, could imagine her thoughts adding together, ever calculating, never missing an opportunity to wring a man's pockets or find a new girl for her collection, like she'd found me.

Was it the redhead's facial expression, or the man who reminded me of Chey, or the way a note led the melody into a subtle variation, even though I knew the music inside out? There was no telling.

Sometimes, memories rushed back, unbidden, unwelcome. Shards of my past unfolding against a backlit screen, images racing by like a drug trip. Vivid. Painful.

The faces of my parents the last time I saw them alive. Waving to me as their car faded into the distance down the dirt road that led away from the agricultural institute where they lived and worked. I was five years old. My father ran the institute and my mother worked in the laboratories and experimental gardens as a researcher. That was how they had initially met and fallen in love. Or at least that was what I was told later by relatives.

He had been an engineer from St Petersburg, she was a local girl from the Donbass region. He had been posted to Donetsk on a temporary secondment, which became permanent once he married and they had their first child. Their only child. Me.

I know I was wanted and loved, and now it hurts like hell that my memories of my early years and of my parents are fading to oblivion as the past recedes. I think I remember a vegetable garden, some of the toys I played with, but what escapes me is the sound of their voices, the soothing lullabies my mother would sing to help me fall asleep. *Lubachka*, I think she called me. But now those memories, those songs, are buried far and deep and I can no longer retrieve them, nor can I picture the smile on her face or the severe, professorial demeanour of my father.

I don't even know the colours of my parents' eyes. And the false memories created by the few photographs I retain of them are all in black and white.

I was told that the driver of the lorry who hit their car on the Moscow Highway was drunk. The articulated lorry he lost control of was carrying a cargo of building materials. It was no consolation to hear he also died in the collision, crushed in his cockpit by massive blocks of concrete that had cut loose from the back of his vehicle. All three died instantly. It was the middle of the night.

I was taken in by my aunt, my mother's sister. She was divorced and childless, and also lived close to Donetsk. Once she had wanted to be a ballet dancer and she made it her life's work to see that I followed in that path, encouraging my dancing and sacrificing much in the way of money and leisure time so that I might realise her ambition and be successful where she hadn't been.

I was enrolled in the local dance academy, and attended classes after school three times a week and then again at the weekend. In order to pay for my lessons, my aunt was obliged to give piano lessons every Saturday in our apartment, which meant on those days I had to make my own way on foot to the academy buildings over three miles from where we lived, through heavy snow, sunshine or under the rain, whatever the weather. I had to make this journey increasingly regularly, after school, as her old used car was beginning to fall apart and she was unable to pick me up.

It afforded me much time for daydreaming.

Of course, like most little girls in the USSR, let alone the Ukraine, I dreamed of making it as a prima ballerina and I was repeatedly told that I had the necessary natural talent. But did I have the discipline, the ambition?

The answer to that was less evident.

I was lazy and unwilling to learn the classical steps, hated their rigour, preferred to lose myself in the music and improvise movements that just came naturally and were not part of any of the choreography our stern teachers were trying to drum into our small skulls.

'Lubov Shevshenko,' they would shout at me time and

time again, 'you are incorrigible. What are we going to make of you?'

I think I was eleven by then, and I managed to pass the final set of exams and was invited to move to St Petersburg, my father's place of birth, to attend the prestigious School of Art and Dance. I had no known relatives living there any longer and, as an orphan, was granted a menial bursary to cover my living expenses, although I had no choice in the matter and would have to live in a dormitory for other provincials similarly adrift in the city – an old secret police building that had been converted into a school for the disadvantaged.

The prospect of living on my own wasn't daunting, as life with my aunt had over the years become a series of silences and misunderstandings. She had, since the day she took me in, treated me as an adult, when I still wanted to be a child.

Being thrown in at the deep end and having to share in close proximity an eight-bed dormitory with other kids, most of whom were a few years older than me, was something of a traumatic experience. They hailed from Siberia, Tajikistan, a couple were also from the Ukraine and others from the Baltic States, with their perfect complexions, high cheekbones and rotten teeth. I quickly realised I had little in common with most of them. Only two of us attended the same school, while the others were scattered across a variety of different institutes, none of which had artistic aspirations, so we stood out like a pair of sore thumbs, Zosia and I.

I couldn't even pretend we became close friends. At best, from the advantage of her sixteen months seniority and the fact her breasts were already growing, she tolerated me, found my presence convenient as a messenger, factotum and facilitator. Luba, junior assistant when it came to anything illegal or forbidden, like smuggling cigarettes into the dormitory or concealing other's banned make-up under her mattress – that was me. My early training in criminality . . .

A few years into my time in St Petersburg, Zosia fell pregnant. She was seeing a boy from the physics institute, and I would, of course, cover for her absence on the occasion of her forbidden assignments. She was only sixteen at the time. When she was found out, the process was decisive. One day she was here, and the next day she wasn't. Thrown out of the school and shipped back like a dirty parcel to her family near Vilnius. We were told that there had been a grave illness in her family necessitating her return home, but we knew better, we knew the truth.

Almost two years later, in my final year at the School of Art and Dance, just as I was thinking that when I graduated I would take up a place in the corps de ballet in one of the city's lesser dancing troupes, I received a brief letter from Zosia out of the blue. She'd had a little boy, named Ivan, and was now also married to an older man who worked in the local state council. She said she was happy and enclosed a photograph of her family. It had been taken in a garden where the trees looked like skeletons and even the grass was sickly green. Zosia by then was approaching nineteen, but to me she already looked like an older woman, at least years older than she actually was, eyes sunk, hair dull, the sparkle of her youth gone for ever.

That was the day I swore to myself that I would neither marry nor have children.

*

During those years, we had our normal classes in the morning: Russian grammar, Russian literature (my favourite), arithmetic and later mathematics and geometry, history, geography, civic duties and others I daydreamed through with arduous distraction. Our afternoons saw us learning, rehearsing, practising and dancing at the school. We each had three dancing outfits, one to be used only for actual performances, when the ballet piece we had been working on for months was finally allowed to see the light of day at a gala performance. I was never given a solo and it looked as though I would always be a baby swan in the fluttering ensemble of the corps de ballet. Though I felt more like a flouncing duck. Oh, how I hated Tchaikovsky!

Ballet classes extended to the Saturday, so the only free day we were granted was the Sunday, but then most Sunday mornings were occupied cleaning our clothes, ironing, darning and bringing the dormitory back to tidiness, which left only Sunday afternoon as truly our own. Mostly we attended the local cinema house and the nearby ice-cream parlour. And had the opportunity to meet boys, before our curfew: 8 p.m. for the under fifteens, 9.30 for the older girls. The curfew was strictly enforced, and any defiance or breaking of the rules was always punished by a loss of weekend privileges.

Boys . . .

How could I not become interested in them, living for years on end – and teenage years do feel as if they last for ever – with seven women, a world of sly confidences, tall stories, raging hormones and peer envy? We monitored each other with the fierceness of hawks, purring with curiosity, brewing jealousy as if there was no tomorrow. Who was the prettiest, the tallest, the one whose breasts developed faster?

Some concealed the onset of their first periods, while others proclaimed them loudly to all and sundry. I was no ugly duckling in their midst, the orphan from the Ukraine. I was not the tallest, the most opulent, or the first or last to bleed, but in my head I always knew I was special. Realised that, unlike my fellow students, I had ambitions to see the world while all they could think of was the immediate future, some form of academic success and the prospects of a good match. Everything in my surroundings whispered to me that there was more to life than this.

Sex . . .

Another popular topic of conversation during the dark nights in a girls' dormitory. An endless chatter that extended to dressing rooms, rehearsal rooms, shower areas and the red-brick wall at the back of the building, which we knew none of the staff ever bothered patrolling in earnest and where all of us would take turns to smoke when, by hook or by crook, we got our hands on American cigarettes.

Being one of the youngest, I became a voyeur in the house of lust. During those years, all my dormitory companions flowered but, despite all the ballet classes and arduous exercises I was prescribed, I initially found it difficult to shed the puppy fat of my childhood. They would all say that I had a lovely face, but my body was slow in emerging from its cocoon. And so, in the communal showers, I stood like a spy, the water dripping down my body, endlessly watching, envying the other girls and the way their hips curved, their breasts hung, their arses spread, while I was still just a pack of bones surrounded by flabby skin, lacking definition and grace.

Oh, they talked a lot after the lights were out, about the boys they had met and the ones they would meet, and the things they would do. Silently, I listened, trying to distinguish the truth from the lies, sometimes shocked to my core, at other times burning inside with every bit of taboo knowledge that filtered my way. Always confident that one day I would join their ranks. Become an adult, become a woman.

The ice-cream parlour on Lugansk Avenue was the place where we hung out, an old-fashioned relic from the Stalinist years. On nine visits out of ten, all they could offer was vanilla flavour, and even then it wasn't natural and left a bitter chemical aftertaste in the mouth, but the two old babushkas who ran it, on behalf of the State of course, did not mind us girls lingering there for hours on end, exchanging scurrilous gossip, swapping make-up tips, meeting the guys from out of town who traded in nylons and often pressured the older girls into stolen kisses, not in lieu of payment – as that was always inescapable – but almost as a tip that guaranteed they would return another time and consent to sell us stockings that were unavailable outside the black market.

And then, as we got older, some of the girls began to boast of the fact they had granted the men more than just a kiss.

I couldn't afford nylons anyway so the whole subject was academic, but from the time of my first period, every time I visited the ice-cream parlour on Lugansk, I think I blushed as a curious buzz raced through my lower stomach and my imagination ran wild. It also made the taste of the ersatz vanilla palatable.

The year after Zosia's sudden departure, the girl occupying the nearest bed to mine was a girl from Georgia called Valentina.

Valya was a wild one, always getting into trouble, not so much out of any inherent sense of evil but mostly out of mischief and provocation. She was the one who instructed me in the art of giving blow jobs, which she insisted men liked and provided us girls with a direct path to their hearts or, as I discovered later, their loins. She kept on joking that I would never be a true Russian woman until I knew how to suck a man's cock. She even stole bananas from the kitchens on the rare occasions our esteemed Cuban friends shipped boatfuls of bananas over to the motherland in exchange for the moral support we were providing them with, according to the newspapers and the Central Committee.

Initially I was more interested in the blissful taste and consistency of the bananas than in their shape, but Valya insisted I practice for evenings on end until she pronounced I was ready to do the deed.

His name was either Boris or Serguey. I still can't recall his features in much detail, or his name. Because after Boris (or Serguey) came Serguey (or Boris) a few days later, as I quickly became a recidivist. He studied – well, they both did – at the nearby Technical Institute. I was sixteen and I guess he was just a year or two older. Valya had engineered our meeting, advertising the fact I was willing and, no doubt, pocketing a few roubles for the service. We met at the ice-cream parlour. I remember it was a day when they had additional flavours, and I chose to sample the wild strawberry alongside the classic chemical vanilla. He paid. Later, we walked hand in hand to the red wall behind my school and Valya acted as a lookout. He undid the belt circling his thin waist and pulled his frayed corduroy trousers down to his knees. His underwear was halfway between white and grey. He looked me in the eyes. He seemed even more terrified than I was. I gingerly extended my hand down to his crotch and took hold of his penis through the cheap cotton. It felt soft, limp like a piece of cheap meat. He froze. For a moment, I suddenly didn't know what to do next, however much Valya had rehearsed me in preparation for this moment.

Then I remembered. I got down on my knees. The ground was cold. I pushed the material aside and saw a man's cock for the first time. The spectacle was both frightening and fascinating. It was not what I'd expected. Smaller, maybe. I took a deep breath. A musty smell reached my nostrils, the smell of man.

I now took Boris's (or was it Serguey's?) cock in my hand. It jerked. I could feel his pulse through it.

I opened my mouth, steadied it, and presented his cock to my lips.

I extended my tongue and first licked his stem, and then traced the vein downwards to his balls sack, something Valya had recommended should he not be hard at first sight.

Again, a tremor coursed through his penis.

Finally, I took a deep breath and placed the mushroom-like head of the cock inside my mouth.

Within seconds, before I could suck, lick, grip or anything, I felt it growing, filling me.

It was a revelation.

As my lips took a firmer hold on the quickly hardening cock, I felt its smooth solidity, its sponge-like, resilient texture.

He was moaning, even when I did nothing.

My mind was geared to overdrive, storing the experience,

noting the sensations, dissecting the conflicting emotions. It was like entering a whole new world.

But the moment barely lasted for more than a minute before Boris (or was it Serguey?) brutally withdrew from my mouth and spurted a white stream of ejaculate across my chin and the top half of my dress. He looked at me quickly, mumbled an apology and pulled up his trousers. He turned and fled, leaving me on my knees like a supplicant, my mouth still open, my mind still abuzz.

'So how was it?' Valya asked. 'Exciting?'

'I don't know,' I told her truthfully. 'It was interesting, but it all happened too fast. I'd like to try again.'

'Really?' Valya said.

'I don't think I was doing it wrong,' I added. 'Maybe it was him.'

The next morning when I was brushing my teeth, I took a long hard look at myself in the mirror and I saw a new person. The child had gone. I finally looked into the eyes of a woman. Now, I know the transformation does not take place overnight, but it was as if a metaphorical bridge had been reached and crossed, triumphantly conquered.

I realised that I had achieved a distinct sort of power over the young man's cock and I was the one who had enjoyed the sensation most, contrary to expectations and tradition.

The second one, who could have been Serguey, was already hard when I pulled him from his trousers, and his penis was even more beautiful, straight like a ruler, a beautiful pink hue, unmarked by veins and with heavy balls hanging low beneath it.

He even tasted different.

Over the next year or so, led by insatiable curiosity and a deep attraction to the world of sex, I would come across a whole variety of cocks. I had no interest whatsoever in the men they belonged to. They were typically local, so often uncouth, inarticulate, clumsy, heavy drinkers for the most part, quite uninteresting to me. But they were the only sort around.

In my dreams, I imagined bad boys with more sophistication, elegant men with a sense of the wicked who would seduce me in all impunity and weave their evil ways around my deflowered innocence. I wanted the big league players, the men whose voices could make your knees tremble and electrify the senses. I knew that somewhere they existed and were waiting for me, ready to plunder and excite me. But until they came my way, I had to satisfy myself with the provincial boys who just weren't bad enough but nonetheless gave me a taste of the forbidden.

Once the rumour spread in our limited circle that I was willing and available – at any rate for blow jobs – they came running. Few were satisfied with just that, though, and invariably sought more, but I made the rules very clear. My body would retain its mystery and any attempt to breach my limits would result in immediate dismissal from my favours. Of course they tried it on, but my will was implacable. I would suck cocks but nothing more. And, of course, none of them were ever allowed to touch me, either.

The young Russian men I had the opportunity to meet seemed cut from the same unattractive pattern, but the rumour was that foreign men were another species altogether. Nina, one of our seniors, who had once had the privilege of travelling abroad as a replacement in the corps de ballet of a minor touring company had informed us girls in the dormitory that foreign men not only had bigger cocks but also were poets.

In my own naive way, it was a quest. How mistaken I was! And to compound my unease, my willingness to entertain the boys gave me a bad reputation and I found it difficult to make friends. On one hand they were jealous of me, while on the other they feared I might one day steal their men. The minds of young women do work in mysterious ways.

But even though now I no longer remember the faces of any of my Russian bad boys, I still recall with a smile on my face – call me mischievous, if you will – the cocks I serviced in the interest of my worldly education. Ah, my bad boys! But quickly I tired of them and their lack of originality and vocabulary and their clumsiness, and longed to meet bad men.

I resolved that I would move overseas at the first possible opportunity.

But without Valya to line up men for me as she had boys outside the school wall, my sexual discovery came to an abrupt end when I left St Petersburg.

Until Chey.

My first real lover. The first man who had entered me, owned me.

And he was a man, not a boy like the ones from the ice-cream parlour. He had known exactly what to do with his cock and, better still, what to do with me. Life with him made me selfish in bed, bored with other, inferior men.

My relationship with Chey had marked me, with lines as permanent as the ones I later had etched onto my flesh in the form of a tiny smoking gun, only an inch or two from my inner thigh, a place that most women kept secret, for only the most intimate friends and lovers to see. But by then

I had become a nude dancer, and Chey's gun was displayed to a roomful of people night after night. I saw when their eyes alighted on it. The initial curiosity, as they wondered what it was, perhaps a flower in bloom, and then the shock when they realised that I had a weapon burned onto my skin, pointing directly at the most powerful weapon of them all, my cunt. And then the hunger from men and sometimes women who saw it as a sign that I was wanton, dangerous in bed or looking for pain. A bad girl.

But I wasn't a bad girl. I was Chey's girl.

I remembered the day that we met. I was nineteen, and I'd just arrived in New York.

Encouraged by a well-meaning older tutor, I'd auditioned the previous year by videotape for a scholarship with the American School of Ballet, in the Lincoln Center.

My application was declined.

Another girl in my year got in, but she had wealthy parents, a father who had made quick money buying up steel and fertiliser plants for next to nothing in the economic collapse of the eighties while the rest of the population starved.

She was blank faced with limbs as thin as a bag of matchsticks, but she had grace and an obvious pliability, a uniformity to her movements that must have appealed to the scrutineers.

I took her address, and used her as a contact for my visa application after I graduated. Through my aunt, who had distant relatives living in America, I managed to get sponsorship. I was granted a three-month post-graduate stay, long enough to find my way around and build up a little local work experience as a waitress, and when my permission to remain expired, I melted into the back streets of Ridgewood, Queens, a neighbourhood that was full of Eastern Europeans. Slavs, Albanians, Ukrainians, Romanians, they had all come looking for a new life in America and ended up living virtually the same existence on new soil under the shadow of a different set of buildings.

I found a dingy apartment on a quiet street that was fairly cheap and close to a subway line that could deliver me quickly into Manhattan where I had found a job in a patisserie and coffee shop on Bleecker Street. The cafe was run by a Frenchman named Jean-Michel who had just broken up with his wife and didn't care that I was illegal, so long as I was beautiful and applied only the most delicate touch to his pastries. The croissants and petits pains au chocolat he baked were the best in the Village, light, fluffy, their smell a siren call to delicate stomachs, and the mille-feuilles were to kill for, so it was no hardship selling them. I'd always been a patient person, perhaps as a result of having no particular ambition, no maternal clock ticking, no one to hurry me along, no one to report to, so I never rushed the dough, always let the uncooked croissant mixture sit for as long as it needed to before gently rolling it out and over a butter square, turning the dough and rolling it again and again, folding it into towers with each turn, and eventually adding the bittersweet chocolate mixture and baking it in the oven until the shop was filled with the rich scent of two dozen pains au chocolat ready to be stacked on a glass dish in the window. And Jean-Michel's frequently wandering hands across my rump as he repeatedly instructed me in the art of baking according to his style were just a minor inconvenience, as long as I made it quite clear that was as far as I would allow him to venture.

Fall was just beginning to turn into winter. The days

were still bright and the sky blue. Local New Yorkers had started to carry scarves and gloves in their handbags in preparation for frosty evenings, but I was accustomed to much colder weather and I liked the chill that settled on my bare arms as I walked down West Broadway. It was the first Sunday in November, and I was alone in the shop. Jean-Michel was out running the New York marathon, pounding the sidewalk in a desperate effort to stave away the pounds that had inevitably gathered when he'd succumbed to middle age and American servings and his belly had grown in accord with the size of his croissants.

The bell on the door had tinkled, making me jump and nearly drop the tray of pretty pastel macaroons that I had spent all morning making, mixing egg whites with ground almonds and sugar, and piping the sweet nutty paste onto a sheet of paper, ever so careful to make each piped circle perfectly round, smooth and all exactly the same size so that they could be filled once they'd cooled and then packed into boxes with ribbons and sold to city girls who came in looking for a treat, or guilty husbands who couldn't find a florist on their way to the subway.

I'd burned the tips of my fingers and a line across my palm in my rush to right the tray before my sweets tumbled onto the floor, and I was annoyed and impatient when I hurried from the kitchen to the counter to serve my next customer.

Chey.

'You should put some ice on that,' he said, nodding towards the vivid red welt on my hand where I'd been scalded by the hot tray. I'd flinched when he set the coins onto the counter instead of on my waiting palm, in exchange for a chocolate croissant and a cappuccino.

'Yes,' I replied, because I couldn't think of anything else to say.

He was dressed casually, in a university athletics sweat-shirt and a pair of jeans and non-descript trainers, and his tousled blond hair glinted like hay in the sun that flooded through the windows, as though he'd just been out for a walk in Central Park, or on one of the streets that wasn't cut off for the marathon runners.

An all-American look, apart from his eyes, which were evidently sharp, but also cold. He met mine when he looked up from my hand. His were blue-grey, the colour of the sea on a cloudy day, and somehow didn't blend with the rest of his attire, or the sound of his voice. He didn't have a New York accent. It was something else, something I couldn't put my finger on.

He looked out of place in his casual clothes, like someone who had woken up in the wrong house, alongside someone else's wardrobe.

I shivered when I handed him his change. A quarter.

He sat inside on one of the stools along the bench that faced the window, flicking through the pages of a book so quickly that it seemed as though he wasn't really reading it, while I stood hidden between the kitchen and the counter and stared at him, watching as he held his croissant in his left hand and dipped it into the milky foam and ground chocolate that decorated his coffee, leaving behind bits of feathery pastry that floated away and stuck to the sides of the cup.

It was hot in the small shop, warm from the ovens, and soon he pulled his sweatshirt over his head, bringing his T-shirt up with it for a few moments before he shimmied it down again, revealing a tanned, muscled back and a glimpse of a tattoo that wound around his right side. His T-shirt was short sleeved and just tight enough to display taut arms with sinews that rippled as he lifted his cup to his mouth.

He suddenly turned to face me.

And I realised that I was holding my breath.

2

Dancing in the Moonlight

I didn't see him again for a week, and then he came back, wearing a sharp anthracite-coloured business suit, this time with a companion. They sat in the same place by the window with their backs to me, Chey and his fat friend in the zipped-up cream jacket who ordered a second pastry and another cappuccino and stared at the line of my breasts as I served them to him.

'Waitress,' he said, snapping his fingers in the air, as though I would have trouble noticing him only a few feet away and they being the only customers in the store.

As I brought his drink, his hand shot out to the sugar jar, right in line with the tray as I set it down on the bench, knocking his cup of coffee sideways and down the front of my white blouse. I yelped and leaped back as the hot liquid scalded my skin, barely managing to keep my cool and avoid cursing at the pair of them.

The fat man picked up a napkin and moved forward to lunge at me and dab at my breasts, until Chey stood up and pulled him forcibly back onto his stool.

'That's enough,' he said, and his companion had visibly wilted, all the bravado seeping out of him like air from a balloon.

He had spoken in Russian.

The next day a parcel was delivered to the store,

couriered all the way over from Macy's, with a note that simply read: *Apologies. For your blouse.*

It was pure silk, with a fine lace collar, much more beautiful, and no doubt more expensive, than the functional one that I had stained. The French owner raised an eyebrow at me as I tucked the parcel next to my coat and handbag, and made no mention of sending it back. Chey's friend had been rude, and I would accept this gift in return.

A week later, I turned twenty, and he asked me out to dinner.

'How did you know it was my birthday?' I asked him when he came into the store that afternoon to check that I had received his package. My tone was accusatory. The last thing I needed was a stalker – particularly one with clumsy friends – even if he was handsome.

'I didn't,' he replied, smiling. 'Happy birthday. I hope that it fits, and is a fair replacement for the one my friend ruined.'

'Oh. Yes, of course. It's beautiful. Thank you. There was really no need . . .'

'You're very welcome,' he replied.

He was about to leave the store when my curiosity got the better of me and I asked him in my native tongue, 'Are you Russian?'

The question fell between us like a stone, weightier than I had intended. I felt like a fool, and a nosy one at that. Prying was a quality that I disapproved of in others.

'No, I'm not,' he replied in English. 'I speak just a few words. But only for work.'

'That's a shame,' I replied. 'Sometimes I am homesick for my own language.'

He paused, as if mulling something over. I regretted

being so honest with a perfect stranger. I had no close friends in New York and I'd been starved of company for too long, and now I'd made a fool of myself in front of this man. The doorbell remained silent, no matter how hard I wished that another customer would enter the shop and save me from my embarrassment.

'Can I take you to dinner, Luba?' he asked after a long silence. He'd caught my name from the badge that was pinned to my apron. 'I won't speak Russian to you, but I can keep you from being lonely, for an evening. I know what it's like to be new in a city. And it is your birthday, after all.'

I'd been told Americans were more forward than folk in other parts of the world, but Chey was my first sign of it. If a good-looking and pleasant man was going to ask me out to dinner then I would not turn him down without good reason. I accepted.

We ate at Sushi Yasuda, on East 43rd Street, surrounded by bamboo walls and bamboo tables, as if we had stepped into a temple, a world away from the dreary rush of Times Square only a few blocks over. It was the first time I'd eaten raw fish. I wore his blouse, of course, and a simple black skirt with a pair of low kitten heels that I had once bought to attend job interviews. His attire matched mine in formality, which was a relief; just a simple but well-cut white shirt and a pair of jeans.

Chey showed me how to mix wasabi into the soy sauce and I told him about my life growing up in the Ukraine. He told me about his own in return.

His father had served in the army and, consequently, he'd grown up in military bases all over the world, which was where he had learned to speak a few words of Russian, as well as a little German, some Spanish and fluent French and Italian.

He now made a living trading jewellery as an amber merchant, which afforded him many opportunities to practise his Russian, speaking to the dealers in Kaliningrad. Both of his parents were dead, like mine. His father was killed, not in combat but in a bar fight when Chey was fifteen, and his mother had committed suicide shortly after.

Chey had run away from the boys' home in New Jersey that the State had planned to relocate him to until he came of age, and he'd begun working in a pawn shop. A knack for business and an appreciation as keen as a magpie's for jewellery had led him to international trading in precious stones. Later he focused on amber.

I asked him why he'd chosen fossils over other prettier, more popular and surely more valuable gems, like diamonds and rubies, and he told me that the first time he had seen a piece of amber that a Latvian woman had traded in his store when he was sixteen, he had felt as though he'd caught hold of a piece of the setting sun, its colour was so golden and its feel so smooth and silky. The piece had a tiny creature trapped inside, perhaps thousands of years old, and the young Chey had wondered how it felt to be cast inside a prison of light. So his love affair with the gem had begun.

The way he told me the story of his life sounded somehow poetic to my ears, and colouring slightly at the thought, I recalled someone telling me once how poets had nicer (or was it longer?) cocks. I couldn't deny that I was attracted to him. I felt drawn to him, the magnetism of his eyes, the square angle of his shoulders as he leaned forward and spoke to me with an almost confidential air. We sat in the booth and sometimes our knees touched or his fingers brushed against my sleeve as I stretched my hand out to pick up the soy sauce or the water. This was a real man, complex, charismatic and, a small voice inside my head kept on reminding me, potentially dangerous, and I was orbiting around him like a moth to a flame.

When he walked me to the street and paid a taxi driver to whisk me safely home so I didn't need to suffer the discomfort of a late-night subway journey home to Brooklyn, I had waited for him to make his move, to lunge at me and take payment for the meal or his kindness in the way that I was used to men wanting a kiss or more in exchange for their gifts. But his hands didn't stray across my buttocks and neither did his eyes drop below my own, searching to see what secrets I might have hidden under the blouse he had bought to replace the one his friend had intentionally ruined.

Chey kissed me gently on the cheek, politely held the taxi door open and promised to call me, and I went home disappointed, rejected and a little angry with him. I was used to men wanting me, and being more overt about the fact. Over the years, I had come to realise that dating was a transaction, and anyway, the thought of giving him a blow job would not have been an inconvenience – far from it. Chey's cool chivalry left me empty handed, bereft of the usual weapons that I would employ to ensnare his favour.

I became more irritated when I found myself looking out for him in the shop, jumping each time that the bell rang, rushing to get to the counter in case he was the next customer.

Two days later he phoned the patisserie while I was dusting powdered sugar onto the choux Chantilly, careful to tap the sieve very gently so the pastry shells were lightly and evenly dusted, not overpowered and sickly with too much sugar on top.

Would I see him again? I agreed and this time he took me to the movies at the big multiplex off Union Square. I expected his hand to touch my knee or his arms to wrap themselves around me during the film, but he was a proper gentleman and I sensed he wouldn't approve of groping a woman in the dark on a second date.

We had a coffee on University Place after the perform-ance and when we left he pulled me to him and kissed me softly on the lips, not long and lingering, but with feeling. When he pulled away he smiled and raised his arm at a passing cab. He handed me in and shut the door, paying the driver to return me to Brooklyn. I was slightly dis-appointed, hoping that after that kiss he might have taken a step further.

My impatience continued to rise steadily over the next fortnight as we enjoyed a further two dates and again he did not make his move. It was as if he was quietly observing me, judging me, orchestrating the steady rise of my desire. Of course, I didn't wish to appear overeager, but then again my frustration was building. I liked him and it was obvious from his flirtatious manner and soft, sensual kisses at the end of each date that he was attracted in equal measure to me.

It was then he dropped the bombshell.

He had been called away unexpectedly on business in the Dominican Republic, he told me over the phone.

And he wanted me to join him.

When I confessed that if I left the country I would most likely never be able to get back in again, he advised me that he sometimes had a private jet at his disposal and that airport officials would pose no problem. I presumed that this meant he planned to bribe the airport staff who monitored these things into falsifying their records to indicate that their passenger had the appropriate paperwork in order. Both on departure and on arrival.

So I discovered, in one fell swoop, that Chey was a man of wealth, power and influence, to an extent that I hadn't fully realised during our dates.

Naturally, that should have been my first clue that his business in the amber markets was neither as humble nor as law abiding as I had automatically presumed. But I grew up with the black market, in a world where bribing the police was simply a part of life. As for the money, Chey was so casual about it that it was easy to overlook. Day to day, he rarely flashed his cash, always dressing well but in understated fashion and never orchestrating unusually expensive dates. If he had wealth hidden away that he took for granted, then I could not find a way to hold that against him. Or to ask him how it was that he came by the money. An inheritance, perhaps, a successful investment or even a lottery win. Whatever it was, I resolved to remind myself that he had never lied to me about his income, and if it turned out to be more than I had expected, then that could only be good news for me.

I was not about to let an opportunity for an overseas holiday escape. Unless I managed to secure a Green Card, or intended to leave the States for ever, I might never get one again.

So it was that I accepted his invitation and arrived in La Romana with just a few belongings in a carry bag. I'd used some of my meagre savings to buy a swimsuit – a tiny gold bikini that glittered in the light – and a pair of sandals with a thick wedge. I had a cotton dress, a skirt and the white blouse, and if that wasn't enough for me to fit into whatever ritzy establishments that he had planned, then he'd need to buy me more things.

A car and driver appeared to collect me at the airport. Chey was apparently in a business meeting and unable to come in person. I sat alone in the back seat of the sedan with the window open, enjoying the warm air brushing my skin and the sweet smell that wafted on the breeze from the sugar factories as we raced along the wide streets lined with palm trees towards his private villa on the resort, which was so large that when we pulled in I had thought the ring of airy white stone buildings with their thatched roofs by the oceanfront comprised the entire resort, where we would have one bedroom. In fact, the driver explained that all of this was Chey's and mine, at least for the next few days.

I was shown upstairs by a uniformed maid who led me silently to a vast unoccupied room overlooking the villa's private beach with its endless shore of golden sand. I dumped my bag on the king-size bed and briefly admired my surroundings.

The floors were marble, polished and shiny, and the balconies offered a perfect view of a glittering ocean on one side of the villa, and an oval-shaped pool on the other. I had never come across such luxurious surroundings before and almost felt as if I didn't belong here. The fittings were elegant and devoid of ostentation, but spoke of taste and wealth.

I stripped off in one of the expansive bathrooms, revelling in the feel of the cool slate tiles against my feet. I washed away the dust from my travels, donned my bikini, and made my way downstairs to the pool. I ordered a fruity cocktail from a barman who had seemingly come out of nowhere the moment I appeared. Drink in hand, I pulled my book from my bag and settled in to wait by the pool, marvelling at the strangeness of life and how a girl from Donetsk had ended up in a place like this.

Chey arrived just as the sun was setting: an enormous orange orb that had flung its flame-like tendrils into the sky as if in an attempt to stop itself from falling. Shades of pink and tangerine as bright as the mango that had decorated my drink glowed brightly against the deep blue of the ocean.

I didn't see him come out to the pool, but I felt the warmth from his skin as he perched on the side of my deckchair, leaned forward and kissed my cheek. I looked up. He was shirtless, dressed in just a pair of cream board shorts and sandals. His skin was a rich bronze colour, no doubt the result of several days lounging in the Caribbean sun before I had arrived.

'Would you like to go for a ride?' he asked.

Without waiting for my reply, he threw me the loose cotton dress I had hooked over the back of the chair and took my hand, leading me out to the front again, where a scooter was parked on the grass. He climbed on and I slid up behind him, wrapping my arms around his strong, muscled waist. I hung on as we sped down to the seafront at La Caleta, passing a row of ugly concrete buildings that contrasted strangely with the straw-thatched roofs and colourful painted walls of nearby tropical-themed bars and shop fronts where bunches of bananas were piled alongside fishing gear and signs advertising various tourist activities.

Chey hired a boat at the marina, a small white speedboat with *Valya* painted on the side in faded black. It felt like an omen to me, seeing the name of my old friend, the girl who had set about my sexual awakening. I wasn't sure if it would turn out to be a positive or a negative omen, but I felt instinctively that it would lead to sex.

And it did.

We flew over the water in *Valya*, my hair whipping back behind me in the wind and the taste of salt in the air like a kiss from the sea.

'This is La Isla Catalina,' he said, when we docked the boat at a small marina dedicated to the resort and he helped me to jump overboard. The sand was almost white and the water clear and pure as crystal as we waded to the shore.

We walked across the dunes, under palm trees and passed other little bays with no more than a smattering of people dotted across the hot, thin sand. Children playing with plastic buckets and swimmers spread out in the water, bobbing in the gentle waves. He led the way, and so I was able to get a better look at the tattoo that covered the right side of his back, bare apart from the thick strap of the hold-all bag that he carried, which obscured my view, but only partially. It was a cat of some sort, etched in golden ink. A leopard, I thought. Its sleek body rippling along with his muscles as he walked; its head invisible to me beneath the fabric of the bag strap.

I had further opportunity to investigate when we arrived at a secluded beach with a ring of trees blocking the view from anyone who wandered nearby. Chey bent down in front of me and pulled a blanket out from the bag, exposing his shoulder and the head of the leopard, its eyes black and teeth bared in a fierce growl.

'I'm a pussy cat, really,' he said with a smile, when he turned and caught me staring at him.

He sat on his haunches on the blanket as he pulled more things out of the bag. A bottle of champagne, two glasses, some bread and cheese.

We ate, and talked. Little about him, more about me.

'So what do girls in boarding schools do in Russia to pass the time?' he asked, with a suggestive smile.

'You mean when we weren't bribing the boys for cigarettes?'

'Yes. Why did you come to America? What did the little Luba want to be when she grew up?'

'A prima ballerina, like all Russian girls. But I wasn't good enough. I was too lazy.'

'Now that I don't believe.' He poured more of the chilled champagne into my glass. 'Do you still dance?'

'Never. Not even when I sing in the shower.'

'Will you dance for me?'

Perhaps it was the champagne that had so swiftly gone to my head, along with the cocktail that I had finished earlier, or maybe it was the dream-like setting that was straight from a Hollywood movie, or the fact that I felt like I owed him something for bringing me here, and I always paid my debts. But I got to my feet, and began to move on the sand, swaying gently in time with the movement of the trees and the rhythm of the waves cresting and falling behind me.

I was aware of the effect that I was having on him. My body was close to nude in the tiny bikini, my nipples visible through the thin gold fabric now that the air had begun to cool.

Chey's eyes glittered, fixated on me.

My world turned still for a moment under the intensity of his stare and I was filled with a rush of adrenalin, just as I had experienced by the red-brick wall in the school yard in

Donetsk. But instead of a provincial Russian boy, here I was faced with a beautiful and generous man, and one who obviously wanted to watch me. The thought of exposing myself to him and revelling in his gaze set my whole body simmering.

I reached a hand behind my back and flicked the small clip that held the strap of my bikini top, letting the fabric drop down to the sand as I raised my arms over my head and continued to dance.

'And the rest,' he demanded, the path of his gaze travelling from my exposed breasts down to the gold triangle of my bikini bottoms.

The pants were fastened with strings tied into a bow on each of my hips so I was able to cast them aside with just a few tugs, and then I froze, not out of fright but purposefully, allowing him to examine my body as I stood still under the bright light of the tropical moon.

'You're a mermaid,' he said. 'You move like the sea.'

He took my hand and pulled me towards him, and I sat astride his waist, shifting my body a little so that I could feel the hard bulge of his cock straining under the fabric of his shorts and enjoy the feel of the rough material against my skin.

Before Chey I'd only been kissed by one boy. One who had found his way to me and the red brick wall at my school through Valya. The only one who hadn't wanted his cock sucked, who preferred a little tenderness. Or maybe he had just been shy. His name was Sasha, and when I fell to my knees and moved my hands to his trousers, he pulled me up again, and instead pressed his lips to mine.

Now Chey pulled me lower and kissed me. He tasted of champagne. His lips were firm and his tongue probed my mouth gently. He held my chin in his hand, directing our kiss. Then ran his hands over my shoulders, caressing my arms, my breasts, stopping at my waist. I shimmied down in one sudden movement and began to undo the tie and button that held his shorts together so that I could show him my trick, the only trick that I knew.

Chey laughed when he realised what I was trying to do.

'No, my mermaid, allow me,' he'd said, pulling me up and flipping me over so that I was on my back, staring up at the stars that shone like fireflies in the night sky as he dropped his face between my legs and pressed his firm tongue to my pussy.

I gasped in shock as a wave of pleasure coursed through me.

It had never occurred to me that a man might return the favour so quickly, and I'd never had any cause to wonder how it would feel if he did. In the dormitory back in the Ukraine, we had gossiped feverishly about many things, but this had always been one of the most shocking for us somehow. The girls boasted about their skill at taking cocks into their mouths, but the idea of men going down on us had been unspoken, shameful.

Of course, I had touched myself many times and orchestrated a whole palette of pleasure in the process, but all so often in the dark, beneath the sheets and the bed covers, straining to remain silent. I knew the geography of a penis like the back of my hand, but I'd never had the opportunity to see myself in the light, had never imagined what it might be like for the boys learning to pleasure women. If that was part of their high school education, if they came hoping for more than just their trousers pulled down and if they left wanting.

So the touch of Chey's tongue against my nub was like a stab to my heart. Electrifying. The physical experience immediately transmuting the psychological one and setting off a blazing fire at the core of my being.

It felt like falling into the sun and I closed my eyes and abandoned myself to the sensation of his strokes, sometimes quick and sometimes slow, short and sharp or long and languorous, moving in time with the rise and fall of my body as I responded to each new caress.

He followed with his fingers, and that too was a revelation. I'd never used a dildo. I wasn't too embarrassed to be seen in the shops off Broadway with their pink, red and purple window displays and tacky lingerie on plastic hangers, but I budgeted each dollar I earned with military precision and had just enough for my rent, food, subway fares, emergency savings and books, the one luxury that I allowed myself. Spending money on sex toys would have been a ridiculous extravagance.

Chey's dance with his tongue had made me wet, and his finger slipped in easily, moving inside me, exploring, teasing, and he soon followed it with another.

'God, you're tight,' he breathed, as I thrust my hips against his hand, wanting him to fill me more, go deeper. I'd been a virgin long enough, I felt, and this was the last hurdle that I had yet to breach on the road to womanhood.

I hadn't been saving myself for marriage. I was far too practical for that. I just hadn't wanted it to be with one of the boys against the red-brick wall, or some man in a bar with fierce alcoholic breath who would leave me with a baby and no future, like Zosia in the yard with the skeleton trees. What better opportunity would there be than handsome Chey under the light of a tropical moon? And if the sand beneath the blanket was a little cold and hard compared with the king-size bed in the resort, then that was an inconvenience that I was prepared to put up with.

I reached down, eager to feel his cock in my hands, to discover what sort of man he was. It had been a long time since I'd felt one and I missed it. I wanted to weigh his balls in my palm, wrap my fingers around his girth, trace my fingertips along each bump and crevice.

'You're impatient,' he told me, and batted my hands away, as he continued his own explorations of my body.

He slipped a finger into my anus, penetrating both holes together as he continued to stroke my clitoris with his tongue and the sensation was blinding. Better than anything that I had experienced before, multiplied a hundred times over, and I forgot him entirely as my own pleasure consumed me. I gripped his hair with my hands, and pushed myself upwards, impaling myself on his tongue and trapping his head against me in case he thought for a moment that he might move away or stop or breathe, for any change in his rhythm might ruin everything. Then I came in one great rush like a wave from the sea behind us peaking and crashing and then fading away.

As the sensation subsided and my movements slowed, I was suddenly acutely aware of the rustle of the trees, the firm press of the sand against my back under the blanket, the occasional snapping of twigs that might have been an animal or even a person spying on us, the gentle breeze that brushed my skin and the sheer number of the stars that glowed in the sky like silent witnesses to my adventures beneath them.

He pulled himself up to lay alongside me, cradling my

body against his, until the warmth that filled me subsided and I relaxed into his arms.

'Shhh,' he said, rocking me back and forward as though I was a child.

It was the first time that a man had ever given me an orgasm.

He didn't protest when I pushed myself up to my knees and fiddled with the catch on his shorts, then pulled them down and tossed them onto the beach alongside my discarded bikini. His cock was still hard as a rock and as bronzed as the rest of him, as though he had spent weeks sunbathing nude.

He moaned when I lowered my head to his groin and licked all the way along his shaft to his tip.

'Oh, Luba,' he said, shuddering as I took him into my mouth.

Chey tasted wonderful, and his cock filled my mouth in a way that I had never experienced before. I took my time over it, my tongue darting along his glans and circling his head as he continued to moan my name and wrap his fingers ever so gently in my hair. But I wanted to abandon all sense of duty and technique and simply feel him sliding in and out of me, thrusting to my depths.

He shuddered, and withdrew, gently caressing my chin as he did so.

'Luba . . .' he said again, reverently.

'I want to ride you,' I replied.

I had waited long enough, and now I wanted to know what it would feel like to have a man inside me, filling me to my depths. But I didn't want to end up carrying his child, and though I knew that I could take pills afterwards to stop that from happening I had no idea how to get hold of them here, so I was relieved when he reached up to his rucksack and pulled a box of condoms out from the pocket, and more relieved when instead of handing one to me he tore the wrapper open himself and rolled the thin rubber down to the base of his cock. Getting hold of bananas to practise blow jobs was one thing, but being caught with condoms in the dormitories, even if we could have got hold of them, would have meant immediate expulsion.

I was still wet after my first orgasm and aching to sate my arousal. I climbed onto him, lowering myself slowly onto his hardness, stifling a cry when he reached my wall which had not yet been broken, and a sharp bolt of pain shot through me. The pang lasted only a moment, and then I realised that this was it, I was having sex. The sensation was disappointing at first in comparison to the feeling of his tongue against me, and I briefly wondered what all the fuss was about.

Then I began to move, and he put his hands on my hips and rocked me back and forth, slowly at first, then gradually faster. I discovered that I could stimulate myself even more if I leaned forward a little and ground my clitoris against his stomach muscles. I watched the expressions of pleasure and abandonment flit over his face and I decided that all the blow jobs in the world were nothing compared to the power a woman had when she was straddling a man.

Chey didn't lose himself within minutes like the school-yard boys. When I'd begun to tire of thrusting against him he flipped me over again with one swift turn of his arm so that I was on all fours, staring up the sand dunes into the line of palms swaying in the distance, feeling his heavy ball sack smack against my thighs with each thrust, revelling in the sound of his moans as I pushed myself back against him, bringing him to climax.

Then he came, gripping my shoulders with his strong hands and driving his cock impossibly deep inside me until he was spent and I could take it no more and we broke apart panting, ecstatic.

For a while we lay tangled in each other's arms, wishing that we could be transported magically back to the resort without needing to go to the bother of the long walk and boat ride ahead of us, romantic though both would be in the moonlight.

He ran his hands along my body, over my stomach and then my thighs, pausing when he found the streaks of blood that decorated my legs.

'It was your first time,' he said, his voice full of wonder. 'I didn't know.'

'I have a lot of catching up to do,' I replied, and he laughed.

'I would be very happy to oblige.'

For the next few days we made love at every possible opportunity, until we both felt raw and exhausted. Making up for lost time.

'Your body is made for fucking, Luba,' Chey told me one day as we lay on the silken sheets of the king-size bed. But by then I already knew. All the years of ballet training and my vivid imagination had just been a stepping stone to this point.

But our holiday could not last for ever, and after five days we returned to New York. At the airports I witnessed Chey passing wads of banknotes to sundry officials and we were effortlessly ushered through the VIP channels and never importuned.

I loved New York with a vengeance, but on arriving back,

it felt so dull and grey, albeit not as much as the depressing concrete vistas of Donetsk.

I was driven back to my Brooklyn digs and Chey assured me he would be in touch again. Soon.

He was true to his word and two days later as I completed my shift at the Bleecker Street patisserie and walked out of the door, there he was, standing on the sidewalk waiting for me, dressed in his regulation off-duty uniform of blue jeans and a white T-shirt. He took me back to his apartment.

'I want you again,' he said.

But it wasn't long before he had to go away again on business. A few days here, a few days there, each absence longer than the last, with little notice or explanation. And not once did he ask me to accompany him again.

It wasn't that I was possessive – being brought up as an orphan quickly tames that particular instinct – but after the initial glow of our relationship, I quickly began to resent Chey's continued absences, the cancelled assignments, the broken promises.

He had, alongside his first gift, given me a wonderful amber brooch in a delicate steel frame, which I now wore daily. He had handed it over to me before the car had dropped me off in Brooklyn after the return trip from the Caribbean. Later he left me a pair of keys to his apartment in the Meatpacking District on Gansevoort Street.

It was in an old brick building, once used as a storage depot, which had been converted into large individual units, and even the bathroom was larger than my modest Brook-lyn digs.

The apartment was a symphony of black and white, straight from the imagination of a minimalist designer. Every sleek item of furniture and domestic implement, especially the well-equipped kitchen, all stainless steel and shiny surfaces, sprang from the pages of a glossy magazine. It looked and felt expensive and, for the first time, it made me wonder where Chey's income came from. Surely the amber business was not that profitable.

My realism was stronger than the romantic side of me and I knew that whisking me away on a whim to the Dominican Republic must have cost him a fortune. He said I was always welcome, but all too often when I visited impromptu, he appeared to be away.

On one occasion, I had undressed and draped myself naked across the immense bed in which he slept and waited for his arrival, only to doze off and wake with the morning sun on my bare skin, still alone and feeling something of a fool.

Irritated by what I considered a personal rebuff, I took one of his impeccably ironed shirts from his closet, slipped it on, and began an exploration of the apartment. Only to find that past the drawers and cupboards in which he kept his fabulously expensive clothes, suits, shirts, ties, shoes, everything else was locked. Which only made me more curious.

But it was easier to remain blind and enjoy the moment. Whenever we were together, the sex was fantastic and Chey, despite all the things I knew he was keeping back from me, was everything I'd always wanted from a man. Strong, attentive, ironic, decisive.

Then, at the patisserie one day, Jean-Michel's roving hands lingered a bit too long and we ended up having a flaming row. I had no choice but to leave the job. I had no intention of going, cup in hand, to Chey to ask him for either moral or financial support. A girl has her pride. Not that it would have done much good as this coincided with his longest absence from Manhattan.

The last time I'd seen him we were in bed and I'd noticed a faint set of bruises across the knuckles of his right hand, and had dismissed it, knowing he would clam up if I even asked, as he had always done when I'd enquired, back in the Caribbean, about the provenance of the parallel scars that ran across his shoulders, and the significance of his cryptic leopard tattoo. I knew that veteran die-hard prisoners in Russian prisons had many tattoos with a varying degree of significance but his was not of the same ilk.

His scars and tattoo increasingly attracted my fascination and, when we made love, I would drag my fingers across them in a forlorn attempt to both map them and draw out their significance. Oh, how I loved to explore his body, the flowing surface of his skin, the rippling muscles concealed beneath the surface, how every piece of him connected with the other and turned him into a perfect machine to make love to me, every nook and cranny adapting to my inner rhythms, the savage movement of his thrusts as he dug deep inside me, the fragrant breeze of his staccato breath as he fucked me, the rigid engine of his buried cock.

Now I could forget all the Russian boys and their lack of subtlety and sophistication. Chey was a man, one who didn't have to be told how to hold a woman, rein her in, set her loose at the right moment and watch her journey from lust to drained satisfaction.

I loved how his fingers journeyed across my skin, teasing, playing, hurting me even, and taking me to the edge until that magic moment when release finally came. With him I felt like a flower; and I opened myself up for him like never before. I'd been a cocoon, a larvae, and now I was a butterfly and I soared.

High.

And when I came I would whisper his name.

Chey.

And then fall asleep in his arms, safe, protected, warm and soft, my limbs akimbo, washed by the release of desire.

One morning when I woke up, he was gone. There was just a hastily scribbled note on the kitchen top telling me he had to go away at short notice, didn't know how long he would be, but assuring me that he loved me to the moon and back. I smiled. It was an expression we'd heard someone on a TV series say and we had both burst out laughing at the same time. It had become a private joke between us ever since, though I was beginning to feel the truth of it.

In the note he suggested I stay on and look after the apartment while he was away. Big deal, I thought, annoyed that he could leave me so easily. To cool my frustration I walked all the way to my job on Bleecker and straight into the fierce argument that led to my losing it.

My savings lasted just three weeks and without a visa getting another job was far from easy. And there was still no sign of Chey. I had no alternative but to relinquish my sub-let in Brooklyn and move my few belongings into Chey's Meatpacking District apartment, somewhat fearful of what his response would be when he found out. But still, six weeks later, there was no sign or word from him and his phone was no longer taking messages even.

One morning I had scraped together some change I found on Chey's desk and was having a coffee at the nearest Starbucks, gazing ahead at the rusting steel columns of the

High Line and pondering my limited course of action, when someone called out my name.

'Luba!'

It was Chey's fat Russian friend, the one who had deliberately spilled the coffee over my blouse. His name was Lev and, when we had been introduced by Chey a few months ago, he had profusely apologised for his earlier behaviour. He was visibly scared of Chey, who held the upper hand in what I assumed was their business relationship. We never spoke together in our native language and Lev had a pronounced East Coast accent.

I greeted him with a distinct lack of enthusiasm, my anger at Chey's absence colouring my attitude to his acquaintances.

'So, how are things?' he asked me.

'So, so,' I replied. 'You wouldn't know where Chey has decamped to, would you? Or how much longer he will be away?'

'He never tells me anything,' he said.

'Typical.' I swore under my breath.

Without being asked, he sat himself across from my table. I glanced over at him. His shirt was bursting at the seams, its front buttons screaming in agony as his stomach forced itself forward and was barely contained by the material. How could such a lump of a man be associated with Chey?

He misinterpreted the scorn on my face for sadness.

'What's wrong?' he asked me, with a look of concern.

'Your friend Chey; that's what's wrong,' I replied. 'One day here, the next day elsewhere, without a single word of warning. It doesn't make things easy,' I protested.

I then explained what had happened at the patisserie and

how I'd lost my job and was now in a precarious position. He offered to let me have a few hundred bucks, but I just couldn't accept them. Not from Lev. He would expect a return payment in one way or another, and that was something I was unwilling to give him. Instead, I brushed off his offer and told him that I had to find a job, and why it wasn't as easy as it appeared.

A broad, goofy smile illuminated his face.

'I'm illegal too,' he declared, as if it was something to be proud of.

'Congratulations!' I exclaimed bitterly. 'I'm proud to be a member of the same club . . .'

'But Chey, he tells me you are a wonderful dancer. You trained in Russia, didn't you?'

'I did. But that was a long time ago now. And I wasn't that good, not technical enough.'

'What's technical about dancing?'

'I don't think you'd understand,' I pointed out, taking a sip of my rapidly cooling coffee.

'If you wanted to dance again, for a job, you know. I think I could help. Until Chey returns, if you want.'

'Tell me more,' I said, although I already suspected it wouldn't be at the Lincoln Center or with the New York City Ballet.

He explained.

Initially, I was dubious.

'You sure you have no idea when Chey will be back?' I enquired, hoping this wasn't my only option. How could I dance naked for other men when I knew, deep in my heart, that it was only Chey I truly wanted to dance for?

'No. It's impossible to know. Business, you see.'

'Take me, then,' I said.

49

The name of the club was the Tender Heart and it stood, all steel shutters, graffiti-laden walls and discoloured pink awning, at the top end of the Bowery, close to Lafayette Street. It had once been a popular rock club during the glory days of punk, I was later told. The walls of the basement area still dripped with several generations of alcoholic sweat and I almost gagged as Lev guided mc through the narrow foyer to a recessed area where the offices were.

'It's better when the air conditioning is on, from late afternoon when the club opens to the public,' he pointed out to me. 'Barry, who runs the place, is always trying to save money so he has it switched off when the joint is closed.'

Barry was a diminutive Brit with an old-fashioned and dubious moustache and thinning hair. During the course of any conversation, he wouldn't fail to remind you several times every hour that he hailed from Liverpool. But he looked nothing like any of the Beatles.

He sat at a rickety desk that had survived every world war you could think of, facing piles of untidy ledgers. Just a glorified accountant, I assumed, and no hint as to who the club actually belonged to. I briefly suspected Chey, but the place was just too downmarket and lacking in class, I decided, to be associated with him.

Lev had called ahead to warn him of our arrival.

'So, you're Chey's girl?' He grinned.

'I'd rather you called me a woman,' I said. 'I waited long enough to become one, so I'm rather fond of the title. And I don't belong to anyone.'

'And feisty at that,' he concluded with an amused smirk. He probably thought he looked ironic.

'Yes, they breed us tough in Russia,' I said, thickening my accent on purpose.

He looked me over, like a butcher appraising a cut of meat.

'Our common friend has told you what we do?'

'He did.'

'You dance?'

'I did. Although not the sort of dance you have in mind.'

'Is that a problem?'

'No.'

Barry gave Lev a glance and the fat Russian acolyte stepped out of the crowded office.

'Can I see you?' he then asked.

'See me?'

'Your body. Naked. In this sort of job, you understand, it's what I'd call' – he searched for the right word – 'a prerequisite. You see, the customers must have something decent to feast their eyes on.'

'OK.' I nodded.

He sat back in his leather armchair and kept on staring at me.

I undressed.

His eyes lingered over every square inch of my skin, moving from part to part, area to area, almost examining me forensically, assessing, judging.

I just stood there facing him, feeling the oppressive heat floating throughout the room, seeping in under the door from where the club's public areas were, my legs ever so slightly apart, trying to retain a modicum of modesty and elegance as I was being perused.

'Very nice,' he finally stated.

I lowered my eyes.

'Breasts are small, but real, high and firm. That's good. Dancer's legs, thin but strong. Turn round,' he ordered me.

I obeyed.

'Lovely arse. A true work of art,' he proclaimed. 'Turn again,' he asked me.

Again, he looked me up and down, his eyes lingering on my crotch.

'That'll have to go,' he said.

I looked down at my naked body, perplexed.

'All that hair,' he pointed out. 'Nice colour, matches your head. So rare, real blondes these days. All comes from a bottle. Some of the girls in other of our establishments even colour themselves down there, but it looks so fake, I always feel. Even though some of the punters are taken in by it. But at our location, we've always made it a point of honour that the dancers are smooth . . .'

Maybe I still looked puzzled.

'Shaved,' he continued.

I confirmed my agreement. It wasn't something I'd ever done. Back at the dormitory it had not been allowed by the monitors. Later, in St Petersburg at the School, we were required to trim on the sides so no unseemly hair could be seen peering outside of our leotards, even though we always wore thick tights for both practise and performance.

The vision of my nuder-than-nude cunt flashed across my mind and the idea gave me a perverse thrill.

Smooth . . . All part of the new American me.

I snapped out of my brief daydream as Barry's voice droned on.

'There are some rules and they are never to be broken,' he explained. 'You never show pink. You never speak to members of the audience unless they request a lap dance.

You are allowed to turn lap dances down, but don't make it a regular occurrence. What you do after hours and outside the club is your own affair. Clear?'

It wasn't totally at this stage, but I nodded my approval, regardless. I needed the job but also something was building up inside me that made me already look forward to the dancing, the stripping. The intuition that not only would I enjoy it, but that it would give me a sense of control. Over life. Over men. It was the same realisation I'd reached after my initial, amateurish blow jobs and the night I had lost my virginity. A feeling of power.

Barry's Liverpudlian tones chattered on.

'I'll take it as a given that you can dance, and as you're a friend of Chey, you won't have to pay the house a fee for every set like the other girls do, so all the money you make, from tips and private dances, is yours to keep. But please don't tell the other dancers about it. It would cause bad blood.'

Again I nodded.

'So when do you want to start?' he finally said.

I began my life as a stripper the following day. Lev fronted me a few bills so I could acquire a costume, which I improvised from various items I found in the market stalls that occupied the old parking lot next to the building that used to house Tower Records on Broadway, just a few steps away from Shakespeare & Co where I loved to go and browse the latest books. I also hunted for the right music and spent hours deciding what I would dance to. My first thought was to select something classical, Russian even, but I thought that might be an artistic step too far for the Bowery. I finally opted for Counting Crows' 'A Murder of

One'. There was something melancholy about the music that appealed to my Russian soul.

By the time I had packed and unpacked my bag for the tenth time that afternoon, checked that I had everything I could possibly need and heard the lock mechanism in the apartment door click shut behind me, I was almost ready to run back to the patisserie and offer Jean-Michel my arse to grope again so long as it meant that I didn't need to climb onto the stage that was waiting downtown for my approach like a block awaiting its next condemned man. But not quite. I was far too stubborn to allow a puny thing like fear get the better of me, and when my turn came I stepped out from behind the shabby dressing-room curtain with its beer stains and cigarette burns, squared my jaw and vowed to get on with it.

All the most important things in life, birth, death, losing one's virginity, seemed to involve the removal of one's clothes at some point or another and for me, stripping was just another one of those experiences to tick off, something that I had been building up to from the moment that I decided to skip ballet rehearsals in favour of pleasuring boys from the ice-cream parlour by the red-brick wall at the back of the school. As the music switched on and the familiar lyrics poured out of the loudspeakers, I wondered what kind of bird I had hidden inside, what manner of creature I would unleash when I dropped my flimsy costume and unveiled my nudity to the punters who were barely visible beyond the beam of light that I stood beneath.

I felt instinctively that I had crossed a Rubicon, selected a fork in the road that there would be no reversing from. No matter what I chose to do in the future, there would be no erasing this moment.

I raised my arms overhead, like wings, and began to dance.

3

Dancing with the Ponies

Initially, at the Tender Heart, I was distracted by the rundown grunginess of the club and found it awkward to reconcile my intentions to be graceful as well as sexy. The downbeat atmosphere of the principal auditorium, with its cheap wall hangings barely concealing old torn posters advertising long-gone appearances there by Patti Smith, Richard Hell & the Voidoids, and Television, combined with the tawdry disco tunes my fellow dancers performed to during their sets were a sharp dampener to any attempt to remain above the fray.

On my first night, apart from the fact I felt so terribly self-conscious and ill at ease in my unveiled skin, I made the mistake of shedding my minimal bikini and the assorted thin silk scarves I had thought would combine well with it and provide me with something to work with, leaving me standing at centre stage halfway through my music, totally nude and with nothing to do. Finding myself there, isolated, confronted by the vacant gaze of half a dozen bored customers whose facial features were all indistinct, I felt more like a mannequin than a dancer. I attempted an *entrechat* and nearly fell to the ground as my feet had no grip on the polished wooden stage. I quickly gave up on the idea of a few ballet moves for fear of appearing even more ridiculous.

I shimmied a bit, did a few turns, smiled as best I could. Then I repeated the feeble movements again and again, hoping for the tune to come to an end. I steered well clear of the rigid metal pole that dominated the stage and which all the other strippers that night had teased with, danced around, and embraced with pseudo-erotic abandon.

The hiss of silence in the loudspeakers came as a profound relief, as did the darkness which I took advantage of to quickly bend over and gather my scarves and shiny bikini and an orphaned five-dollar note that one of the spectators had deposited on the edge of the stage.

Later, some of the other girls, a varied bunch with a rapid turnover, one day here, another day gone, taught me how to dance around the pole, but it was never a discipline I took to.

I wanted to be different.

I also learned to time my effects and the stages through which I revealed my body, my assets. Since Chey and I had returned from the Dominican Republic where my blonde hair had bleached quite significantly in the sun, I had not had it cut and it was the longest I'd ever worn it. He liked it that way. Enjoyed gripping its ends hard when he rode me from behind. Now it was long enough to cover my breasts when I pulled it forward, an extra element of tease which the anonymous men who watched me, and the regulars I began to accumulate, seemed to like, my nipples winking through the curtain of falling hair.

Watching others, I also saw how they withheld the final reveal, only allowing the customers a brief, limited glimpse of their pussy just before the lights went out and the music climaxed, like a final tantalising treat. Surely, I felt, this was cheating; wasn't it what they had come for?

Now that I had shaven, I delighted in the spectacle of my smoothness and a small fire invariably lit in my belly before every set at the prospect of unveiling what was the most intimate part of me to all these strangers, knowing all they could do was look and not touch, wonder but not taste. It gave me the feeling I could lead them anywhere, make them do my bidding, just for a sight of my cunt.

'You're getting better and better, girl,' Barry remarked after watching my final set one evening, a few weeks after I'd begun working at the club. 'You were certainly clumsy at your first attempts, and I wouldn't have kept you on had you not been a friend of Chey's and had such a beautiful body. But you've come on in leaps and bounds.'

'That's nice to hear,' I replied.

'In fact, you're too good for this place. You should be dancing somewhere they have an appreciation of class. You're wasting your time here; you should be uptown where they tip better.'

It was true, the financial offerings of the Tender Heart's miserly spectators were far from impressive. And some of them were so unpleasant and uncouth that, by my second day, I'd decided to turn down private lap dances, and had formally informed Barry of this as a take-it-or-leave-it option.

He gave me some names and I went for interviews and auditions. There was still no news of Chey.

Once I made it clear I was in no mood for casting-couch antics and just there to dance and keep customers enter-tained, I was quickly offered the opportunity to perform in a better category of establishment and even had the chance to choose where I did so.

I began alternating between two private members-only clubs on the Upper East Side, which both catered for upmarket locals and the mostly foreign clientele staying at the four- and five-star hotels dotted around the Central Park area.

The gratuities were considerably better, and I soon settled into a routine, sleeping into the afternoons and working late nights and weekends, at Sweet Lola's or The Grand, where my classical background was admired and even encouraged, as two nights a week they had a pianist in and the girls did slower numbers to live music, in a cabaret style. I'd brought the house down and gained favour with Blanca, the beautiful Czech woman who managed the dancers, with a rendition of 'Makin' Whoopee!' that involved so little dancing and so much writhing on top of the piano that I felt as though I'd hardly had to work for that night's tips at all.

I even agreed to the occasional lap dance, as the punters at both of my new clubs were so much more upmarket than they had been at the place Barry ran, with their expensive suits and endless parade of dollar bills that they were only too happy to throw around at the slightest provocation. One man wanted me to do nothing more than remove my shoes for him and show him my bare feet. He would pay princely sums in exchange for just a glimpse of my toes, and even more if I allowed him to press his face close to my ankles as I stood *en pointe*, though I never allowed him to touch me. I was too afraid of losing my now comfortable position to risk stepping outside the management's rules for the sake of a little extra money.

The girls and I tried to split cab rides home wherever we could for safety's sake – we'd all had a scare when Gloria, one of the dancers who I worked alongside regularly, had been approached in the alleyway behind Sweet Lola's by a crazed fan who had taken a swing at her after she had spurned his advances – and also to save money. I was earning more than I'd dreamed possible at the Tender Heart, but I was still frugal with it, and so that night I'd asked the driver to stop once the meter totted up to the amount of change in my pocket plus a small tip and I'd walked the few blocks home from the corner of West 14th Street and 11th Avenue. It was 6 a.m. on a Sunday morning and the usually busy streets near the West Side Highway were quiet so I took a detour, walking up to the great steel arch of Pier 54 and watching the water of the Hudson River continue its gentle flow, glinting in the light of the rising sun. A local dance troupe ran performances and lessons here and I'd often thought of tagging along, perhaps even making some friends.

Things were going well for me now in New York, but even though I was used to my own company, I sometimes felt terribly frustrated and lonely without Chey. It wouldn't have been so bad if he'd only told me where he was going and when. I didn't want to appear a nag or a shrew, and I was perfectly capable of surviving without him, but I had been born into a world of straight lines, uniformity and precision and I resented the chaos that his unexplained and unscheduled absences lent to my arrangements. I wanted to impose some kind of order on my existence, cement the feeling that, pitiful though it might be, my life must have some kind of purpose.

I was in a reflective mood when I arrived back at the apartment, and still tired from that evening's exertions, so I didn't notice Chey's blazer hanging over the back of the chair in the second bedroom that he used as his office, the folded-up newspaper on the kitchen bench or the gentle hum of his space-age washing machine.

I had already begun my post-work ritual – tossing my hold-all costume carry bag onto the sofa in the lounge, to be unpacked when I was awake again, switching on the kettle to pour hot water over a tea bag and add a slice of lemon, reminding myself of the home country, splashing a little cold water on my face in the bathroom to wash away my night-time, dancing self from the regular, everyday person who kept her clothes on, most of the time – when I noticed him in the bedroom. I was by no means unobservant, but Chey moved like a cat, graceful, quiet, always like a coiled spring ready to be released. He could have crept up on a flock of pigeons without sending them skywards.

My initial pleasure at seeing him was quickly replaced by other, stronger emotions when I remembered his abandonment, and how this time I had planned to lay down the law, and tell him that I wouldn't be treated this way. Then I noticed what he was sitting next to. A colourful pile of chiffon and lace. The outfit that I had hastily tried on and discarded in favour of another as I packed my bag for that night's shift.

He took one look at the mixture of guilt and defensiveness that spread across my face and his expression hardened.

'I thought you only danced for me,' he said. 'Is this how you now dress at the patisserie? I went there to look for you, but learned you had left . . .'

'Then you thought wrong,' I replied haughtily. 'I dance for me. Not anyone else.'

That much was true enough. Until I had completed that first shift at the Tender Heart, I hadn't realised how much I missed the rigour of the steps, the flow of the music, the pleasure that I took from the applause of a satisfied audience, how I enjoyed watching all eyes fixated on the rhythm of my body.

'Why?' he asked. 'Did you not think that you could call me, that I would look after you?'

'I'm not your pet,' I told him peevishly, 'not some mail-order bride who just wants to sit at home and wait for you. Spending your money and fucking you in return like a whore.'

'You know I don't think of you like that,' he replied, visibly aggrieved.

I straightened my shoulders and set my jaw, prepared to argue to the bitter end. My independence had always been hard won, and consequently it was something that I valued highly. And if Chey didn't like it, then I would leave him, and use the money from my dancing to make my own way in life.

'I enjoy dancing. I missed it. And I won't be beholden to you, or to anyone.'

'You know that you're no prima ballerina in a place like that, Luba.' He waved a card for Barry's joint, which he had found crumpled up inside my bag.

I sighed. 'I'm not there any more. I've already moved to a classier joint, more in line with my style. And don't act like I'm a common stripper,' I insisted. 'You haven't even seen me perform.'

Eventually, we came to an agreement. He would watch one of my sets. If he liked it, he'd let me carry on. If he didn't, I'd give up dancing for money, though only if I could find another way to keep my mind and body occupied and earn a living of my own.

That night, he made love to me like a man possessed. As

if the ardour and the calculated hardness he inflicted on me as he thrust repeatedly inside me was a way of deepening our bonds at a primal level.

I'd never known Chey to be as tender and as rough, and it was a combination that both delighted and scared me, as if I was encountering the real Chey, a new 'him', and he was all of a sudden both a Prince and the Devil in human form.

Looking into his eyes as he relentlessly fucked me, his hands grasping my arse cheeks as I lay on my back and cushioned the savage need of his assault I could see that he was already imagining the way I looked naked for other men when I danced and this was his attempt to mark me as his once and for all and keep me from others' clutches. A form of jealousy, but one that made him so much more imperious, a lover like no others could ever be.

I spent even longer planning the first set that Chey would witness than I had planning my first ever dance at the Tender Heart. What would he enjoy, what would he approve of? True, I knew I didn't owe him anything, and I could do whatever it was that I pleased. But I liked Chey, and from the two alternatives available to me, continuing the status quo but with his blessing was undoubtedly my preferred option.

I felt, instinctively, that he would like my dance, just as he had on the beach. He would enjoy watching me. But I wanted to make absolutely sure that he would see that what I was doing was different. I wasn't merely a showgirl, shaking my titties for the tip jar. There was more to it than that. An art. I wanted more than his approval. I wanted his respect.

So I went out of my way to make sure that every detail of

my routine would appeal to his taste, from the stage lighting – white, not red – down to my outfit – a plain, floor-length gown, white cotton, like the one that I had worn on our holiday, which I could simply slip off my shoulders, without any elaborate strip tease. I went on stage barefooted, and performed my full set to one side, with the centre pole in darkness. For my music, I chose one of his favourite songs, something that I had heard him play in his office on the few occasions that he'd been at home, working on his computer. 'Devil in the Details', a home-grown American song by the Walkabouts, a track with a slow start rising to a more athletic crescendo that gave me a chance to start gradually, with more delicate movements, working into the more brazen steps. It was also my sign to Chey that I didn't forget him when I was dancing.

He came to my next set at Sweet Lola's. And when he told me afterwards that I was good, I flushed with pride.

His next comment, though, was like a slap across the face.

'But you could be better,' he added, just as he tapped the key code into the gated entrance to his apartment building.

I bristled immediately, but stopped myself from snapping back at him, remembering that my plan was to gain Chey's approval and support for my new venture, and if there was one thing that I had learned about men, it was that they liked to feel as though they were in control, even if they weren't.

'Really?' I responded with all the sweetness I could muster. 'Do explain.'

If Chey noticed the acidity in my tone, he didn't mention it.

'Classical steps should be set to classical music.'

'I did consider that, but thought it might be a step too far for the club. The Grand allows me a little classical—'

'Leave the clubs to me,' he replied firmly.

'Okay . . .' If Chey could broker me even more sway with the Madams, then so much the better. I wasn't too proud to accept his help, if it meant that I would have more creative freedom.

'And there's a wildness about your movements.'

'You're starting to sound like my Russian ballet teachers.'

'Well, your Russian ballet teachers were right. You would benefit from more restraint.'

Initially, his plans to influence my routines were entirely physical. He introduced me to his Dojo, a martial arts school on West 27th Street where I knew that he trained when he was in New York, keeping his body fit and his muscles taut, a habit that I in no way planned to discourage, as I would not date a man who allowed himself to get fat like his friend Lev.

Besides my dancing, I had never had any need or desire to take any formal exercise. Saw all that sweatiness as somehow ungainly and unnecessary; as once I had dropped my adolescent puppy fat, I had always been naturally slim. Even my daily breakfast at the patisserie – a pain au chocolat or choux Chantilly and frothy coffee – had not added a pound to my trim frame.

Chey led me through the reception area, tapping in his membership card and signing me in the guestbook as I surveyed my surroundings, the scent of dried sweat and damp towels, the few men and occasional woman in cheap and dishevelled exercise wear, and wondered how he thought that this might improve my dancing.

We passed an acquaintance of Chey's, who was wearing

only a pair of brightly coloured satin shorts and protective straps on his hands, mock-fighting himself in the mirror and I stifled a laugh as he preened when we walked by. He and Chey locked eyes in a gesture of recognition, and then the other man ducked his head, like a dog in a pack that knows he's just been cowed.

I was pleased to find that in Chey's company, no one ogled me; no one stared or seemed to find my presence unusual. I felt as though I stuck out here as much as I had when I first appeared on a stage, but Chey's naturally confident bearing and slightly fierce expression seemed to deflect the attention from me, which was nice for a change. I didn't like to be peered at unless I had explicitly granted the viewer permission, as I did when I was dancing.

He demonstrated some stretches, and basic movements. Muay Thai, he called it, and I found to my surprise that my dancer's body was naturally suited to the exercises. My legs and abdomen were strong, and my balance practised, so that when we moved onto the bags, I could kick and strike with ease and surprising power.

Next, he showed me a variety of basic hand-to-hand combat techniques, fitted pads onto his hands, and invited me to hit him, while he ducked and blocked to avoid me.

He was obviously allowing me to land most of my strikes successfully, and holding back his own strength to avoid hurting me, but even though I knew he was letting me win, I found myself revelling in the familiar stretch of my muscles, the dance with Chey as opponent instead of lover, the impact of my body on his body, the way that he looked as he dived and side-stepped to avoid a blow from my elbow or foot, the glow on his face as a slight sheen of sweat began to gather, highlighting further the definition of his muscles.

I paused momentarily to catch my breath and he leaned forward and kissed me, biting my bottom lip so hard that I nearly cried out in shock.

'You should have blocked,' he teased. 'You weren't paying attention.'

'I saw that coming from a mile off,' I insisted. 'Just didn't want to stop you . . .'

He lifted me straight off the ground and I wrapped my thighs around his waist, trapping him into a leggy embrace as he walked us over to the wall and pressed my back against the mirror.

'But the door's open. Someone will see . . .' I whispered, knowing that I didn't really want him to stop. Pressed between Chey and the smooth, cold mirror I felt my arousal growing. We were in one of the smaller studios, which held mats for stretching and a couple of punching bags, adjacent to a larger room that sported a full-size fighting ring, several bags attached to rings in the ceiling and a weight-lifting area.

'I don't care if they do,' he replied, lifting up my vest top and displaying my breasts, nipples already erect, to anyone who chose that particular moment to enter the space. 'Besides, no one will disturb us. I made sure of that.'

I wondered only momentarily what Chey had done that made the rest of the gym inhabitants seem so afraid of him. Perhaps he was a particularly strong fighter. Maybe he owned the Dojo. But all of those thoughts scattered from my mind when he lowered the elastic of my leggings and slipped a finger inside me, and then another.

'You seem to have enjoyed our session more than you let on,' he said, fingering the wetness that had seeped between my legs, in response to both the physicality of the situation and the vision of his firm body as he moved alongside me.

'So. Will you let me train you, mermaid?' It had become his name for me, ever since the dance on the beach.

'Yes,' I replied.

'Good,' he said, with an infuriating grin.

He lowered his head to my ear and pressed his lips against my lobe, his breath hot against my skin.

'Your first task is to learn to wait.'

He was teasing me, and my profound irritation at being so powerless in the situation was overwhelmed by the enormity of my arousal. I was so desperate to feel his hands all over me again, to feel his cock inside me once more and to enjoy whatever it was that his vivid imagination cooked up this time that I allowed him to simply unpeel my legs from his waist and rearrange my clothing into a semblance of order.

I felt stunned, drugged with desire, as he led me by the hand to the exit, totally aware and enjoying the fact that my nipples were visible through the thin fabric of my T-shirt.

But as soon as we returned to the apartment he was called away again, and amid apologies that he would make it up to me once more, he was gone and I was left alone, to eat, dance, sleep, and wait for him to come back again.

A week or so later, I came home to find an unusual costume laid out on the bed. I hadn't seen any of the girls in the club wearing anything quite like it before. A series of leather straps, metal buckles, and a pair of clips with bells attached that I guessed were designed to be attached to my nipples.

I'd seen one girl at Sweet Lola's perform a routine in a leather corset, black lace-up boots and a whip that she cracked with each pirouette, but her costume hadn't been quite like this, and neither was it the sort of outfit that I had guessed Chey had in mind for me. In my view, leather, PVC and the like were trashy items, the type of thing that hung in sex-shop windows, better suited to the sort of girls who needed something ostentatious to distract from the fact that they couldn't really dance at all, merely rub themselves against the stage pole and hope that no one would notice how dead their eyes were or how clumsy their steps.

Alongside the costume was a note: *Try it.*

Chey understood my temperament well. We were not so different at our core, each of us stubborn as hell and only liking an idea if we thought it was our own.

I fingered the straps. The leather was thick, but soft. It wasn't cheap or scratched. The buckles gleamed in the light, and the whole thing was well put together, as if it had been made by an experienced leather worker, not a factory that spawned cheap garments by the dozen.

I had to stand in front of the mirror and have a few tries before I worked out how to strap myself into it, but when I did, I was pleasantly surprised. The costume formed a harness which outlined each of my breasts and my pussy in a diamond shape, with a strap at the back that gently pulled my shoulders up, affirming my posture.

When I turned, Chey was standing in the doorway, smiling.

'You look good,' he said. 'I like it.'

'It's not what I expected. Not . . . classical. You think I should dance in this?'

The harness wasn't tawdry, but it was very different to my usual understated style for the stage, which I felt drew attention to the delicacy of my movements and underscored the fact that my performances weren't about sex. Or at least, not just about sex.

'Only for me,' he replied.

He lifted his hand to display an addition to the costume. A pair of long black platform boots with no heel at the back and a metal ring on the base, so they resembled a horse's hooves.

I lifted an eyebrow in question.

'They're good for balance,' he said. 'But very difficult to walk in. Or so I hear.'

Chey left the strange-looking boots at the bedroom door and glanced at me a moment longer, then began to loosen his tie and walk towards his office.

The idea of dressing like an animal seemed a little foolish to me, but I responded immediately to the prospect of a challenge. My dance teachers had criticised me for many things, but never my posture or my ability to stand *en pointe*.

The boots were made from a thin, soft leather with a camouflaged zip on the inside that ran three-quarters of my long legs, ending halfway up my thigh. At first, I had to hold onto a piece of furniture for support as I tentatively pushed myself up to standing, balancing on the platform of the shoe so that I could take a few short steps. It wasn't quite like a ballet step, as I couldn't straighten my foot completely, but with a little trial and error, I was able to adjust my posture so that I felt reasonably stable, if not as graceful as I would prefer.

To make the vision complete, I picked the clips up from the bed covers, with the bells attached, and fastened them carefully onto each of my nipples. The sensation wasn't painful, unless I knocked or jarred them. I took another look at myself in the mirror.

The effect was rather beautiful, if a little odd. I'd often been told, by Chey and by others, that I moved like an animal, and with my long legs and thin body, I supposed that I most resembled an equine. As a final touch, I brushed my blonde hair firmly into a ponytail which sat high atop my head like a horse's mane.

Then I walked, carefully, in short steps to his office to show him the finished result.

Chey looked up from his computer screen and grinned wickedly.

'Beautiful,' he said. 'Come here.'

I moved unsteadily towards him until I stood directly in front of his office chair, where he was reclining, now bereft of both his business shirt and tie and wearing just a pair of loose-cut jeans that sat low on his hips, exposing the V of his lower abdominal muscles.

'Spread your legs,' he said.

I complied, revelling in the fervour of his gaze, the appreciation with which he was admiring my body.

He tested my slit with his fingers, checking to see how wet I was, and then moved his fingertip around my clitoris in tiny circles, beginning slowly and then speeding up as I began to relax and press myself against him. My legs wobbled and I almost lost my balance as his caresses became more vigorous and I let out a low moan, inviting him to continue the dance of his hands on my body. He caught me as my thighs buckled and spun me around, pushing his papers out of the way and clearing a space on the desk that I could lean against.

The peculiar cut of the boots meant that my stance was

skewed. Within the shoes I was standing on my toes, my buttocks pushed into the air and my back arched, my forearms resting on the table. I could hear his breathing behind me grow ragged as he surveyed my form, and I imagined how I must look in the thigh-high boots with his leather harness framing my backside and restraining my natural movement. Each time I shifted forwards or back, the bells on the nipple clamps tinkled, reminding him that I had condescended to dress this way at his request, a fact that he seemed to enjoy as much as the way that I enjoyed his appreciation.

He grasped a handful of flesh from each buttock, pulling, kneading, then holding me open, spreading my arse cheeks wide and then testing the tightness of my anus very gently with just the tip of his finger.

I heard the sound of his office drawer rolling out, the click of a bottle lid, and then he resumed his ministrations, slipping one finger, and then a second inside my arsehole, while he continued to tease my clit with his other hand.

My knees were aching from the forced pressure of the awkward position necessitated by the boots, and my nipples throbbed beneath the clips, but all of those things faded to nothing as the pleasure from his touch swamped my brain and every thought turned to sensation, as if whatever part of me was conscious flooded out of my head and into my body.

'That's it, relax,' he soothed, and I felt myself opening up to him more, allowing him in, and I pushed back, feeling the head of his cock pressing against the nub of my arse.

If there was one thing that was sure to draw a stunned hush to any of the late-night dormitory conversations in my dreary state school in Donetsk, it was a mention that a man's cock might fit not just in a woman's pussy, or her mouth, but in another place as well, the most intimate and taboo of all: anal sex.

But once I had recovered from the initial shock of Chey's desire to explore me there, I found that I loved it, or, at least, that the feeling of his fingers inside me as he fucked me or played with my clitoris was certain to send me rocketing to an orgasm. Now I wanted to feel more, to feel his cock inside me, to allow him to possess all of me, fill me to the brim.

I gripped his desk with my hands, holding back a wince as my opening struggled to allow him in. He stopped, waiting for the initial discomfort to subside, stroking my back, caressing my neck, touching me softly in encouragement until I relaxed further and pushed back again, stretching to accommodate every last inch of him.

Then he began to thrust, at first gently and then harder as I moaned in pleasure and encouragement. He took hold of my hair tightly, wrapping its length around his wrist and pulled, guiding my movements as I bucked against him until I felt him stiffen and then release inside me.

I straightened my back, preparing to turn and kiss him but he held his hand down on my lower spine, directing me into position.

'No. Stay there,' he said softly, dropping to his knees so that I stood over him as he teased me with his tongue, licking my clitoris, delving deep into my lips in exactly the way that he knew I preferred, then flickering his tongue until I came with a cry. His face remained pressed against me, as though he wanted to drink in my orgasm, lap up every last ounce of pleasure that I expelled.

I was unable to support myself any longer and when my knees gave way beneath me he caught me in his arms and lowered me onto the floor, pressing his lips against mine in a slow, passionate kiss.

He knelt over me and removed the nipple clips gently, then unzipped each boot and eased them from my feet, massaging my ankles and toes as I felt the blood rushing back and my normal circulation returning.

'Why are you smiling?' I asked him, watching the look of amusement pass over his face.

'I wasn't sure if you'd do it. Wear the costume I bought you. Thought it might have been a step too far.'

I considered his comment.

'I wore it for me,' I said. 'To see if I could. To see what it would be like. Curiosity is my motivation for many things.'

'My curious cat.'

I half expected him to continue in the same vein and buy me a catsuit next, but he didn't. Instead, he gave me a tiny silver chain that fastened around my ankle, with a charm attached, so small that you would not have been able to identify the shape without looking at it closely. A horseshoe, fashioned from amber.

It was one of many gifts that he had bought me, each carved from the same stone. Those magic rocks he allegedly traded in, those stones from the depths of time on earth.

The next time I danced, I imagined he was riding me, that I was his pony girl. The dance was wild, excessive, animalistic; the colours in my cheeks so scarlet that for my second, later set of the evening I had to borrow some white concealer from another of the dancers or I would look like Snow White. After she'd been fucked by Prince Charming, of course.

Blanca, the Czech madam, tut-tutted as I left the stage,

but there was a complicit glint in her eye, as if she knew point by point what Chey had done with me the day before. I blushed even more as I passed her on my way to the dressing room.

'No pink, Luba. No pink.' And she wasn't referring to my cheeks. In my abandon, I had displayed too much to the men in the audience.

Not that any of them had complained to the house.

Until I met Chey, I never knew amber could come in so many shapes and colours.

Back in the Dominican Republic, in response to some of my initial questions about his trade, he had taken me to a small private museum sited in a run-down commercial centre, which housed an incredibly varied amber collection. He had explained how these stones had evolved from dead fossils into rare pieces and how the amount of cloudiness and shade affected their value. I had never worn or owned amber before, and my first gift from Chey was a large stone, which he had a local artisan set inside a steel locket. It was too heavy to wear as a necklace, so Chey suggested I might wear it as a bracelet that same evening, around my arm. I had spent a long time in the sun and discovered that I tanned with remarkable ease without burning, despite the natural paleness of my skin, although I had of course taken the precaution of rubbing much in the way of strong lotions and skin moisturising products into my shoulders and arms. He marvelled at the supernatural way the colour of the stone combined with that of my skin, in a mini-symphony of brown and orange where the demarcation line between live flesh and dead blurred. The dress I wore was white.

A few days later, he gave me a smaller amber piece,

almost milky in appearance, and presented it to me in bed, waking me from an afternoon slumber, ordering me to lay down on my back and almost spreadeagle myself across the crisp sheets, as a gentle breeze rustled the open curtains to the balcony that lead to the adjoining beach. Gently, he deposited the stone in the pronounced hollow of my belly button.

'It brings out the lioness shade of your cunt,' Chey said, pointing out to my pubic thatch and drawing a finger between the moistness of my opening in appreciation of my charms. I tried not to blush. And, of course, one thing quickly led to another and we were late for dinner. That night he had convinced me to sit at the table of the exclusive restaurant in which he had booked us, pantieless and my pussy still raw and screaming silently from the repeated assault of his caresses and his vigorous thrusts.

In New York, he added to my collection of amber pieces with exaggerated generosity, each piece tailored to my mood, the clothes he bought for me or the shades my body passed through when he fucked me and turned our lovemaking into a ceremony that bordered on the holy.

I could swear that whenever I danced within a day or less of being fucked by Chey, every anonymous male gaze in the audience knew all about it, just by watching the way my breasts swayed, my cunt gleamed or my arse shone in the target of the spotlight. The thought excited me. Wildly.

I was wanton, I was a woman. I was Chey's woman.

If only he wouldn't keep disappearing without warning, refusing to tell me where or why he was going. My heart and sex called out for him in the middle of the night in the large empty bed, and those nights went on for ever, my whole soul missing him, my body in the grip of withdrawal symptoms, my need to be filled like a hunger that could never be sated.

It was after another of those long nights that the worst happened.

I had been celebrating a record evening for tips with Alice and Maya, two other Russian dancers who worked the same circuit as me, at the bar of the Algonquin on 44th Street, dressed in all our finery, which by then I could afford. We were leaving the hotel and hailing separate cabs to drive us to our respective homes, in my case the mostly empty Gansevoort Street apartment that I shared with Chey, when I caught sight of a familiar silhouette lumbering across the opposite sidewalk. I hadn't seen Lev for weeks, since he'd introduced me to Barry and the Tender Heart.

I called out for him and he looked over, a furtive, embarrassed air about him at seeing me. At first, it seemed that his initial instinct was to flee from my presence, then he did a double take and waited for me to cross the road and join him by the steps leading up to the Royalton Hotel where the Philippe Starck bar was one of Manhattan's classy joints.

'Luba.'

'Hi, Lev . . .'

'You look . . . good . . .' His eyes seemed to be avoiding mine.

His nose was bulbous and distinctly misshapen, there were black and purple circles beneath his eyes and the way he stood betrayed a limp or some pain in one of his legs.

'What happened to you?' I asked.

'You didn't know?'

'No.'

'Chey didn't tell you?'

'I see so little of him, but tell me.'

He hesitated a moment then looked me in the eye. 'He did it. He beat me.'

'Why?' I asked, incredulous.

'Because of you.'

'Me?' What had happened? I was genuinely perplexed. Had this been Chey's immediate reaction, I might have understood it. I guessed that Lev or Barry must have told Chey how I found my way to the Tender Heart, and his anger was unsurprising. I knew men could be jealous. But I had now been dancing for weeks, and after his initial shock, Chey had seemed accepting of my profession, even proud of me and the way that I danced. I could feel myself beginning to boil inside, adding this to the long list of things that Chey kept secret from me, that he lied about.

'Well, he was unhappy that I suggested you should go . . . dancing. He was furious. I've never seen him so angry.'

'He did . . . this to you?' I appraised his bruised features. He was unappealing at the best of times, but now looked like a recovering gargoyle. I remembered the way that the men at his Dojo had avoided Chey's gaze. No wonder, if this was what he did to his friends at the slightest provocation.

'The nose has been reset,' Lev said. 'The marks will go, given time. And my leg will get better.'

I was furious. Lev was just a passing acquaintance and not someone I would choose to spend much time with. But he had been there when I needed him. How could Chey not only have done this but also kept it from me?

'He's a jealous man, Luba. It's just that you don't realise the power you have inside you. It can do that to men, you know.'

The yellow cab I finally caught couldn't race down 5th Avenue towards the Meatpacking District fast enough for my liking. I was seething inside and absolutely determined to have it out with Chey once and for all and discover who he really was, whether it would suit me or not.

Of course, when I arrived, he was not at home. Worse, his closet door had been left open and bore witness to the fact that he'd packed in a hurry and at short notice. Which meant he would be away for at least a week, if not longer.

On my bedside table, his idea of a parting gift was yet another piece of amber. The tenth, by my reckoning. But I was determined not to let him get away this time. I jumped into the shower and, full of rage, scrubbed myself clean, as if I was washing Chey away from my skin.

Later, wandering across the vast apartment in darkness, and unable to compose myself enough to go to bed and find sleep, I noticed a drawer in his study had been left open.

Inevitably, as it was always locked, as were so many other areas in the apartment, I approached and snooped.

Sheets of uninformative shipping documents in a variety of languages, a surprising amount of paperclips and elastic bands and beneath this mess, a gun.

Black and shiny.

Smelling of oil.

My heart jumped.

I gingerly picked it up and looked at it closer.

A Sieg Sauer.

It looked dangerous but beautiful.

Like my lover.

My heart sank.

After fleeing Russia, had I ended up with an American bad man, an American gangster?

4

Dancing with the Guns

When I found the gun, my whole world went cold.

I knew that America being America, it was relatively common to own a gun. But not one like this. Chey's gun, like almost everything else he owned, looked expensive. It was sleek, steel grey, recently polished and easily accessible in the top right-hand drawer of his desk where most people would keep the things that they used most often, their spare pens and paper clips, perhaps a diary. Not a lethal weapon.

I might have invented excuses for him, pretended that he kept it as protection against burglars, if I hadn't then found the silencer alongside. I'd never seen one before, other than on television, but the long, slim, metal attachment could not be anything else. And no one uses a silencer for protection. A person defending their own home would surely want to make as much noise as possible to alert the neighbours to call for aid. Only the hunters needed silencers, not the hunted. The people with something to hide. Like Chey.

I pieced it all together.

The lies. The long and unexplained absences. His association with Lev. His wardrobe of ill-matching outfits with no particular style, designer suits hanging alongside athletics team sweatshirts advertising universities I knew he hadn't attended. All the money, the bribery, the expensive lifestyle and business meetings held in odd locations all over the city. The locked drawers. The papers on his desk in a myriad of languages, notes written in his hand in much more complex Russian than he purported to speak.

He was some kind of gangster. Of what sort I didn't know, drugs or weapons or something worse. Whatever it was, I didn't want to know. I'd seen enough Hollywood films and knew enough about the black market from the boys who made a living selling nylons and cigarettes to young Russian girls to realise that the more you knew, the more likely you were to end up floating in the Neva River, or, in my case, the Hudson.

I should have rolled the drawer shut right then and walked away but Chey's gun called to me like a siren song, deadly and beautiful, and my hands slipped into the drawer and stroked the length of hard silver before any rational thought could pipe up to tell me to leave, to run, to pretend that I had never seen it.

It slipped into my hands as though it was made for me, the barrel as sleek and svelte as the body of a woman and the trigger just begging to be touched, held, caressed.

I held the gun with my arms straight out in front like I had seen in so many action films and paced through the house, spinning one way and then another, pirouetting suddenly to turn and aim at an imaginary enemy. I caught sight of myself in the bedroom mirror, where I had last stood and observed myself trussed up in his pony harness, before we'd had sex in his office. Right alongside the drawer with the gun in it.

My pose was confident. Arms fully extended, elbows locked, abdominal muscles tensed, eyes gleaming in an expression halfway between lust and violence.

At that moment, I felt as though I understood him at last.

The animal in him, the attraction to danger, the survival urge inside that overpowered every other instinct even when it meant hurting the people who loved us.

Then the pain hit me like a fist, with anger gearing up behind it for a second blow.

A ball of hurt, upset and betrayal grew deep in my belly, and then flew through my limbs and down the barrel of the gun.

I swung.

Lifted my arms.

And fired.

There was a loud bang. And then a smash, and a crash, as the glass front of his forty-inch flat-screen TV shattered onto the floor. I reeled backwards across the room as my shoulder nearly blew straight out of its socket from the sheer force of the cartridge moving through the barrel.

My ears were ringing. So much for the silencer, and all the movies I'd watched that had promised nothing more than a barely audible 'phut'. The sound of the shot alone had reverberated like an avalanche through the apartment building and in my imagination, must surely have roused all the neighbours, not to mention the shattering of the TV screen over Chey's polished wooden floors.

I wasn't going to wait around to provide an explanation, to Chey, to the neighbours, to the police or to anyone, and in doing so, reveal the fact that I was now aware of his secret. The authorities might think that I was an accomplice. Chey's enemies, of which he no doubt had many or else he would have no need for weapons, might think I was their enemy also. His friends might think that I had information that made me dangerous. Chey himself might think that I had discovered some secret that I couldn't be allowed to keep.

And so I fled.

Gathering all of my possessions into the tote bag that he had bought for me to keep my work things tidy, I disappeared onto the streets. I always felt safest when surrounded by people, so I walked towards the bustle of Times Square and Midtown. I knew that I would be invisible amongst the tourists and commuters that packed like sardines onto the sidewalk, all moving in silent rhythm, faces transfixed on the surrounding screens playing their ceaseless procession of music clips and adverts, hands busy tapping into smartphones or fiddling with other gadgetry and no one paying the slightest attention to me.

At first, I was too afraid to be upset, or even angry.

Each footstep too close to my own, the clang of metal on stone as a dog raced by, its lead scraping the sidewalk and its owner struggling to keep up, the honk of horns as the yellow cabs vied for space on the surrounding streets made my pulse race and the blood hum in my veins.

I stopped to buy a cold drink and a bag of pretzels from a street vendor so that I would have something to do with my shaking hands, then I found a vacant bench to sit on and consider my options.

My insides were in turmoil, every nerve, muscle and sinew coiled and ready to spring, as though I was permanently waiting for the next beat in a song that was stuck on pause. My thoughts scattered like pigeons in the wind, tears streaked down my cheeks as my sadness mixed with anger and I wasn't sure whether I wanted to punch him or kiss him.

So this was how it felt to have a broken heart.

I tossed a piece of pretzel onto the sidewalk in front of me and ground it into dust beneath my shoe, imagining all the things that I would shout at Chey if I had the opportunity to tell him exactly what I thought of him, how much better off I would be without him, how little I needed him.

But moments later I would remember all the things that I had loved about him, and my heart would break all over again.

A kid with a purple Mohawk flew past on a yellow skateboard and spat, nearly hitting my leg with his spittle. I yelled an obscenity in Russian at him and he laughed and rolled away to join his friends, all of them smiling encouragement at him and yelling back at me.

This added provocation mixed with the nugget of fury that had settled in my chest and it grew and grew, overtaking my hurt and my broken heartedness and reminding me of the present and my new reality. I had no Chey to call on. I was on my own, and the first thing that I needed was a safe place to stay tonight where I could plan what to do next.

Blanca was the first person I thought to call.

The only person.

She was the lead hostess at the Grand, and the woman that I felt the most affinity with. Perhaps because she was also Eastern European and had left her homeland behind for New York. Most of the other girls at Sweet Lola's and the Grand were American, and I had little in common with them. Selma and Santi hailed from Mexico and Gina was from Argentina, but they were new and had barely spoken a word to me and I to them. I supposed I ought to make more of an effort to be friendly but I saw little point when others were not inclined to be friendly to me, and when most of them didn't last more than a handful of shifts anyway.

Blanca appeared on the doorstep as I approached her loft apartment in Williamsburg, Brooklyn, not too far from my old quarters in Queens, but much more upmarket. She did okay for herself, I thought, as she showed me through to the kitchen with its shiny stainless-steel fittings and the airy living room adjacent where I would be sleeping on a fold-out couch. Probably scooped off some of the dancers' tips as well as her own wage and the house fare that the other girls paid for each set. But, as far as I was concerned, she was worth every penny, for making sure the Grand kept its upmarket feel and not lowering standards as the other bars in the area had done for the sake of cheap girls and easy money.

It was the first time I'd seen her outside of work, where she usually dressed in long, flowing gowns with her ample cleavage displayed like two plump white bread rolls begging to be taken into a willing mouth.

Today she was wearing a pair of jeans and a plain white blouse, her auburn hair scooped up into a loose bun on top of her head. She was about the same height as me, but in contrast with my thinness, Blanca had a full-figured, ample form. I guessed she was in her thirties. I knew that she had danced for years at the Grand before taking over as the girls' supervisor, and it showed; her figure was round in all the right places but also firm and meaty and when she turned to show me around the apartment my eyes drifted down to admire her buttocks, perky and wonderfully fleshy, sculpted tight beneath the denim fabric of her trousers.

As I watched Blanca's arse sway with each step, it occurred to me that I might have another option besides men. My relationship with the male species had always been a matter of give and take. One asset exchanged for another. A matter of rational calculation, cold hard logic. Romance, sure, but more than that was the matter of survival, of sex in exchange for safety and comfort. Not that I didn't like the sex. But even that was a transaction, my body for his, one orgasm granted in return for another experienced.

Maybe it would be different with women. Less of a power trip and more of a meeting of equals.

For the first few nights, I distracted myself from the pain with a mixture of fury and lust, remembering all the ways that Chey had hurt me and all the reasons that I had to hate him, or by wondering about Blanca's voluptuous body standing nude under the hiss of the shower water in her tiny bathroom, questioning whether her nipples stood erect parting the flow of the droplets that ran over her skin as she massaged herself with soap, and whether her pussy was still shaved like a dancer's or if she had allowed her hair to return, covering her inner secrets like a curtain. I would ease myself to sleep by slipping my hand under the thin blanket and caressing my own smooth mound until an orgasm sent me to my dreams happy and light headed quicker than any drug.

But Blanca didn't give me any reason to think that she returned my affections, and her arse remained firmly zipped into her jeans for the duration of my stay. Worse still, I wasn't the only girl that she provided a refuge for, and I was soon sharing the fold-out couch with Dee-Dee, a Jamaican girl who had just arrived in New York City and walked straight into the arms of a Lev or a Barry who had upgraded her to Blanca once they realised that she had some rhythm in her long legs and breasts good enough to appear in a lingerie catalogue.

With the sleeping Dee-Dee snoring alongside me and her thick limbs taking up most of the bed, my episodes of nightly self-pleasuring disappeared and my dreams turned darker, full of bullets and steel barrels that I pictured in all different forms. Sometimes I was inside the gun, dancing like a Bond girl, sometimes the gun was pressed to my forehead with Chey holding the trigger, and sometimes it was inside me, the icy length of the Sieg Sauer filling me to capacity and leaving me at the edge of a climax that was both terrible and immense in its pleasure.

Trying to keep the thoughts of Chey out of my head and the subsequent pain out of my heart was like trying to dam a river with clay. Certain to fail. I still missed him, although I tried to pretend that I didn't. Missed his mind, missed his company, missed his hard body and his cock and all of the wonderful things that he did to me on the rare nights that he was home.

It was painful to know we lived in the same city and that, at any moment, our paths could cross. On the street, in a bar, anywhere. I kept away from both the Meatpacking District and Chey's apartment, as well as the Upper East Side where the clubs he knew I had worked in were situated. I knew that if I came across him, I might not be strong enough to resist his attraction and I would listen to any old hoary story that he might conjure up to justify his periodic absences when we had been together, and the presence of the gun in the drawer.

Part of me begged for the opportunity of a fortuitous encounter, however unlikely the chances were in such a vast place as Manhattan, while the more sensible side of me feared such a thing happening and the way I might react.

Chey was under my skin.

He knew I liked to spend much of my leisure time browsing in bookshops, and in particular Shakespeare & Co on Broadway where the staff didn't mind my hanging around and casually flitting from book to book reading a page here and a page there before normally settling an hour or more later for a cheap paperback. So I had to avoid the store and moved my allegiances to the Strand where I could lose myself in the heavy crowds. Moving between the aisles and floors or leafing through volumes there, I would sometime feel the gaze of someone looking enquiringly at my back, and every single time I thought it would be Chey, and, heart buzzing, I would turn round only to find it was just another man attracted by my looks and unaccustomed to seeing a foreign-looking blonde in a bookstore who didn't fit the identikit pattern of female readers.

A couple of months went by and Blanca informed me that there had been no sign of Chey at either of the clubs attempting to track me down and that maybe I should return to work. Possibly, with a few weeks at places down on Long Island or out in New Jersey first, to get my dancing mojo back into gear and allay my nervousness at performing again in the city.

I agreed and began to peruse realtor's lists and windows with the thought of finding myself a small place to live, a rental, maybe in the West Village. Alone. I wanted my own space, the opportunity to think, lounge, slob at will, and the past weeks staying at Blanca's with her and the revolving door of other dancers with whom I had little in common was beginning to prove tiresome. The conversation was limited and I was growing weary of being asked to share some of my clothes and, invariably, make-up with them at the slightest opportunity. I needed breathing space.

I declined the out-of-town option.

'No, I want to work the Grand again,' I told Blanca. 'If they'll have me. I like the place and no man is going to stop me doing what I want. Anyway, they have sturdy bouncers . . .'

'Oh, that they have, my dear,' Blanca said.

My resolve had returned, and together with Blanca, we plotted my grand return to the dance floor. I perfected a new routine. Fine-tuned the music. Acquired the perfect outfit and discreet accessories for the occasion.

'Luba's Grand Return to the Grand.'

We giddily devised a small leaflet advertising my initial appearance and it was decided that following my one-off set on the Saturday night, I would only grant a single lap dance. To the highest bidder.

I was defiant, confident Chey would not dare come along and get involved.

And if he did, I would flaunt myself with every wanton sinew in my body, show him what he was now missing, provoke him even, display to every man all the things I would never grant him again. To prove I was no longer just his pony girl, but a woman every man desired.

There was a big corporate IT convention on in town, at the Javits Center, and the club that night was packed, lines of limos parked at the kerb, powerful engines roaring softly, chauffeurs at the ready, and a multitude of sharply dressed and suited executives lining up to enter the premises once they had satisfied the scrutiny of our bunker-sized bouncers.

While the other dancers did their thing, I sat in the

dressing room, all dressed up, made up and with nowhere to go, with a posse of butterflies doing the tango inside my stomach. Still wondering whether his eyes would be in the audience, watching, lusting after me, missing me, maybe?

There was a resounding hush as the lights went out and I took my place on the dark stage.

The loudspeakers awoke and released my spoken intro-duction: 'My name is Luba . . .' My voice, my Russian lilt, my huskiness. It had taken me over an hour to perfect those four words as an overture for the Debussy music. I'd wanted to sound mysterious, remote, alluring, the very essence of me.

The performance went by in a dream.

It felt as if I was the only person present.

Buried deep within the cocoon of the dance, a prisoner of the searing spotlight, a white body connected to the red-hot circle of a private sun. I'd even got the management to dismantle the dance pole so that nothing obscured the sightlines or distracted the men's implacable gaze while I performed.

I was flesh incarnate. I was the queen of the night. I was sex, breasts, cunt and arse. Every moment I had rehearsed was planned so that every single man present would desire me with a vengeance, would gasp, pant, grow hard like rock, lust uncontrollably for me with every atom in his body. I wanted them all to yearn, to want me more than they had ever wanted anything in their life before I had walked on the Grand stage and opened their eyes.

But, at the same time, I also danced for myself, alone, ignoring the waves of sexual greed washing across me, as they journeyed from the audience in sheer red heat across the stage, my domain.

It worked.

As I flew from the stage when the darkness returned and provided me with a safe harbour, sweat pouring from me, my cheeks burning, my scalp itching in sympathy, my insides literally on fire with sexual need, Blanca gave me a sideways glance and whispered, 'That was on the borderline of totally obscene and beautiful, Luba . . . You keep on surprising me . . .' And she winked at me in complicity.

The other dancers gave me curious looks, as if I had overstepped the bounds or personally offended them. It did not bother me. For them, dancing was just a job. For me, it was now an extension of who I was.

Over the Tannoy, I could hear Blanca back on stage enthusiastically orchestrating the auction for my unique lap dance.

His name was Lucian and he became my first millionaire and my second fuck.

From afar, in Russia, or more specifically in a shithole like Donetsk and the Ukraine, California was an unreachable paradise. An idealised place where the sun shone continuously over a landscape of blue seas, palm trees and ostentatious affluence. Much like the Caribbean, where Chey had taken me, but without the inescapable, surrounding poverty. A promised land that only gangsters and their molls could reach outside of their dreams.

And now I was there.

Courtesy of Lucian, my software geek extraordinaire.

I don't know how much he paid for his private audience with me in the club's lap-dance room; later Blanca just handed me a wad of notes which I didn't even bother counting, not only the proceeds of the auction but also the barrage of green bills that had been thrown onto the stage by appreciative male members of the audience at the end of my set. I never bothered to stay around and pick up these tips, as I found it both undignified and degrading to have to crouch there still naked with the glaring lights back on and gather the notes. Blanca always took care of that for me. Said it gave me a sort of unapproachable mystique, another aspect of mine the other dancers heartily resented.

The lap dance was unexceptional. He did not attempt to touch me, and I barely ground against him as he seemed satisfied just watching me shimmy and squirm a few inches away from him, wearing my white bikini and my pale skin, allowing my own hands to travel seductively across my breasts, belly and thighs in a form of self-loving that I knew men appreciated, his eyes agog in a parody of worship, not even a faint smile on his closed lips. The music I had selected – a track by the English trip hop group Archive – faded to a halt and I stepped back from him. In the semi-darkness there was no way he could conceal the pronounced tent of his erection inside his khaki slacks. He wore his old-fashioned heavy-framed glasses slightly askew.

'That's it,' I said. 'I hope you liked it.'

'You really are Russian?' he stated.

'One hundred per cent.'

'I think Russian women are beautiful,' he said. 'Different.'

'Exotic?'

'No, that's not what I meant,' he added. He paused, as if struggling for words. I came to his rescue.

'We are all different. Like women everywhere, you know. I'm actually from the Ukraine. Girls from the other republics sometimes look very different. Some of us have very long legs, others have prominent cheekbones and those from the Asian borders can have slightly slanting eyes and low-slung arses. There is so much variety. You mustn't generalise.'

'I realise that,' he said. 'But . . .'

He fell silent. I was about to walk away and he called after me.

'Is Luba your real name, or just a stage one?'

'It's my birth name, yes. Actually, it's a diminutive for Lubov, but no one uses that much.'

'Luba,' he said, as he if was savouring every letter of the name on the tip of his tongue like a culinary delicacy.

He was in his mid to late forties but looked, and dressed, ten years younger, had made his fortune developing software and then licensing it to some of the leading corporations in the field. He had then invested some of the proceeds in other start-ups, including Google and Facebook, and no longer needed to work for the rest of his existence. He spent much of his ample spare time devising role-playing games, mostly for his own edification, seldom bothering even to take them to market. He had a large, rambling canalside house in Venice Beach where friends and hangers-on came and went at leisure. His soul had never grown up and he was still a worshipper at the altar of beauty and found it difficult to relate to women.

Quite the opposite of Chey. Who, right now, had left me scarred and empty and must have been, yet again, out of town on some illegal errand or job, or he would have otherwise been in the audience at the Grand tonight and made himself known, if not begged me to return to his fold.

'Would you dance for me again?' Lucian asked.

'Not tonight?' I said. 'It was a one-off. I must stick to the rules.'

'Tomorrow, then?' he asked.

'I don't work every day,' I replied.

'I'll pay,' he added.

'It's not a question of money,' I said.

'Oh . . .'

He was just a man and right then I knew I was a puppet mistress.

'Where are you from?' I asked.

'Omaha, Nebraska,' he said. 'But I now live in California.'

As he said that, all of a sudden New York felt like a sad, cold and grey place, full of the memories of Chey and everything that hadn't worked out, and I had a hunger for something new.

'I will dance for you there,' I said. 'Take me to California and I will.'

His eyes lit up.

'Two conditions,' I quickly improvised, noting his reaction. 'We go tomorrow and I cannot promise that I will sleep with you. Maybe I will, maybe I won't. We'll just see. Play it by ear, but we can always be friends.'

He gulped.

He was a nice man, but a voice inside me was whispering maliciously in my ear that good men would never prove enough and that only bad ones could now fill me and my soul. But Lucian, right then, was the next best thing and I was damn well seizing the opportunity.

I knew he'd proven the highest bidder for the lap-dance auction, but never even guessed how wealthy he was.

I only found out when we passed through the VIP terminal at JFK and were driven to a private hangar where he'd leased a private jet that stood in waiting for us.

I stayed true to my word, and danced for Lucian in the enormous lounge in his Venice Beach house that overlooked a quiet canal. Every night.

I became his private dancer.

Daytimes, while he was working in his study at the back of the house, I would go for a walk along the boardwalk, sometimes reaching as far as Santa Monica, where I'd invariably reward myself with an ice-cream at the end of the pier. On every occasion, a different set of flavours to break up the monotony.

I became a tourist in La-La Land. One of thousands of pretty women.

After every dance, Lucian would leave a wad of notes for me, keeping our relationship as a strictly businesslike transaction.

Behind his glasses, he watched me move like a kid in a candy shop, ever embarrassed by his erections. I told him he could touch himself if he wanted, but he was too shy to do so in my presence. After a week of this, I went to his room one night and slept with him. I owed him that.

Lucian was adequate but no more. Tenderly clumsy, affectionate, annoyingly verbal, although every time his babbling flow of words became too soppy and sentimental I would promptly bring my fingers to my lips and quiet him.

Apart from the sex, it felt as if I was living with the brother I'd never had. Once I'd moved into his bedroom, I continued dancing for him in the evenings, but refused to accept his money. It didn't feel right any longer.

But I was not made out to be a woman of leisure and the blandness of California and Lucian's gentle personality soon began to tire me.

'I'm a dancer,' I told him as we were sipping mojitos on the terrace of a plush restaurant on Figueroa Boulevard one evening. I'd spent the afternoon shopping downtown but even the clothes in California failed to enthuse me. 'I need to dance, for an audience, not just for one guy. Or I don't feel whole . . .'

He sighed, as if he sensed what I had in mind.

'It's your life, Luba. I won't stop you.'

I made him swear he would not try to come to the places where I might find work. Explained how I wanted to keep our private life and my professional dancing strictly apart. He reluctantly agreed.

I found a gig at the White Flamingo near Burbank. It was a dive, and the tips were poor, but I could lose myself in the dance. The shady operators who ran the joint couldn't keep their hands to themselves and insisted I play more cheerful music. I didn't kid myself: it was stripping, not dancing any more.

It was like living in two separate worlds, both carefully insulated from each other. The gaudy lights of the Burbank club at night and the peaceful byways of Venice Beach and Lucian's house throughout the day. Any girl would have yearned for the latter, but something inside me was madly attracted to the danger and glamour of the former.

Lucian had to go to Canada for a conference in London, Ontario, and I accompanied him to the airport. He had arranged for the hire limo to drive me back home after we'd parted. Barely five minutes away from LAX, the driver had just come off Airport Boulevard and had taken a minor road that would lead us to the coast when I spotted a large ramshackle building on our right. A sign outside flickered feebly in the daylight sun. 'SIN CITY' and below the capital letters: 'Dancers Badly Needed'. It was more of a sprawling shack, with whitewashed walls and a corrugated-iron roof. I asked the driver to stop, got out and dismissed him.

The manager was Russian. His accent was from the Baltic regions.

'You know how to dance?' he asked. His breath smelled of vodka.

'I do.'

'Ah, Russki . . .' There was no hiding the fact once I opened my mouth.

'I'm in America. I speak English here.'

He nodded and gave me a familiar look. I stripped and faced him.

'Small tits,' he remarked, grabbing hold of one and checking its firmness. His hand was strong and calloused. 'The Americans, they like bigger. If you want, we can pay for operation, and then you pay back over a few months, no?'

'No,' I said. 'I stay this way. Big is not my style.' I stared at him defiantly.

'You have a name?' he asked.

'Luba.'

He purred in appreciation, and recited the house rules. For what they were worth – apparently almost anything went here.

The devil in me wanted to know how low I could stoop. Would I go full circle and end up giving blow jobs at the back of the club against its whitewashed walls?

I agreed to start the following day. Final shift of the day. There was a bus stop round the corner of Sin City, and the bus took me all the way to the Venice Beach seafront, with its gaudy parade of T-shirt stands, parading roller skaters and run-down bars. I was about to take one of the streets that led inland to the canals and Lucian's house when my attention was caught by the imposing silhouette of a tall blond man in running gear exiting a store. For a moment my heart stopped, but I focused my gaze and realised he was nothing like Chey, just the same height and build.

As my breath returned to its natural rhythm, I noted the colourful images spread across the shop window. It was a tattoo parlour.

Had it been a sign? A further indication that my life was about to change? For good or for bad.

I walked in.

'I want a tattoo.'

The guy, all long hippie hair in dreads, looked up at me.

When he asked where I wanted the tattoo, my response was immediate.

I knew I was a creature formed by sex and that it would always be a part of me.

I slipped out of my skirt and panties.

'Here.' I pointed to the area of my cunt.

He was not taken aback in the slightest and handed me a sheet of possible illustrations.

'Most popular images there are roses or dolphins. You choose the size. I'll price accordingly.'

I declined the examples. 'I know what I want,' I said.

And fell silent.

'What?' he asked.

'A gun,' I said.

I sat in a worn leather chair at the back of the store,

which reminded me of a dentist's. But the rest of the room was surprisingly light, clean and sterile, almost high tech in its clean lines. I had expected something sordid.

It hurt like hell. Like nothing I had ever felt before.

A little like how it might feel to have a scalpel slowly cut across heavy sunburn. Halfway between the pain of severe heat and severe cold. But it also felt terribly erotic, and the wetness spread between my legs as the skilful but apparently indifferent tattooist went about his job, his touch as light as feather and delicate.

He stepped back and handed me a small rectangular mirror in which my naked cunt stared back at me.

And the closely adjoining new tattoo.

The minuscule gun.

It even looked like Chey's Sieg Sauer.

I was whole, no longer empty, and Chey was forever a part of me.

The tattoo opened something up inside me. It was as if the tattooist had tapped into a vein, marked my soul as well as my skin.

It was a tiny drawing. A gun, unremarkable from a distance. To the patrons who sat at the tables metres from the stages I danced on, it could have been anything. A Chinese symbol, my star sign (I was an Aries), a flower. But any man, or woman for that matter, who got close enough would recognise the barrel of the Sieg Sauer that pointed directly at my sex.

I noticed a change both in me and in my customers from the moment that I was inked.

My movements became more athletic, riskier. I chose darker music, danced to Radiohead's 'Creep' and Jimi

Hendrix's 'Voodoo Child'. I sashayed like a femme fatale, twisted like a woman possessed and showed as much pink as I damn well pleased, and if management didn't like it, they soon changed their tune when I became the star performer every night.

The men at the bars and downmarket clubs I now found myself dancing in loved it. I was the dangerous one, the wild girl, and the more wild they believed me to be, the wilder I became.

Inevitably, Lucian began to bore me. He fucked in one of the same three ways each and every time: missionary, doggy style, or me on top. Always in the bedroom at the same time three or four evenings per week with the same feeble expression on his face and he thrust only until he was spent, never bothering to check whether I had also orgasmed.

I didn't fake it, like the girls in the dormitories had always insisted was the polite thing to do if you wanted to keep your man happy. I didn't give a damn. Instead, I waited for him to roll off me and fall asleep and then I turned over and teased myself to climax, wetting my fingers with the seed he'd spilled inside me and then performing a familiar dance across my clitoris until I felt the customary fire surge through my loins and into my mind and heart.

When I wasn't dancing, or masturbating, I felt vacant. California was too sanguine for me. Once the fun wore off, I found the city and its inhabitants vacuous. I missed the cold winters and the melancholy of New York, and even of St Petersburg. And, not being able to drive, I was forced to use cabs everywhere, which, despite Lucian's generosity, irked and cost me.

I was empty.

Naturally I could have turned to drugs and alcohol like

the other girls at the clubs who numbed their senses before and after every shift to make the time pass and the undressing easier, but I pitied them, and then began to find them pitiful, snorting their earnings up their noses each night to get them through the next.

But very quickly, the whole bright Californian tackiness got to me badly, the flat light, the anomie, and I realised that even my dancing was suffering and I was all too often going through the motions and, possibly, stooping to the vulgar levels of the other dancers. I was on a downwards path.

The men I was beginning to accept into my bed whenever I felt in need of something more substantial than Lucian weren't even exciting any longer. Or bad enough. They were just indifferent.

Maybe it's something about being Russian.

You become philosophical about things, pragmatic even.

I knew something would come up.

And it did.

Following a run-of-the-mill set performed to a house full of surfers and leather-clad bikers and mechanics in a joint close to LAX, I met Madame Denoux.

She'd been in town scouting for talent in the classier places off Beverly Hills and Hollywood, after a fruitless trek through the silicone-infested stages of Orange County, where the girls were getting younger and more artificial by the day. Her flight back to New Orleans had been delayed due to bad weather conditions in the north-west and, put up in one of airport hotels, she was killing time visiting the nearest clubs in the area for want of anything better to do.

I'd already showered and dressed after my dance, the club was only half full by then with most of the surfers in search of an early night to catch the prime dawn waves and the bikers back with their wife and kids. I was heading for the exit, clad in just an old T-shirt and a pair of cut-off shorts when I heard a woman's voice calling out to me.

'Hey!'

I stopped in my tracks and faced the older woman standing at the bar, nursing what looked like whiskey or bourbon.

'Yes?'

'You're Luba, the Russian?'

I nodded.

'You're wasted in a place like this, girl.'

She had an unusual accent, American but with a slow drawl, which I would later find out was not only Southern but from New Orleans. She was fifth-generation Cajun.

Her form was voluptuous, held tight inside a green velvet dress, plump white breasts spilling from its elegant sheath.

'Don't I know it?' I said. 'So what?'

Was she hitting on me? Recently, it had been happening more and more. Was it a West Coast thing? On occasions I had been tempted to experiment, but as most of the other women who'd taken a shine to me had been baristas at the various clubs or, more rarely, other dancers, it would have made matters awkward. Never mix pleasure with business, someone had once told me.

'I own a place. Down home in the French Quarter, in New Orleans,' she said. She handed me a card. It was pale red with the type in black italics. All it said was 'The Place', and listed a telephone number. I raised it to my eyes and gave it a quizzical glance.

'It's very exclusive,' she added. 'Not open to the general public. Usually by invitation only. Classy.'

I waved at the late-night bar attendant and ordered an iced tea.

'You have my attention,' I told Madame Denoux, after we'd formally shaken hands and she'd told me her name.

'Luba. It's a great name. Real one?'

'Yes.'

'There were rumours floating around about you, you know. You were in New York, mostly danced at the Grand, no? Then you just vanished off the face of the earth. My good friend Blanca was distraught, I hear. Any reason?'

'I had my reasons,' I commented.

'It's usually man trouble, no?'

'How perceptive of you.' I grinned.

'Anyway, none of my business. But dancers are my business. What a coincidence to find you here . . .'

I smiled. 'We Russians believe in fate. Always have.'

She set her glass down on her counter decisively.

'I would like you to work for me,' she declared.

'The Place?'

'Yes. We're in a quiet, discreet area in the Vieux Carré. One dance per night, only four days a week. Say a three-month contract. We'd certainly make it worth your while. After that, you might wish to stay or I have international contacts if you intend to move on. You have class, although I don't think you were at your best tonight, were you?'

'I wasn't. Just dancing? No obligatory extra-curricular business?'

'The occasional lap dance, for certain clients. There are added possibilities, but that's something for a later discussion. I think you have class and realise that what we provide can also be artful. So much more than just nudity.'

She looked me up and down, not like a butcher assessing a piece of meat, but like a connoisseur in search of intangible things.

One week later I was in New Orleans, my clothes and handbag full of amber pieces stored away in the rickety bamboo cupboard of a clean bedroom in a family-run bed and breakfast in Métairie.

When I informed Lucian I was leaving him, he didn't appear surprised. It was almost as if he was expecting my departure. I think that, deep in his heart, he'd always known I was just passing through and that I had only stayed with him this long because of his money. He wasn't entirely wrong, of course, but I held him in much affection nonetheless. He had been the right man at the right time, but the times had quickly changed and my demons had taken over, acknowledging the fact he was not my future. He generously gave me his blessing and wished me good luck. We agreed to stay in touch, but never did.

Once again, I was living to dance, reverting to my classical ambience and music, no longer even trying to titillate, at ease with myself and what I was doing.

It was New Year's Eve, just a few hours into the last day of December. I could almost touch January. I was ending my set, the music slowly fading, impressionistic, like isolated dots in a landscape. I awoke from the dream of my past and my eyes fell upon the pretty redhead sitting with her man amongst the sparse audience. And I saw the way she looked at me, as if I were a mirror.

5

Dancing with Lovers

She had the demeanour of an animal straining on a leash.

She was a simmering and barely contained pool of energy, an arrangement of chemicals just waiting for an igniting spark.

I had no further time to play spy, as the final notes of Debussy drifted out of the loudspeakers and into the ether, and the spotlight plunged from bright white into black.

A hush spread through the audience as it always did in response to the erotic physicality of my set, its abrupt ending and the sudden darkness that seemed to move from the stage and across the small audience like a fog, surprise muffling speech for a few moments as I scooped up my dress and quickly ducked behind the backstage curtain, careful not to make a sound.

Madame Denoux was waiting for me in the wings with just the white beak of her mask visible and shining through the shadows like an ominous beacon. She covered my nudity with a leopard-print cape, my cue to scurry onto the stage again for a round of applause as her voice whispered through the public address system as mysteriously as any New Orleans voodoo queen's: 'Show your appreciation for Luba.'

It was another marker that set me apart from the other

girls, who each remained onstage after their dances, lit up by the spotlight to receive the audience's claps and cheers.

Rather than suggest that I change my style to fit expectation, Madame preferred to highlight my points of difference. She believed that a second brief vision of my body draped in the animal skin and lit up for just a flash would emblazon my image into the patrons' minds – wanton, wild, unique – so that they would inevitably return, primed for another dose of their favourite drug, Luba.

It was a strategy that I was happy to adhere to, not least because I basked in that brief but intense tribute, all eyes focused on me and aglow.

Tonight I used the opportunity of my final few seconds onstage to catch a last glimpse of the red-haired girl and her handsome man.

They were now entirely consumed by each other. Her expression was animated, her excitement palpable in the small circle of onlookers. She practically radiated, her pale skin gleaming and opalescent against the fire of her mane.

He watched her face with a mixture of hunger and satisfaction, as if he had been waiting for some kind of signal from her that he had now received. They were barely touching, but the strength of their desire for each other was so obvious that the vision of the two of them sitting close together, modest in dress but evidently immodest in thought, was almost pornographic.

Darkness returned just as the applause faded and I paused for a few moments longer in the shadow of the stage wing, greedy to observe the couple. Their response to my set seemed important.

From my shadowy corner I could see that they were deep in conversation, but I could not make out a thing, try as I might to fix my eyes on their lips curving sensuously around the shape of each silent word.

Madame Denoux approached and addressed the man. They engaged in a brief exchange at the table, which caused the girl to blush a deep scarlet.

He and Madame stepped away from the table and out of my line of sight. I continued to watch the girl, as her skin shifted into a myriad shades and her stance contorted to match her response to the situation. Red with shame, pale with fear, tense with mounting excitement and straight backed with pride.

The Place dealt in only one add-on service that I was aware of: lap dances, though Madame called them 'private dances', which she considered a classier title.

Had the couple booked me for a private set? That would explain the girl's demeanour and the man's disappearance with Madame. She always processed a customer's credit card before coughing up the goods.

Normally the private dances bored me and I completed them on occasion merely because the tips were good, it was expected and acquiescing helped to secure my employer's favour.

But the thought of going with the man and the girl sent a slow thrill up my spine.

His fierceness. Her pliability. The vision of the two of them madly embracing. The way that they each might taste.

My heart tripped wildly as I imagined the possibilities en route to the safety of the dressing room, which would now be bereft of all its inhabitants, the other dancers having evacuated down streets or into homes in pursuit of either quietude or celebration before New Year's Eve began in earnest.

I returned to my seat at the mirror to wipe my skin and relax my mind, seeing little point in speculating on the habits of my mystery admirers. If they had requested a more intimate set, I would soon be advised of the fact, and as Madame Denoux strictly forbade any kind of sexual contact between punters and dancers, then fantasising about more than a lap dance with the intriguing couple could only lead to frustration.

Empty of its usual hum of activity, the room appeared to be holding its breath, lonely until the next evening's girls arrived and with them a steady hubbub of gossip flying from mouth to mouth, flimsy costumes rustling, jewellery rattling, cosmetic purses snapping open and shut.

The rare quiet suited me and was one reason that I always volunteered for the later shifts.

I wore minimal make-up, but always completed a cleansing routine before changing into the most casual of outfits for my journey home. It was my way of shifting from my working persona into what I felt was my regular self. The more I grew to love dancing, the more the two blurred, until I wasn't sure where the day-time Luba ended and the night-time Luba began, a fact that made my little ritual seem all the more important.

Dabbing at my face with a cotton pad did not provide the distraction that I had hoped for. The storm of fantasies and memories continued, an endless procession of images dancing across my mind.

First, Chey and I, entwined in every possible position under the sun, then the girl with her hair like fire and the man who lit her fuse, their bodies twisting, turning, fucking so violently that it was hard to tell whether they were completing each other or destroying each other or perhaps both at the same time.

I had felt that way once.

The heat between Chey and I had never cooled, probably because we hadn't spent enough time together to grow tired of each other.

Those early days and nights spent in his apartment on Gansevoort Street or in the resort in the Dominican Republic had been like a marathon of ceaseless fucking. We'd left the bedroom only when we absolutely had to eat or bathe and such bodily functions could be put off no longer.

Even then I had sat through meals knickerless or wearing whatever device Chey had purchased for the occasion, an exquisite glass anal plug or a remote-controlled dildo that buzzed inside me each time he pushed the button that he kept in his pocket.

I had been certain that we'd be thrown out of a bar in La Caleta when he had insisted on sitting alongside me in the booth seat where we perched drinking cocktails with pink umbrellas and his arm appeared to be merely draped over my shoulder but in fact was stretched all the way down my back with his fingers inserted deep inside the rosebud of my arsehole as the other tourists sat around us remaining totally unawares.

I caught a flicker of movement out of the corner of my eye. It was Madame Denoux again, still wearing the long blood-red gown and mask. The velvet fabric of her dress blended so well into the décor of The Place that she was able to appear out of nowhere like a ghost, as if she was not the owner of the establishment but rather a part of the walls. Even at home she retained an air of mystery and a hint of the macabre that made me worry that if I stayed in this business long enough I would become like her and be unable to separate one self from the other.

She looked extraordinarily pleased with herself. I had learned to judge her moods beneath her costume and even the thoughts that flitted through that unusual mind of hers by the peculiar way that she tensed or relaxed her body.

Dancing had made me more in tune with not just my own physicality but others' too. The cause of Madame's good mood was undoubtedly the couple and I imagined the large sum that she had managed to extract from them for services presumably yet to be rendered. But she had not asked if I would agree to a private dance and did not seem to be on the verge of verbalising a question.

No. She was holding onto another secret, and whatever it was, I resolved to find out.

The only weak spot I had found in the impenetrable armour of Madame Denoux's discretion was her pride. She liked to brag of her triumphs.

'A very striking girl,' I said to her, stoking the furnace of her ego. 'Fascinating.'

'Don't try to be subtle, Luba. It doesn't suit you.'

'I am merely curious. Human nature, no?'

'Well, if you are prepared to be patient then you will see,' she replied smugly. She had given me the option of an early dance so that I could go out and ring in the New Year, but I declined. I was not superstitious, and the passing of one moment to the next meant little to me.

I paused, knowing that she would fill the space of my silence if I waited long enough.

Eventually, she continued. 'I was certain that he was going to ask to buy some of your time, you know. But all he wanted was to see his own girl dance. Strange. Just when you think you have the men folk all figured out, they continue to surprise you.'

I was vaguely hurt that he hadn't asked for my company. He was so clearly entirely wrapped up in her. But I was intrigued by his request to have her dance instead. In public. Nude. I remembered Chcy's reaction when he first discovered that I was working. His shock and anger.

What sort of man, I wondered, would actually pay for his woman to undress in front of an audience?

The sort of man that I would like to get to know, I decided.

'So they will return, tomorrow? And she will dance?'

'Yes. At two a.m. on New Year's Day.'

'The dance of a new beginning, or an ending?' I mused aloud, fascinated by the psychology of the two strangers who were now embedded in my thoughts.

'You can be so melodramatic sometimes, my dear . . . it's a habit that leads to ruin. Curiosity killed the cat, you know.'

I briefly wondered whether or not the redhead would go through with it. But I knew instinctively that she had already made up her mind, as I had the first time, long before I stepped out onto the stage. The challenge and the possible humiliation were all part of the thrill.

I abandoned my cleansing routine, packed up my few belongings quickly and headed for home. It was close to 4 a.m., that muted time of the morning when the air feels thin and the atmosphere stretched, as if readying itself for the birth of the sun.

Most of the rest of the day was spent in glorious respite.

Napping in bed or sitting in the chair by the window, immersed in my book.

But I was again unable to sleep, and as the afternoon bled into evening, I grew restless, abandoned the worn paperback and returned to work.

I was not well accustomed to being idle, and since I had a few hours to kill, resolved to spend them planning costumes from the wall-to-wall racks of outfits that Madame Denoux had collected over the years, and rehearsing a new routine. It would be the first dance in which I had seriously embraced a prop. I planned to dress as a dove, and perform in a gilded cage suspended from the ceiling, before breaking free from the restriction of the bars and pirouetting as if in mid-flight, attached to an invisible harness. I was rather proud of the choreography which I had devised in one of the many sleepless nights that had me turning in bed feverish with nightmares or awake and plotting something, anything to take my mind away from Chey.

Time drifted by. Voluntarily trapped in my bird's cage in the dressing room I felt as though I was part of another world, a hazy world where my mind inhabited the space between sleeping and waking, dancing and stillness and my memories were just a jumble of images that could have filled the Kama Sutra. I barely noticed the muted sounds of fireworks in the distance and the cheering that filled the bar as the act that Madame had planned for the big finale reached its crescendo and the New Year officially arrived.

The girl's voice disturbed me from my daydreams.

'I prefer to dance naked,' she said, visibly straightening her back in an attempt to add height and authority to her posture.

Madame was trying to get her into one of her elaborate

costumes, but the girl wanted to appear fully nude from the outset. It appeared that the redhead considered herself a cut above stripping.

She would dance naked, but she wouldn't take her clothes off for anyone.

I wondered again what sort of relationship it was that she shared with the man who had arranged for her to dance for him. Her pride and his apparent desire to own her seemed a strange combination.

She might have won round one, but she had under-estimated Madame Denoux, who was as stubborn as a bull and would never allow a dancer to take the upper hand. Without so much as a blink, she had produced the box, inlaid with velvet, that I had seen sitting alongside the costume jewellery and even considered making use of myself, but never had, fearing it too daring, even for The Place.

'You will wear these. Your benefactor prefers it.'

From my refuge in the corner of the dressing room where, I knew, she could not see my face, I watched with bated breath as Madame Denoux supervised the redhead's preparations. I saw how she flinched when Madame clipped on the body jewellery contained within the wooden box – the rings to her nipples, the thin metal chains to her labia – and, finally, decisively, as she inserted the butt plug. As Madame led her to the empty stage, I left the dressing room and tiptoed on bare feet through narrow corridors towards the back of the performance room where I stood in the deepest pit of darkness. I was beginning to tire. It had been a long night, and my limbs were growing stiff from spending too long in the cage, but this was something I dearly wanted to watch.

I could see the strong shoulders of the young woman's companion silhouetted against the muted light of the stage as he sat towards the front, and regretted I was unable to conceal myself in the stage wings and observe both his reactions as well as her dancing.

The heavy velvet curtain slid open.

Her face displayed a mixture of fear and pride as the strong glare of the spotlight erupted, highlighting her loneliness on the desert island of the stage.

The fierce red fire of her pubic hair was like a target to which my eyes were drawn.

She stood hesitantly for a second or more until the sound system came to life and a look of panic spread across her pale face, as she realised she was still immobile.

The music the young woman with the red hair had elected to dance to was classical. I'd heard it a thousand times over but at first I couldn't place it until, out of the blue, my memory focused and I pictured the record sleeve housing its vinyl version back in the rehearsal rooms at the ballet classes in St Petersburg. A pastoral image, medieval-looking, probably from the Dutch school, with peasants toiling in a field and plump-thighed nymphs gallivanting on the edge of a forest. Vivaldi's *Four Seasons*. We'd never danced to it as it had never been part of any repertoire.

It was not music to dance to.

I wondered why our guest performer had chosen it. Perhaps the man she was with had chosen it for her.

Her first movements were tentative. Nudity came easy to her and she stood straight, firm-backed, almost defiant, confident in the power of her body, but there was an initial clumsiness in the way her arms moved, just out of sync with her legs, her pelvis swaying softly to the melody. There was no doubt she was musical, but it seemed she had no dance training to fall back on as she tried with all the dignity she could muster to follow the sounds and combine elegance and eroticism while controlling the plug that filled her remorselessly and limited her motions as she clinched her arse cheeks to hold it in, not that she needed to as those implements have a talent for staying put.

Of course, we had actually never been subjected to anal plugs in our ballet training, but there had been one particular instructor, a thin, malevolent pony-tailed woman who worked us to the bone, who had often ordered us to imagine we were thus encumbered. We had all blushed deeply, but the concept had stayed with many of us, a perfect vade mecum when it came to maintaining one's posture with a touch of grace.

She began to relax, her movements loosening as she abandoned herself, and her body, to the flow of the music and the moment.

Her face was a whirlpool of emotions as she grew into the performance, moving from her initial apprehension to resigned acceptance and then fully assuming the dictates of her lust, as the juices inside no doubt began to flow and irrigated her soul and the deep well of her desires. Each gesture became softer, less edgy, gliding on the borders of obscenity and beauty as she kept her eyes fixed on the man in the audience she was exhibiting herself to, more than nude and exotically adorned, undressing the very core of her heart to him as an offering, a sacrifice.

I recognised all those stages. I experienced them when I danced. Pretending it was for Chey.

Opening myself.

The temptation was too great. I furtively stepped past the

bar, keeping myself bathed in darkness, and adopted a new position where I could finally observe the man – Madame Denoux had let slip his name was Dominik – as he watched the red-haired girl dance and succumb to the giddiness of her most secret emotions.

He was hypnotised by the spectacle of her dance, his mouth half open, his breath on hold, his handsome features etched with cruelty and yearning, as much a slave to her as he was controlling her.

I knew that look.

I briefly closed my eyes and pictured Chey's face when he used to ride me, the elegant sway of his torso, the sharp angle of his hard cock, the faint aroma of his breath and his heat.

And I understood that every time I performed on stage, ever since I had fired that gun and fled from the harbour of his arms, I was calling for him to take me, fill me, spread me open until I gaped and the increasingly pornographic way I deported myself on all those stages was just a desperate cry out, a substitute for the sex that defined me, that made me whole.

The red-haired young woman finally came to rest, her legs parted, her chest heaving, the small rings clipped to her nipples shaking imperceptibly as the memory of her swaying persisted, her clamped labia puffy and swollen as all the blood in her body had moved to her erogenous zones.

She padded to the side as the spotlight was switched off.

Now I was jealous of her.

Because I knew that when she left The Place and returned to whichever hotel room the fascinating couple would retreat to tonight, the man, Dominik, would take her, fuck her, imprint his soul on her in savage fashion and I wanted to be her, wanted it to be me in the arms of a forceful man, a bad man even, arousing me, punishing me, cruelly playing with me, satisfying me.

The following morning I rose early, and went down to the Mississippi shore, walking from Jackson Square all the way to the big mall, alongside the Aquarium, the Imax Theater and the berths for the large tourist steamboats, the *Creole Queen* and the *Natchez*. The air was full of spices as the long barges lumbered their way down the mighty river like prehistoric monsters. The New Year's festivities were being cleaned up, although the smell of beer still lingered in the Bourbon Street gutters. The sky was grey and I had to wear a sweatshirt. Gulls hovered over the waters. When I could walk by the banks of the river no more, I turned and retraced my steps to the Café du Monde, outside which a clown was inflating sausage-shaped balloons. I cut into the square and, intersecting Dauphine, made my way to the club. Madame Denoux was also an early riser, and I found her checking the accounts in an old-fashioned double-columned ledger – she had no truck with computers.

'Isn't it your day off?' she queried as she saw me knocking at the open door of her office.

'It is,' I confirmed. 'I wanted to talk.'

'That sounds ominous.'

'Not really. Just a chat.'

'Tell me, child,' she said, finally putting down the ledger and giving me her full attention.

'I think I need a change of scene,' I said.

'Ah, you Russians, always on the move. Fallen out of love with New Orleans, then?'

'Not at all, I love this place. It's so unique. I could spend a lifetime here. It's . . . me. Somehow the dancing is not enough. I need more. Not that I really know what,' I explained.

Madame Denoux smiled.

'Can I come back with a proposal, Luba?'

'Of course.'

'Promise me you won't be shocked, or offended.'

'Don't you know me well enough by now?' I said.

I was aware Madame Denoux was well-connected. Her frequent absences from New Orleans on business and the shadowy daytime guests we performers saw visiting her while we rehearsed, all tucked away in her office, confirmed that impression.

'You like men?' She looked me straight in the eyes and it felt more like a statement than a question.

'I do,' I answered. 'But I will not whore myself. That is totally out of the question,' I added.

'Good,' she noted. 'Because that's not what is involved.'

'Get to the point,' I demanded, annoyed that she appeared to be skirting around the subject.

'Yes,' she continued, 'there would be sex involved, and in a way it could be construed as sex for money, but in our eyes, yours, mine, it will be sex as beauty, an art. That's what our clients already pay for, don't they, when they come to watch you and the other girls dancing. The illusion of sex. Well, the idea is to provide with them with so much more than an illusion, to take matters a stage further, beyond sheer titillation. And there are men who will pay veritable fortunes for this.'

She was appealing to the artist in me. Because even when I danced and became a driven creature of sex and untold desire, I also considered myself above the fray, expressing myself in the dance without abandon. Others would not recognise it as art, but I did, or at any rate that's how I justified my involvement in the whole game to myself.

'You would go with men,' she said. 'Like you, they are equally beautiful, their bodies masterful and elegant and made for love. And rich people will pay to watch you together. No artifice, no trickery. Like your dancing, it would take place in the very heart of the spotlight for all to see every movement, every bead of sweat, to listen to every sound you make, to observe every tremor running across the surface of your skin as you fuck, are fucked. I know you, Luba, you would be perfect. They will love you.'

I held my breath, crazy fantasies already racing behind my eyelids as I tried to reconcile myself with the concept.

'Interesting' was the only word that, implausibly, came to my lips.

'There is a network in place and I'm plugged into it. My establishment has, on a few occasions, hosted such entertainment for a small coterie of exclusively invited guests or by invitation only, but the performers were always shipped in. Such a specialist area of expertise.' She licked her lips as the memory of these events rushed in front of her eyes. 'Twice I've proposed dancers I'd discovered or brought under my wing to the Network. They were both willing but didn't make the grade.' She sighed.

'Is it safe?' I asked.

'Absolutely. Every performer is tested regularly, whether male or female. It's indispensable. The criterions are exacting and not every one is chosen . . .'

She fell silent for a moment, and I saw a well of regret clouding her impeccably made-up features.

'What is it?' I asked, sensing her change of mood.

She took a deep breath and confessed. 'I was once on that circuit. Myself. When I was younger. Just a few years. I have no regrets. I earned enough to acquire this establishment when I retired. I will never forget those years . . .'

Outside her office window a typical New Orleans down-pour was descending on the French Quarter, washing the city's sins away under a curtain of water as thick as a stage curtain.

'What do I have to do?' I asked her.

The training school was in Seattle, an old warehouse space that had been renovated and converted into a private dance studio just a short walk from Pike Place Market and the long descending stairs that led to the waterfront.

This was where I learned the rest of my curious trade and met the three men who would be fucking me over the next eighteen months as we all travelled the world separately and met up by public demand to do the deed on an assortment of hastily built stages and places in alternately obscure and often glamorous locations for an audience of few.

I was never told their names, and I never asked. Neither did I meet the other female performers who also formed part of the Network, the Pleasure Network as I amused my-self calling it.

I was accommodated in a tall, modern hotel, from the top floor of which I could see some of the distant islands in the Puget Sound. It was just a short walk from the studio where I reported daily at 9 a.m., like an office drone. I was weighed, measured, medically inspected and then photo-graphed from every possible angle and perspective. After a few days, I was allowed to express an opinion as to which photographs of mine should be included in the Network's catalogue. My only interlocutors throughout the Seattle sessions were two middle-aged women invariably dressed in severe grey business suits and white blouses buttoned up to the neck. They looked so alike I called them A and B.

The catalogue, once a new version had been printed to include me, also featured six other young women, but none of them were based in Seattle or visited during my stay. It seemed once you had been trained, there were no refresher courses needed. They were all beautiful in their own way, some exotic, others minor pictures of perfection, one Asian girl appeared to be so small you could fit her into an overnight bag. I wasn't the only blonde, but I was the one with natural breasts and a tattoo of a gun in a strategic place. Only one of the other girls had a visible one. It read 'A Spy in the House of Love' in gothic letters across the small of her back. Our names were listed but I guessed most of the others were using stage names. I remained Luba. I didn't want to be anyone else. The businesswoman in the grey suit who asked me under what name I wished to be listed as just grunted when I told her.

I was not allowed to keep a copy of the catalogue. Its distribution was quite confidential, displaying photos of all of us, clothed and nude, our statistics and other verifiable information, together with a choice of three scenarios.

Only three men were listed at the back of the catalogue. None had names. Once I had been accepted into the Seattle training programme, I was given a day or so to come up with specific scenarios that would culminate with me making love in full public view with each of the individual male performers. My two guardians also came up with a welter of suggestions, just in case I lacked the imagination. Some of their ideas were outrageous, other boring and still others puzzling in their lack of potential eroticism. But they had years of experience and seemed to know what the rich clientele of the Network wanted or was into.

Accordingly I came up with three acts.

And the man I would perform each act with when called to do so (and the prices listed for each act in the catalogue were out of this world and bordering on madness, I felt), would forever be named after the story we would inhabit.

There was the Tango.

The Inca Priest.

And – how could I waste all those months of training back in Russia? – the Ballet School Instructor.

I also insisted that each scenario begin with me dancing and that I should choose the music. I wanted it to be more than just a live, and terribly expensive, sex show. Give the punters value for money.

Having established these parameters, each of the men who were to fuck me were summoned from wherever they were in the world, and we were given forty-eight hours together to perfect our act. With our two grey-suited ladies watching and making notes and even intervening if they felt we were not up to scratch.

I began with Debussy. The clear notes of the music, so reminiscent of the indolent rhythm of the ocean, always reminded me of Chey. And that memory firmly lodged in my consciousness would be a partition, as impenetrable as any castle, ensuring that the anonymous sex would remain a job and not a study in intimacy. I would give the men my body but my mind would remain my own.

First, I would demonstrate the Tango.

It was one of the only partnered dances that I was at least

somewhat familiar with. By its nature so wild and erotic, the tango had seemed a natural choice.

In St Petersburg we had learned what one of our workbooks called the Russian tango to records by Pyotr Leshchenko. He was still considered a counter-revolutionary by some and the tutor who played his songs and taught us the steps only did so when the other tutors, with their stiff backs and flint-like stares, were busy elsewhere writing up class notes or demonstrating the fifth position to groups of younger students.

To me the voice of Pyotr Leshchenko was a sound full of sadness, a yearning for lost love, and as soon as I became aware that the records were forbidden then of course the movements and the music were immediately branded into my brain. It was a learning fuelled by the fire of rebellion and therefore never forgotten.

According to the catalogue, my partner was versed in a slightly different, Argentinian style and I knew that for the duration of our set I would be required to follow his lead in adherence to the emotional tradition of the dance and also in order to keep up.

But I intended to follow in body alone. He would not, could not, control me. Years of ballet training had given me the impervious posture of a poker and I knew that in this room I could hold my own. I was a slave to the dance and not to the man. He was an accessory. A vision of carnality. A prop, nothing more. Tango was my show, and he was simply here for the ride, one of a dozen men who had been chosen merely on the basis of their physical attributes and suitability for the role.

I held my pride aloft like a mental shield.

Assessors A and B appeared unmoved by my solo

performance. As the sound of the sea faded, the tango began, a rhythm as different from the Debussy piece as night is from day. Moving from one beat to the next was like travelling from the cool waters of Northern Europe to the hot beaches of South America and the change in temperature raised the pulse of my heart in expectation of what would come next.

My partner appeared from the dark recesses of the stage wings like some kind of demonic shadow brought to life. The man who would fuck me. It was the first time I had seen him, having purposefully flipped straight past the photos in the catalogue in order both to preserve the theatricality of our act and to avoid developing any notion of attachment to him. He would just be the Tango.

His expression was fierce, his stance implacable, as he stepped into the glare of the spotlight.

He grasped my hand. Pulled me towards him into an embrace with a grip as strong as iron. Had I wished to push him away, the pressure of my fists would have been as effective as the paws of a kitten against the chest of a bulldog.

Fear swam into my lungs and my heart hammered, but with it came arousal. Studying the catalogue, mentally working through the steps, erecting psychological and emotional barriers and hours of self-talk: *It's just a job, it's just a job*, meant nothing when I came face to face with the first stranger that I would fuck in public.

He was young, beautiful, a symphony of tanned skin and muscled limbs. He was the colour of burnt caramel and looked as if he might taste as sweet. He was Chey, ten years younger, but with a much crueller set to his mouth.

All of my carefully thought-out and ever so rational

assertions melted away, tossed aside as quickly as a day-old newspaper when I discovered that I was attracted to him. And with that attraction came release. I entered into the spirit of the music, of the dance, as if I had not been paid to do so.

I knew that I was safe here under the gaze of my two score holders, and within the parameters of the boundary that their presence created I was free to dream of surrender. Of letting go, of being taken. Of the fantasies of my girlhood that inevitably involved pirates or vampires or highwaymen, visions in which I would be overpowered, relinquishing my will to some handsome and frightening stranger and yet I would remain unharmed, waking with my body and mind intact. Just an idea to play with, but a hopelessly seductive one and once my imagination was set alight my body followed.

My breasts pressed firmly against his chest, his cock nestling between my thighs. The furrow between my lips was moistening, his erection twitching, growing.

Like the quiet before the storm, the music flooding through the loudspeakers slowed imperceptibly, each note leaving a question in its wake.

Would I? Could I?

He took my jaw in his hand. Assaulted my gaze with his own.

We stood locked together, engaged in a silent battle of wills, a wordless conversation in which his intent was clear.

His eyes were brown and as dark as the deepest river. His pupils dilated as the blood of his arousal rushed to his extremities.

A pen squeaked against paper, the rasp of the ball scratching its trajectory of judgement in slow upward and downward motion. Whether Madame A's or Madame B's it was impossible for me to tell as he still had my chin and with it the direction of my stare trapped in his hand.

The speakers flared to life once more and I was swept away by my golden boy, my feet following his as inevitably as summer follows spring, our bodies coiling together for the first time like two flames pushed inexorably towards one another in mutual combustion.

He danced with skill, grace, precision, his steps quick and sure, his legs long and elegant, engaged in a complex series of kicks and flicks between each of our open embraces.

With every turn I was swung powerfully to and fro, away from him, towards him, in perpetual staccato motion. It was the dance of the conqueror, the rhythm of the hunt and the hunted.

His cock had grown to fullness and its length and girth was like nothing I had ever seen. The sheer size of it made me expel all the air in my lungs in one quick gasp. A hot flush spread like a forest fire from my loins to my chest and face, suffusing my skin with a pink glow, causing my pulse to quicken, speeding the flow of the juices that were gathering like a tide in the valley of my cunt ready to embrace him.

He pulled me tightly to his torso again. His penis now completely engorged and pressed hard against my abdomen. Out of place, waiting for entry. I resisted the immediate desire to drop to my knees and take it into my mouth. To run my tongue over his shaft, from its base to its tip, to feel every ridge and each prominent vein, to choke on his length, to bring him to his climax, filling my throat with his hot fluid.

My body responded to his touch in animal fashion. An instinct as natural as any other. My nipples were as hard as his cock and throbbed painfully, seeking the comfort of his hot lips and the ferocity of his teeth. I was wet with desire.

Another turn, another spin, another jump into his arms in vigorous gymnastic style.

The control was mine when the moment came and I raised my leg to achieve a vertical split, allowing him to follow with a thrust so severe it penetrated my very core.

For a few seconds, each as long as an hour, we stood like that, my legs stretched apart into one rigid pillar that followed the line of his torso and stretched above his shoulder into a perfect airborne pointe, his rigid cock encased completely by the tunnel of my vagina, which stretched to accommodate him with welcoming hospitality.

We were not fucking but conjoined. Each locked to the other in a dance step that was as old as time. I could not move without breaking away from his shaft so instead I surrendered and he carried me, propelled on the spear of his erection.

His expression remained unchanged throughout. The only sign of his exertion – or was it emotion? – the beads of sweat that gathered on his forehead, reflected in the glow of the harsh stage light like raindrops in a shimmering mirage.

He did not reach a climax. Neither did I. The dance ended when the music came to a dramatic halt and we remained locked together until the assessors coughed in unison, a reminder that we were engaged in a carnal show for the benefit of an audience and not each other. I could not suppress a sigh when he extracted himself from my grip and left me hollow, vacant.

He turned to our judges, gave a slight bow and then strode to the exit without a second glance.

The faceless women acting as judges of sorts did not

express any opinion, but their lips seemed to have moved from the straight geometric lines that they usually sported to a slightly upward expression, which I hoped indicated approval.

I had a day's grace to recover before performing my next act, the Inca Priest sacrifice.

Again I began with Debussy. It was my lifeline, the piece of music that put me at ease in preparation for another unknown fuck.

For this set I had selected a Gregorian chant. The music was not remotely Peruvian, but the heavy, sombre tone suited the ritualistic intention of the show to follow and I found the choir of monastic voices trilling in deep melancholic cadence both soothing and seductive.

My Inca Priest, unlike the music, hailed from South America and he was dark haired, muscled, well hung and as beautiful as my previous partner, though he did not move me to arousal in the same way, and I was glad that on this occasion I had thought to pre-lubricate my entrance to facilitate the passage of what I knew would be another over-sized penis, as being hung like a horse was apparently one of the prerequisites for male members of the Network.

He had a large and ornate cross emblem tattooed on his chest. The cross lay inside a pair of wings like the spine of a bird. It was a half Christian and half pagan motif, which lent another note of mysticism to the show. The Network's assessors had chosen my partners well.

The dance culminated in sex as they all did, but on this occasion I had added an extra element of shock value which I had not described on my check sheet so that it would be as much of a surprise to the two madames as it would to my eventual real-life audience.

When the moment came and the Inca Priest pierced the small bag that I had inserted deep into my pussy and the fake theatrical blood ran down my legs in a parody of Virgin sacrifice, the onlookers' hiss was audible even over the throb of the loudspeakers.

They remained wordless, but I retained no small thrill of satisfaction at having elicited some sort of response from my two seemingly emotionless spectators.

The surprise was all mine when I met the partner in my third and final act, the Ballet School Instructor, and discovered that though identified in the catalogue as male, he had not been born a man in the anatomical sense.

He was tall and slender, his alabaster skin contrasting vividly with his dark, short haircut – a crop that accentuated the delicate line of his jaw and high, cat-like cheekbones. He had eyebrows as fine as a moth's wings and a feminine curve to his chest suggesting the presence of breasts, however slight they might be. He wore flesh-coloured tights that did not in any way conceal the obvious bulge beneath them, but it wasn't until he pulled down the stockinged fabric to reveal a harness and a dildo that I realised I was about to be impaled by a strap-on for the first time.

The experience of penetration was not diminished in any way by the knowledge that the instrument responsible was faux rather than flesh, and again I was impressed by the perceptive examiners who had reviewed the brief description of my proposed act and read into it the mixture of severity and femininity that encapsulated the Russian ballet instructors who had so affected my training.

'You did well,' said Assessor A, or Assessor B, with the barest hint of a smile on her lips when my third act had reached its finale.

And so, with the selection and training rigmarole complete, the next step on my journey began.

I packed my bag again.

Packing and unpacking had become such a regular occurrence in my life that I no longer allowed myself to become attached to the cities or the houses that I lived in or the friends or lovers that I gathered in each. I'd been born under a fickle star, and I supposed that moving from place to place was a part of my make-up as much as my flat chest and long, curly blonde hair. There was no point in becoming sentimental about it. Each new adventure was one of life's seasons, ever changing. I may as well shake my fist at the rain or grow tired of the sun shining for all the good that it would do me to complain about going on the road again.

The Network folk had somehow managed to obtain a convincing set of fake documents for me. With my spurious paperwork I was now able to travel and work around the world to my heart's content, and I began to see myself as more than a dancer. I was a nymph, a creature of the night, a woman of fire, a living promise of sex. Sometimes I wondered whether I was even real, or just the product of someone else's dream. A teenage boy's fantasy gone wild.

My dreams of fancy were abruptly shattered when Madame Denoux confirmed my first booking, in London. Someone there had booked the Ballet Instructor scenario. My departure from New Orleans was not to be in the direction of Paris, Milan, or any of the other glamorous cities that in my mind were places of intrigue and mystique. I knew London was a grey place, but I firmly intended to bring some colour to the place.

6

Dancing Alone

It was raining when I flew into Heathrow.

As it had been raining when I left Seattle, and for almost every day of the eight weeks that I had spent there completing the recruitment process with the Pleasure Network.

The similarity in weather conditions between the two cities brought me a small degree of comfort.

I peered out of the tiny window from the comfort of my plush armchair in first class at the city of London flying up to greet us through a layer of fine mist. It was hard to tell from such a height, of course, but the buildings seemed lower and less uniform than those in New York. The city was split in two by the long silver thread of the Thames River that wound through it. I could make out just one of the landmarks that I was expecting to see: the London Eye glowing whitely in the centre and adding a touch of frivolity to an otherwise sombre tone, an addition that I had always thought odd. Why would a serious town have a piece of architecture that would be better suited to a fun fair or Coney Island as one of its major sights? Such a thing would never happen in St Petersburg.

'Your first visit to London?' asked the woman sitting next to me in a clipped voice that could have hailed from anywhere. She was wearing a cream silk blouse buttoned almost up to the neck and on her feet, neatly crossed at the ankles, a pair of tan loafers. Her scent carried a definite note of tobacco, and lemon zest.

'Yes. I haven't had the chance to travel much through Europe.'

'You will enjoy it,' she replied authoritatively, as if I hadn't any choice in the matter.

She was reading a small book bound in soft black nappa leather with a duck-egg blue satin ribbon bookmark attached to the spine. The type of book that begs to be picked up and stroked. She leaned back and closed her eyes as we dropped through the sky and the plane began to judder as the pilot prepared for landing. I craned forward to read the title: *Scarlett's Allsorts*, printed in brass letters in an old-fashioned font. The woman woke again, and began to read. I caught just half a line over her shoulder: *My body felt like it was singing.* I smiled.

The line set a dozen half-baked thoughts and images freewheeling through my brain, like a flock of birds headed skyward, upset by the arrival of a stone flung into their midst. What did the woman look like naked? I wondered. What type of lingerie did she wear? Not girlish, I considered. Nor old-fashioned. Plain, classic, well made and unfussy in black, cream or beige, perhaps slightly high cut in the knickers.

She stood up and stretched to reach her bag stored in the overhead locker. It was square, plain black with a solid zipper, almost a briefcase. She slipped the book into the side pocket. Her trousers were tailored and sat at her waist, emphasising the straightness of her figure, which lacked almost any sign of feminine curve besides the bulge of her breasts. Her hair was silvery grey and cut into a sharp bob. She flicked the stray locks on each side behind her ears impatiently, displaying the roundness of her lobes, each one sporting a small pearl stud. I guessed that she was in her forties, though she might have been fifty. It was so hard to tell.

'Is this yours?' she asked, holding my black tote. I nodded as she passed it down to me.

I slipped into the aisle behind her, where I stood admiring the length of her legs and tight shape of her backside until the flight attendant announced that we were free to disembark and the short line of people ahead of us began to move.

We were the only women in first class. All the other passengers were men, most of them squat, pallid and uninteresting. They regularly threw both of us curious glances that I ignored, but at least none of them gave me a business card and suggested that we 'come to an arrangement' as the strange man in the seersucker jacket and knotted brown tie who accompanied me on the flight from New Orleans to Seattle had.

'Thank you, Miss Volk,' said the air hostess in a nasal twang that I barely comprehended as I squeezed past her to exit the plane and took my first steps into Britain, barely a step or two behind my silver-haired companion.

Tomorrow night's set would be a breeze. I was booked to perform the Ballet Instructor, and the length of his tightly harnessed hard silicone dildo was bound to slip right in if my current mood was anything to go by. I felt slightly lightheaded watching the pair of loafers ahead of me walking up the ramp towards Passport Control in quick, sharp steps. She wasn't wearing socks, and the flash of her bare ankle was enough to make my pussy throb.

Today I was travelling with a German passport. It would

be the first of many times that I would pass through customs with false papers. The man who checked the photo page and scanned it through the machine asked few questions and barely glanced at my picture before waving me through. He had a pock-marked face and a thick, square-cut jaw like a superhero who had fallen on hard times.

The grey-haired woman was waiting for me by the baggage carousel.

'Are you a woman of the people, Miss Volk?' she asked.

Volk was a Russian variant of the nickname *vovk*, meaning 'wolf', but could be mistaken for the Germanic meaning of the word, 'folk' or 'common people'. Perhaps she was German.

'I would say that I'm more of an acquired taste. Not for everyone . . .'

'Like all the best things in life. And you like books? It is not considered polite to read over shoulders, you know.'

Was she hitting on me or berating me? Women had flirted with me in California, but not like this. The Californian girls had trailed manicured fingernails around the rims of their champagne glasses or giggled in throaty echoes through lipsticked mouths, and never actually verbalised the questions that hung between us, *kiss me, touch me, come home with me, buy me a drink*. Not this frank, ironic tone and straight-backed posture that seemed to be leading directly towards something that I was not yet aware of.

'It looked like a good book,' I replied.

'Would you like to read it to me after dinner?'

A smile played across her lips. She knew what my answer would be before I replied. It was inevitable. Another twist on the river of life and I could already feel the current rising and pushing me inexorably along in the direction of her hotel room. Though in the end, it was mine that we returned to.

We had agreed to eat at Lena, an Italian restaurant in Shoreditch, having exchanged numbers and disappeared back to our respective accommodations to check in, drop off our baggage and shower.

She still carried her almost-briefcase but had changed into a pair of tight leather leggings and another buttoned-up blouse that hung untucked over her hips. It was short sleeved and displayed the muscles on her arms. Her legs were encased in a pair of scuffed-leather riding boots with silver buckles on the heels.

She had an old-fashioned name, Florence, though she said that I could call her Flo. I could not adjust to the shorter version, and continued with the longer.

Florence smoked French cigarettes. One before the entrée, and another after the main course.

'A palate cleanser,' she called it, before stepping outside and disappearing into the shadows so that all I could see of her through the window of the brightly lit restaurant was a single ember glowing red hot in the night.

We shared a lemon ricotta tart with a scoop of vanilla ice-cream, a white ball flecked black with the seeds of the vanilla pod. She ordered coffee spiked with almond liqueur.

She tasted just as I noticed she had smelled when I sat alongside her on the aeroplane. Of lemon and cigarettes, and something else that I couldn't place. I ran my tongue over hers and held her saliva in my mouth for a moment to decipher the peculiar combination that made up her kiss, in the same way that I would consider the particular fusion of flavours in a glass of wine.

Florence was German. She worked as a chemist and academic and was visiting London to give a series of lectures on the advances in anti-malarial drugs. She didn't ask me what I did for a living, or why a woman with a Russian accent was travelling on a German passport and did not speak a word of Deutsch besides *Guten Tag* and *Tschuss!*

We were both in flat heels and it was still early, so we caught the underground from Old Street station to London Bridge and bought a bottle of wine and a packet of ginger biscuits from a corner store at the station. That was the other thing she tasted of, I realised, when she pushed me up against the barrier that separated the Thames path from the river and kissed me again. She caught me unexpectedly, causing the plastic bag in my hand to swing out and the wine bottle in it to clang loudly against the metal railing.

It began to rain again, light drips that misted wetly onto our faces and wrung the curls from my hair. She took my hand and we ran back up to the road and caught a black cab to my hotel on the South Bank, close to Waterloo station and the Royal Festival Hall.

I had a penthouse suite in the Park Plaza. The London Eye seemed almost close enough to touch from the balcony that surrounded the room, and from this distance I understood what the Londoners saw in it. There was a certain light-hearted grandeur and synchronicity in the slowly turning wheel, and a beauty in the bright lights that shone from each capsule like a series of fireflies trapped under glass and set into perpetual motion.

Florence poured the wine, and handed me a ginger biscuit. She hoisted herself up onto the flat top of the balustrade that bordered the balcony protecting the room's inhabitants from plunging to their deaths whilst looking out at the view. She had her back to thin air and a fourteen-storey drop.

'Come down,' I laughed. 'Imagine the mess that the street cleaners will have to clear up in the morning if you fall. They might charge a fee back to the room.'

'I'll make sure you get your money's worth,' she replied. She had opened her legs wide apart and the tight trousers clung to the delineation of her pussy in pornographic style. I could see the slight bulge of her mound and the soft lines of her labia. I had been mistaken about her underwear. She wasn't wearing any at all.

'I doubt you will manage that from there,' I teased her.

'You promised to read to me,' she replied.

'I didn't promise anything. You asked me to. There is a difference.'

There was a challenge in my words, but she didn't rise to it as I had expected. Instead, her expression softened.

'Will you read to me?' she asked, almost plaintively.

'Yes.'

I took her hand and led her back into the room. She pulled the leather-bound book from the pocket of her bag, handed it to me and lay down on the bed. She was still fully dressed, and wearing her long leather boots. I lay down alongside her.

The soft leather cover felt like skin in my hands. I flicked the ribbon back from its place where it marked the first page of a story, *Shoe Shine at Liverpool Street Station*.

I rolled each word in my mouth as I read aloud to catch the feel of the syllables, some quick, some slow, some soft, some low, others harsh, some breathless. Florence closed her eyes as I read. She wasn't wearing any mascara but her eyelashes were so dark they might have been dyed. They were too thick and black for her face and bordered her eyes like bruises, as if something heavy weighed down on her in the night, waiting for her to awaken.

When I had finished, her eyelids fluttered open again, and she rolled over onto her side and stroked her fingers over my lips. I opened my mouth and sucked one of them in. She ran her hand down under the waistband of her trousers and then returned her fingers to my mouth, stopping a centimetre or so away, as if she knew that I was a visitor to a new and foreign land and she was offering me a taste of some local delicacy. I propped my head up to reach, and drank it in.

It was the first time that I had tasted a woman, besides checking the flavour of my own secretions both out of curiosity and to reassure myself when I experienced a shameful sort of fear when Chey went down on me and I had worried so much that the experience would be unpleasant for him although he had laughed at my discomfort and insisted that the opposite was true.

Florence tasted like a sweet kind of nothing. Her scent was a little musky. It was neither pleasant nor unpleasant.

My introduction to the taste of women, like so many other things, turned out to be inconsequential. I was ambivalent. Again, I wondered what all the fuss was about.

Her lips on mine, though, were a joyful press of softness meeting softness and her hands, once they found their way beneath my clothes, were slow and skilful, and all the warm heat of her body against mine made my skin tingle and my clit swell. We were a tangle of limbs together, searching, stroking, pinching, caressing. She held her breath when I popped the buttons open on her blouse and unhooked the back of her bra, releasing her breasts, and moaned when I circled her nipple with my tongue.

I discovered when I removed her bra that she had only one breast. The other had been removed, and in its place lay a slight swell of flesh with a line running across where the nipple would be. The scar was a silvery furrow that ran in a horizontal curve across her skin like an uncrossed crucifix. She exhaled when I bent my head and licked the length of it lightly from one side to the other.

'Let's go outside again,' she said, suddenly. 'I need the fresh air.'

We were both a little drunk, on the wine, on each other. If I kissed her once more I thought that I might be intoxicated enough to climb over the barrier and leap off the side and feel the wind under my arms carrying me down to the ground.

Florence picked up her bag on the way to the glass sliding door and wrestled from it the largest strap-on cock that I had ever seen. It was twice the girth of the Ballet Instructor's and an inch or two longer. She buckled it on over her hips and followed me through the door. It bounced as she walked, heavy with promise. She was naked, and the nipple on her single breast poked out like a berry lonesome on its own island.

I leaned over the rail and waited. I was unsure whether or not I could take it but I was willing to try. I saw no reason not to.

She put her hand on the bump of my lower spine, shifting me into the right position. Her hand drifted between my legs, testing my wetness. Whatever she found, it was not what she was looking for. She shuffled in her bag again and I heard a click of a lid flipping open and then flinched as the lubricant, thick, cold and viscous, was applied to my pussy.

The first stroke did not split me in two as I had feared but filled me to the brim. Her cock was an imprint that travelled all the way from my cunt to my heart to my brain. It made me feel whole, at home in myself. I pushed back against her and heard her grunt. She pushed against me, and we continued in a tug of push and pull until she began to tire, and leaned forward against my back, holding me in an embrace as she rubbed her finger over my clitoris until I came.

We stood there a while longer staring out over the city. Pedestrians wandered the streets below and occasionally looked up at us. Whether they could see two naked women looking back down at them from fourteen storeys above was unclear.

When I woke in the morning she was gone. The only reminder of the night before was the scent of smoke and lemon that still lingered, and the pile of crisp bills that she had left on the glass coffee table beneath an empty pack of her French cigarettes.

One hundred pounds in total. Not even enough for an hour with the cheapest run-of-the-mill hooker. I couldn't decide what offended me most, that she had opted to pay me, or that she had paid so little.

I didn't trust so easily after that. I continued to meet men and women and to fuck them, but I was no longer free with my affections, my mind or my soul. I kept a little part of myself hidden and I threw away the key.

My emotional detachment may not have improved my dancing but it made it bearable. I came to believe that I wasn't fucking at all. I was merely an actress, a purveyor of fantasies, an illusionist selling a dream.

We were not selling sex. That was the job of whore houses and strip joints. The Network's shows were part fantasy and part irony, a visual affirmation that lovemaking was merely an extension of life and not something to be hidden behind closed doors, sneered at or giggled over. Madame Denoux's vision was a dance in which the two partners would join in the most intimate of ways, without drawing any particular attention to the fact. The crescendo, the penetration, would be simply another step in the rhythm of life.

I continued to refuse to meet my partners, Tango, Inca Priest and Ballet Instructor, outside of our set. The only news I had of them in between shows were the regular updates from the Network to confirm matters of scheduling and the health of the members and exchange the certificates that we were all required to complete monthly.

These elements, off stage, added a hint of sterility and matter-of-fact business to the proceedings, but when the music switched on and my partner appeared from the darkness and into the stage light I forgot the organisational and biological necessities and revelled in the response of the audience and the feeling of a bare cock thrusting inside me, a stranger's cock, and the knowledge that we had never engaged in a single conversation besides the most fundamental, the one that occurred between our bodies.

It felt risky and dangerous and endlessly arousing, and cemented my idea that I had become some kind of ethereal sexual being, only half human, the rest a mixture of pheromones and desire, a walking receptacle for lust.

However, off stage was a different matter altogether. I

continued to pick up men and sometimes women and sometimes those who did not identify entirely with either sex but something different again. They were the ones that I was most at home with, the gender benders, the queers and the trans men and women who fucked like anatomy was irrelevant and didn't seem to feel as though their entire being was defined by their genitals.

Most of the time, though, my conquests and the feelings that they inspired within me were unremarkable. I bedded a new person in each city. I collected people as though they were souvenirs, to replace the museums and art galleries that I never visited.

Florence was the only one that I remembered by name. The others I remembered by the music that inevitably reverberated through every room that we returned to, a symphony of tunes designed to relax, stimulate, or simply hide the inevitable noises of lovemaking, the squeaking of hotel-room beds and the slapping of body parts joining in energetic fervour.

In Prague, I met a black girl who penetrated me with a strap-on against a wall in the dark shadows of a club whilst The Cure's 'Lullaby' reverberated through the speakers and the other punters continued to drink beer and eat crisps and stare at each other with glazed expressions completely unaware of what was taking place in the corner of the room where two women who appeared to be engaged in conversation where in fact engaged in passionate lovemaking behind the feeble barrier of a bar stool.

Berlin was old-school jazz, a university student who lived in Neukolln and screwed me slow and smooth to Duke Ellington's 'Mood Indigo' and Peggy Lee's 'Fever'.

Barcelona was a waiter from a tapas bar who called me when I left my phone number on the back of a napkin along with his tip and bought his own playlist of fast and furious Reggae en Español to my hotel room after his shift. Sicily was dark and dirty on the bonnet of a parked car in the back streets of Palermo with Beethoven's *5th Symphony* playing on the stereo. Paris was a local academic who knew all the best patisseries in the Latin Quarter and could only get hard to the sound of Lou Doillon's 'I.C.U.'. Reykjavik was a British expat who had a bag full of phalluses and wanted me to penetrate him from behind while Mick Jagger and the Rolling Stones crooned 'You Can't Always Get What You Want'. In Stockholm a man who wanted me to watch him masturbate while he listened to Johnny Cash reading the New Testament and in Milan a blond German woman on holiday who could have been my double and who licked me to orgasm and then stroked me to sleep to the sound of Ani DiFranco's 'Overlap'.

The songs became more important than the sex and soon it was just a sea of cocks and pussy and the soundtrack that became the backdrop of my life.

When I wasn't dancing or fucking I slept, or wandered the streets and stared at the outside of monuments and museums, enjoying gelato and pizza slices or currywurst or caramelised hot nuts or whatever else was the flavour of the place, and never bothering to go any deeper, to get to know the cities that I passed through any more than I bothered to get to know the people who inhabited them beyond taking one member of the population to bed before finding my way to a different airport and a different city.

And all the time, I thought of Chey.

Quickly a whole year had gone by, I realised with a shock

one morning as I showered and scrubbed on automatic pilot in readiness for another set in front of another invisible audience whose gasps and arousal I could only sense from where I was on the improvised stages, spectators from another world. The travelling had become a quiet routine, a whirl of airports, hotels, dark nights and bodies. I had seen their world but, deep inside, I knew I had seen nothing, just a tourist in the house of flesh.

I had begun to tire of my sex dance. What had seemed a daring performance art in the beginning soon became just another money-earning chore, and when the men I danced with eventually ceased to fill me, and I was left vacant and alone in another hotel room with just the sound of my own thoughts screaming through my mind, I wondered what would be next for me. Where I would go and what I would do when this part of my life too reached its inevitable conclusion?

Next, I was scheduled to go to Amsterdam. But that was still a week away and I was at a loose end so opted for a few days of sunshine further west down the coast in France. Me time.

Another day, another dollar, another dance, another city and another cock.

Or at least, so I thought, before the letter arrived.

It had followed me halfway round the world. The corners of the white envelope crumpled, a slight tear along one side that some postal worker along the line had repaired with a strip of narrow brown tape and a succession of hastily scribbled addresses and stickers redirecting it from place to place.

It had finally reached me, caught up with me, in the

South of France, where I was taking a short break at a small beach resort close to Montpellier between assignments following a well-attended (and well-paid) performance with Tango in the grounds of a remote villa in the hills beyond Cannes during the film festival. I assumed the majority of the audience had consisted of people from the film industry or its attendant financiers, but no Hollywood offer for my services had resulted, just the customary suggestions of sex for money that I had long got used to.

Chey had posted the letter in Miami and addressed it to me c/o Lucian in Venice Beach in California who had redirected it to New Orleans from where it had travelled to Europe and a handful of poste restante addresses I had used as I flitted from place to place on jobs.

At first I did not recognise the handwriting on the envelope spelling out my name. I had never been to Miami and didn't know anyone there. I wondered if it was from another dancer I had somehow befriended in the waltz of dressing rooms I had passed through, but there was something masculine and firm about the script and the slope of the letters.

Even then, I thought it unimportant and neglected to open it for half a day while I busied myself with a late breakfast and a leisurely walk to the beach and a swim. All my communications with Madame Denoux and work-related correspondence took place online as my Mac Air accompanied me everywhere.

I couldn't keep out of the midday sun during the trek back from the beach to my small hotel, and the first thing I yearned for was a shower, but the letter stood there on the bedside table as I opened the door, its haphazard stickers calling to me.

Kicking off my flip-flops I grabbed hold of my nail file and slit it open.

It was from Chey.

By the time I finished reading it and came to my senses, the abundant sweat coating my body had dried unpleasantly across my skin under the sustained assault of the room's air conditioning.

Luba,

I can just picture you reading these opening lines and realising who has written them. I beg you: don't be angry or hasty and tear these pages up without reading them.

Don't.

I miss you . . .

There were another four pages. It was a love letter and the first one I had ever been sent.

A love letter in which Chey never attempted to explain the presence of the gun in his drawer or justify his repeated absences on so-called business or explain where he was while I lingered in New York. He alluded to reasons that maybe one day he would be able to reveal to me, but just expressed sadness that now was not the time.

But what hurt most was having the strength of his feelings for me confirmed in such a naked, emotional way while on the other hand, his words made it clear that he had resigned himself already to having lost me.

With every passing day I just feel you fading away, retreating further from me. It feels like ages since we were together, spoke, touched. And as much as it hurts like hell, it's okay. I am slowly learning to accept it. Your future life is elsewhere and cannot be with me. It's painful, but I have to be realistic about this. To hang on to you would be to do you a disservice. Even if every day I spend away from you is like living a life by only half, a life in which an empty space has taken hold of my body, my heart, your soul.

Ten times every single day at least, I resolve myself to having lost you once and for all, and cry a little inside (or for real if I'm alone), only to find myself minutes later fighting against that resignation, not wishing to accept what is happening or will happen or has already happened. A battle I seem unable to win . . .

Was he unwilling to fight for me?

I remember every single second spent with you and love you even more for it. Every coffee or drink we shared, the walks, the meals, the embraces, the silences. Thank you, Luba, for giving me so much in the short time you allowed me to be yours as much as you were mine (even as a greedy me tries to interject that it was, however, not nearly enough).

Ah, all the places I still wanted to take you too, knowing your hunger for travel, your fervour for new horizons. The cities, the landscapes I could have seen anew through your eyes, the streets along which your wonderful endless legs could have walked down, the thousand private stages I wanted you to dance across for the pleasure of my eyes only, my prima ballerina, my private ballerina, my dancer caught in amber.

There was no mention of the initial displeasure I had witnessed when he had learned that I had begun stripping, no allusion to Lev, and just a bare mention of the gun and what I had done.

By the way, that was a great shot and the TV never recovered . . . Not that it matters, as we never watched it much, did we?

At which stage, the letter, on its second page, became more frantic, his handwriting abandoning its discipline, its regularity, maybe he had been drinking, but his words lost all restraint and it all began flowing like a river bursting its banks, a stream-of-consciousness torrent, in which every wavelet breaking against the dam of my heart felt like a dagger.

Right now, I'm in a small village down South, in a tiny room in a bed and breakfast (there are no hotels here) in which the air conditioning has broken down, so I am sitting dressed only in an old pair of shorts, haven't shaved for a few days. I'm sweating like a pig. I'd describe the bedroom and the view from the window but it would be of no use. I just feel terribly lonely, assaulted by thoughts of you.

I am waiting. Can't even tell you why. And, as you no doubt guessed it has nothing to do with amber, although that side of my life is legitimate, and I have a terrible fondness for it. I hope you still treasure all those pieces I gave you; I saw they were no longer in Gansevoort Street after you left . . .

I slept badly yesterday night. Nightmares or dreams, it doesn't matter what they are if you appear in them, a radiant star of my troubled nights. I had a lustful dream and it still flows through my brain now that I am fully awake. I was revisiting all the times we spent together. Amazed and shocked at the things we have done.

In the dream, we were together again and you stood, naked above me, your legs apart. And then, that crazy sensation of your mouth around me, sucking on me, licking me, protecting me. And the whiteness of your skin and deep green pit of your eyes, of the awesome puckered hole of your arse, the welcoming wetness of your cunt, and the forest of your curls. I close my eyes: the softness of your small, perfect breasts, your hands touching me everywhere, your tongue in my throat, oh my love, you've spoiled me forever for others.

And every vision and colour and sensation of that dream was totally pornographic. But it was also pure, as if we were angels, we were beautiful together. And the thought then returned of how good we are together and not just in bed, the comfort we found in each other, despite the differences in culture and backgrounds we do not share. We were friends, not just lovers, perfect companions, weren't we?

So now I must treasure these memories.

I am a weak man, Luba; I am not noble. I know that the day will eventually come when I succumb to both nostalgia and temptation and try to recreate those joys, that lust, that happiness with others, and I want you to forgive me in advance, because I know that the spectacle of me fucking another with the same abandon and transgressiveness will never equal the beauty we achieved; it will be dirty, immoral, but I fear I am just a man and part of me will want to try again, even while the other half of my brain knows I could never conjure up the transcendence of you again and all others, all other things I will do will be just a vulgar imitation.

I love you so much, Luba. Why couldn't I express it better when we were still together?

Sometimes I make the wish that by magic (pact with the devil, fantasy, the power of dreams . . .) you could live inside my skin for just a day. Then you would feel what I feel and realise how unique and strong it is and what you mean to me. I would kill for you. You now witness the pitiful desperation your decision to end it has caused in me. The madness it provoked when you so suddenly withdrew your love, your affection. It was so sudden that the pain was intense, blinding, like an onset of panic. Words fail me to describe how I felt when you left.

But it's fine. It's okay, my love, my gypsy, my treasure.

Accept my confused clichés for what they are and do not think badly of me.

I love you.

I can write no more words. I know no more words. I've run out of them.

This is where my winter begins, I guess. The years without you . . .

The final pages must have been written on a separate day, later maybe, as the writing was slanted differently, less frantic, just a list he had titled 'The things about you I will never forget'.

Your love
The tenderness in your eyes
The sound of your voice and the charm of your accent
Your occasional awkwardness, your feelings running hot and cold depending on the moment
Your spontaneity
Your impish sense of humour
The heart-wrenching experience of watching you undress
Or undressing you myself
Your quiet beauty, the silk of your skin
The warmth of your mouth against mine
The way you kiss and allow yourself to be kissed until the air in our lungs is screaming for relief
Sharing a bath with you in Gansevoort Street
You walking through the New York snow

Your naked back the evening we went out to Momofuku's

Sitting with you watching a Pixar movie surrounded by little chattering kids

Your hand holding mine in the auditorium and then in the cab going back

Watching you eat, watching you laugh

You singing old Russian lullabies when you don't think anyone is listening

The way you walk, so gracefully, gliding and sexy

The way you would say 'I want you inside me'

The way you would say my name

The peacefulness of your sleep

The way you rode me on the beach the first time we made love

You cuddling against me for warmth between cold covers

The book I was hoping I could write about you, if I only knew how to write

The way your body sprawls across the bed

The velvet feel of your mouth around my cock

Our silences

The delicacy of your small breasts and the colour of your nipples

Your natural pallor

The blonde down in the small of your back

The beauty of us together

The time you cried on the phone because you missed me

Entering you, penetrating you and every time it feeling like the first time, again and again

The look in your eyes when we were having sex

The sheen of sweat on your white skin

Your legs, long and endless

Your Eastern soul

Your emotions

The delighted look on your face when I managed to surprise you

The way your eyes shone with each new gift of amber

How we could argue about the Clash and talk together of books and films, music and life

The way it felt then, like we would never tire of each other and always have something to say

Crossing Washington Square and seeing the dogs, children and squirrels

Walking down Broadway

Sleeping in the same bed as you and staying silent in the morning and watching you wake

Introducing you to Veselka, that Ukrainian restaurant on 2nd Avenue, and seeing you licking your lips in anticipation

Being so proud of being seen with you, with no guilt or doubt

Becoming a better person by being with you

The hope that we could have a future

The terrible dream of having a child together

You not talking to me, sitting on the floor in the corner of the room, childish, selfish, but still irresistible, that time we had our first row

You allowing me to tie your hands together

Your surprise text messages

The dark, untidy forest of your pubes and then your dazzling smoothness, a contrast in worlds

The way you would orchestrate my movements when I went down on you

The view of your most private openings when you got down on your knees and allowed me to take you from behind

My penis moving in and out of you

The way you'd examine my body, parts and whole, perfecting your sexual education
Walking down unknown streets
Searching for restaurants to eat in
Your tongue against my balls
Playfully fighting in bed until I inadvertently hurt your neck
Your tongue against my tongue
Sitting in bars and terraces together, sipping drinks and coffees
Watching you in the shower
Taking you in the shower
The white towels draped across your body after your shower
The single beauty spot on your arse
The sadness in your eyes when you talk of your father and mother
You once going pantieless for me
The way you made my heart sing
How you revived my life after years of sorrow
Your prejudices, your tastes, your likes and dislikes
Your jokes
The fact that you understood me
Walking up the steps in Central Park together
Helping you locate a CD of Russian songs you remembered from your childhood
Exploring New York together
Standing still together at Ground Zero
Your quiet energy and your intense Russian personality
Your quiet moan when you come and the way it lights up the emerald darkness of your eyes
You stripping for me in the corridor

Your playfulness

Fucking on floors and sofas when we couldn't make it to the bed

Being a couple, an 'us'

Watching a World Cup match on the big screen at the Red Lion, surrounded by noisy German fans

Fingering you on the highway when we drove to the Hamptons

Your white skirt

Your flimsy bathing costume top which hid nothing

You undoing my trousers in the silence of the High Line as night fell

Your style

Your exuberant love of life

Your moods

Your defensiveness

Our telepathy

Your dreams, whether wonderful or misplaced

Your wantonness

The vagueness of your ambitions

Your deep love of sex

The honesty of your intimacy

Your body

Your soul

Your uniqueness

Your need

The gentle way you so often said that things or people were 'nice' or 'beautiful' or 'interesting' even without knowing them truly

Your generosity of character and soul

Your intellectual interests and how much they paralleled mine

The fact that we were so good together, we were 'one', we were happy

You

Nowhere in the letter did Chey beg me to return or ask for an answer. He even forgot to sign the letter.

Chey.

7

Dancing with Amber

Chey's letter released a torrent of memories, each of them sweeter and more painful than the last.

A barrage of images and remembrances flooded my mind, as if our relationship could be broken down piecemeal, the moments lining up one after another to break my heart.

The sound of his laugh. The way that he said *Luba*, always extending the *u* sound, as though he was caressing my name with his tongue. His habit of hanging his shirts over chairs when he removed them so that all the furniture in the apartment carried his scent. The way he spread his butter two inches thick. His passion for music. His passion for me. The firmness of his hands and the softness of his lips.

I carried the letter with me everywhere and read it over and over again until I feared that I would wear the ink off the pages. It wouldn't have mattered if I had. I knew the words by heart.

When the express train reached Brussels for the change-over I was moody and impatient, bored of staring out at the interminable green fields flying by outside the window. I couldn't face another minute sitting cramped and still, so skipped the half-hourly connection and walked briskly into the town centre where I wondered why the silly bronze statue of the small chubby boy pissing was so famous. I threw a coin into the water anyway. God knows, I could use some good luck, I thought. Then I picked up a box of the most expensive chocolates that I could find in the nearest tourist shop, filled with caramel, hazelnuts, pistachios and nougat and nestling prettily in a white box tied with a purple ribbon. I returned to the station, settled into a window seat on the next train and shoved the sweets into my mouth one after the other until I felt sick as a thin man in a chequered shirt with a button-down collar stared at me. When I noticed him gazing I ate them two at a time until he looked away.

I was tired of airports, tired of travelling and suddenly uncertain about life altogether. I had chosen to travel by train from Montpellier to Amsterdam just to avoid getting on another damn plane.

By the time I arrived I had virtually decided to hand my notice in to the Network and give up dancing for ever, or at least the kind of dancing that culminated in a public sex show.

The way that Chey had described what we had together was so personal, so private. Reading through the memories of our relationship described in such vivid detail made the contrast between making love and fucking seem like a chasm. An unbridgeable divide.

I had been fooling myself. There was no way for two people who hadn't even properly met to mimic the emotion of coupling on stage. Even in its barest form what I was doing could be nothing more than a poor imitation. And I did not believe that the audience appreciated the skill involved. They did not see the complicated steps and turns. My perfectly executed *entrechat* and *bourrée* went unnoticed. The punters paid a lot of money but they were just there for the fuck, for the cock and the pussy. They were no different from the drunks at Barry's or the stoners who hung around the run-down bars in California. All that separated the exclusive clientele from the riffraff was the size of their wallets.

But I considered myself a professional and despite my misgivings, pulling out of the show was not an option. Tickets had no doubt been booked ages in advance and the discreet venue arranged. Some of those in the audience would have travelled to Amsterdam especially to watch me perform. The Inca Priest, my partner for this act, had a schedule to stick to and money to make just as I did. Whether rain, shine, good mood or bad, even when I was on my period, I still danced. Reliability was a matter of personal pride.

Tonight, at least, we would not be the only show on. We were performing as part of a series of perversions. It was an Amsterdam weekend celebrating the erotic and the exotic and we were just one of the acts on the bill, though as ever advertised to only a select few.

We were performing in the basement of an exclusive art gallery in Jordaan, right in the middle of a gentrified residential area where all the inhabitants were likely at home behind the customary curtainless Amsterdam windows and blissfully unaware of the 'private exhibition' being held just a few doors down.

From the outside, the building appeared to be closed, but the door swung inwards when I pushed it and inside a small handwritten sign painted in deep red letters bore the word *Expositie* and an arrow that pointed to a flight of stone steps leading downwards.

The corridor at the bottom of the steps was whitewashed

and bare. A tall blond man wearing a tuxedo stood outside at the end, blocking another doorway. I showed him the card that identified me as a bona fide Network dancer, and he pointed the way further down the hall to the dressing room, which proved to be an old storage cupboard that had been temporarily converted. I would be paid a princely sum for tonight, but you wouldn't know it from the less than salubrious quarters provided to the performers.

A troupe of dancers were packed into the small room. Each of them naked, and painted like an animal. There was a zebra – black and white from her head to her toes – a giraffe, a panther and a lion. The zebra was wearing head-phones and practising her dance steps. Her footwork was not classical in style but something more foreign to me, a kind of tribal belly dancing. The music flowed through her body in waves as she swayed and gyrated to an invisible beat.

Leading them all was a beautiful dark-haired woman dressed in a ringmaster's costume complete with leather whip and a pair of glittering red stilettos. She wore a curling false moustache, neatly waxed at the ends.

I nodded a polite hello and stacked my tote bag on top of a stack of paint tins in the corner alongside a pile of coats and feather boas strewn haphazardly in a kaleidoscope of colour.

There was a crack as loud as a gunshot behind me and I turned in time to see the ringmaster shooing her menagerie out of the door. She turned and winked at me, an action that took some effort due to the length and weight of her false eyelashes, which were red tipped at the ends and added a menacing arachnid quality to her appearance. The animals filed along ahead of her. They moved as if they were truly inhuman, their bodies swaying like Saharan beasts taking a leisurely trot to the nearest waterhole.

The presence of pseudo animals in a sex show gave a somewhat bestial slant to the proceedings, and curious to see more, I dressed hurriedly, wriggling out of my modest jeans and T-shirt, slipping into the white gown, dabbing a little powder to take the shine from my skin and glancing in the mirror for one final hair check before racing through another corridor to the backstage area where I could hide behind a curtain to watch the first acts.

The stage was decked out like the interior of a jungle. Even the air felt humid, as though we were trapped in one of Amsterdam's greenhouses. The wooden floor was surrounded by a dearth of ferns and tropical flowers in pots in vivid hues of red, purple and orange. Even the sound system had not escaped the jungle theme, as the tweeting of birds and the rush of flowing water permeated gently through the speakers between the acts. The menagerie of animals had settled themselves in to various corners and, rather than dancing, they were behaving as animals would, slinking around trees, nibbling on ferns, staring at the dancers with wide eyes and occasional roars and jumping back when the ringmaster cracked her whip.

The opening act was a contortionist, so flexible that she made my bones ache. The next, a femme fatale in a black silk dressing gown who danced with a gun and ended with a shot into the audience. She was almost making love to the barrel and so passionate was her embrace of the cold metal that I could see myself again in Chey's living room swaying and gliding across his wooden floors with the Sieg Sauer before taking out the television. *Not that it matters, as we never watched it much, did we?*

Chey's words rang in my ears. His letter was tucked into my tote bag and all I wanted at that moment was to be back in bed pressing the sheets of paper to my chest, or better still, lying alongside him, telling him that I was sorry, that I loved him, that we should be together. Tears leaked down my cheeks and dripped onto my gown, sticking the thin fabric to my skin.

I watched the next dancer begin her routine through a watery blur. She was dressed as a unicorn, complete with a slender flashing horn fixed to her head and a sequined harness that glittered as she moved. Her steps were so naturally equine that she made the hooves and harness that Chey had bought for me to wear and which I had been barely able to walk in, let alone dance in seem like a poor parody of an eroticism that was so animal to its core I wasn't sure where the human ended and the creature began.

My eyes were focused on the girl doing her thing but my heart and soul were back in Chey's study remembering how it had felt to lean back against him as he pressed his cock into my arsehole so deeply that eventually I had collapsed onto the floor and he had laid alongside me stroking me back to life.

When she removed her shimmering tight shorts and crop top to reveal a tiny pair of sequined pants that revealed neither breasts nor the demarcation of a vagina or the bulge of a penis but rather a slim and completely flat chest bordered by the straps of the harness it seemed as though she was birthing from a chrysalis rather than taking her clothes off. I had the sense that I was witnessing a creature reveal her natural form rather than a person remove her clothes.

I was accustomed to being the most daring, original and

exotic act on the bill. Up to this point, the Network shows that I had completed were one-offs, just me and my partner performing a single set. This was the first occasion where I was just a part of a line-up. And the girls who I had danced with at The Place, Sweet Lola's, The Grand, or any of the other establishments that I performed in, had simply been strippers of one persuasion or another and varied only in their beauty and ability to shimmy and contort themselves with varying degrees of skill and elegance around a steel pole.

The acts on stage tonight were of a different sort altogether, and for the first time I realised that I was not the only erotic dancer on the planet who could do more than just take off her clothes. I felt like an amateur.

The first notes of Debussy's 'La Mer' penetrated the sound system. I pushed myself to my feet and through sheer force of will moved onto the stage and began to dance. This would be the last time, I told myself. As soon as I was back at the hotel I would call Madame Denoux and tender my resignation. This would be it.

To compound my misery, I had discovered at the last minute that my regular partner had fallen ill and I had to dance with a replacement, a man whom I had not previously trained with and whom I had no experience dancing or coupling with before. He was tall and thick-bodied with a hard look painted across his face. Maybe he was just as nervous as I was and that was what made the angle of his jaw so tight and his expression so fierce.

When we danced he moved a half-beat behind the music and we were never quite in unison and lacked elegance as we went through the motions for what felt like an eternity.

When he finally penetrated me in accordance to the

established scenario of the show I felt dirty and used. And never had I been so glad to hear the final notes that signalled the end of my set.

I felt sickened by what I had just done, not only tonight but for all the previous months now. On the way back to the hotel on Leidseplein where I had been booked into, I couldn't help playing the event over and over in my mind.

I should have taken a cab back and the thoughts would have lingered less, but I knew I needed a shot of fresh air to cleanse my mind before I reached the room and had the opportunity to jump under the shower and wash the infamy away.

It was three in the morning and the city was sleeping. There was just the gentle shimmer of the still water on the Singel in the moonlight and the irregular cobblestones of the canal walk, rare lights emerging from the curtainless windows of old buildings. Passing the dark windows of the neighbouring Athenaeum Bookshop and American Book Center on Spui, I took a detour and made my way to the Dam where just a few stragglers and drunk survivors of unknown festivities staggered by. Then, still in a daze, I took Kalverstraat, a pale ghost amongst its flickering neons, and then yet another canal, which l followed all the way to Leidseplein.

By the time I reached my bedroom, I was exhausted. But also angry at myself. For picking this life, for leaving Chey, for not having the strength to return to him now. The dancing made me feel dirty now, in a way it hadn't before.

I switched on the shower, threw off my clothes and, eyes closed, stepped into the water, turning the heat up until it shocked me back into reality. I stood motionless, letting the water pound against my skin, allowing the steam to envelop me.

By the time I exited the shower cubicle, my body was coloured scarlet red, from the heat and the steam. But my mind still felt dirty. And some of the words in Chey's letter came rushing back to my mind, perverse, beautiful, dirty but so unlike the experience I had just participated in. The contrast was enlightening.

Dawn was peering through the bedroom window, a tentative grey light spreading its day blanket over the Amsterdam roofs I had a generous view of from my top-floor suite.

I lay on the bed, swaddled in thick, damp, white towels but sleep wouldn't come.

Within an hour, rumours of life were creeping up from the street below and I slipped on a sweatshirt and an old pair of jeans and trainers and took the lift down to the lobby. There was nobody in reception, just the sounds of someone vacuuming the back office. I walked out. There was an autumnal chill in the air.

Ten minutes away, some of the floating stalls at the open-air flower market were opening, deliveries being unpacked, displays watered and arranged. The orgy of colour illuminated the grey morning as flowers, bulbs, plants, seeds, accessories and souvenirs were spread out. A young woman with a teardrop tattoo below her left eye and punk-like attire was putting out baskets of cannabis starter kits across the front of the stall's display. Her dyed black hair was cut in an asymmetric bob and I noticed she had identical trainers to mine.

Moving along the quay my gaze was assaulted by the sunshine colours of all the tulips littering each and every stand. It was a flower we seldom had occasion to see back in Donetsk or even St Petersburg. I loved the clean shape of tulips, the serene uniformity of their curves. I somehow found them peaceful. Even though none of the stalls were yet open, I convinced one of the assistants to sell me a large bunch of tulips in a variety of colours, and also treated myself to an immense bouquet of other flowers, roses crowded with lilies, sunflowers and gardenias. I ambled back to the hotel with my armful of flowers, attracting curious stares in the now busier lobby where tourists were trouping in single file from the lifts to the breakfast room.

In the bedroom again, I stripped, and assembled the flowers across the white, crisp bedsheets, orchestrating a deluge of wild vegetation all along the bed's perimeter. I lay down at their centre, my own pale, bare skin now set off by a glowing halo of colours.

It felt like madness. It was madness.

I took a deep breath and extended my hand to the drawer of the bedside cabinet on my right, taking out the small green velvet bag in which I kept my thirteen amber pieces. I scattered them across my skin where most settled in unsteady equilibrium while others slid down into the grave-yard of flowers surrounding me. The largest piece, an almost transparent block of amber, watery-like in appearance but uncloudy, naturally shaped like a heart without the inter-vention of human hands, sat, ready to fall sideways if I moved, halfway below the fall of my breasts and my navel. I took it between my fingers, brought it to my mouth and rolled it around my tongue. Now lubricated I pulled it out and carefully inserted it into my sex, gasping as its unyielding hardness passed my lips.

Then, at random I took another, smaller piece of amber

and placed it inside my mouth where it nestled in the hollow of my cheek.

I was erasing the Inca Priest, the dance, the meaningless sex masquerading as art.

Now I was filled.

By Amber.

By Chey.

And sleep finally came.

I was woken from deep slumber in mid-afternoon. The sounds of Leidseplein were now loud and cheerful, rising all the way up to my window and, when I peered through the curtains, a cold sun was casting its light on the city.

As I came to my senses, I realised it was my phone ringing that had shaken me out of my deep lassitude.

I fumbled for it, spat out the amber piece sitting in my mouth over the flower-laden bed. The other one, I realised, as a pang of fuzzy pleasure shot through my insides all the way to my brain, was still lodged inside my cunt.

'Hello?'

'Luba, you left me a message. What is the matter?'

It was Madame Denoux. It must be morning in New Orleans.

I composed myself as I felt the anger stream back.

'I'm done with it,' I said.

'What?'

'I mean it. I'm in a mind to give up the whole dancing thing, Madame,' I continued. 'I enjoyed it before. But now it makes me feel terrible.'

'You just have to be more dispassionate about it all, Luba,' Madame Denoux said.

'Dispassionate!' I shouted. 'That's not what I signed up for . . .'

I brushed some of the flowers surrounding me from the bed and they fell to the carpeted floor, scattering in improbable patterns. My finger swept slowly across the smooth ridges of one of the amber pieces lying there, and it felt comforting and peaceful.

'You are so talented and beautiful, my dear Luba. This is just a blip. You cannot give up your dancing. Everyone is talking about you as your reputation spreads. It took me years to get where you are already, you know.'

But I'd made up my mind.

'I want out,' I said.

'Surely not?'

'I do.'

'Please reconsider.' Madame's voice was pleading now.

'No.' I was adamant.

'So what will you do?'

'Maybe just normal dancing, I don't know.'

'The rewards will not be so significant, you realise that?'

'I do. But I've saved a lot already. Maybe I'll take a long vacation. Then I'll see.'

I could almost hear her thinking.

'Yes, that's good. An extended break. Excellent idea. Refresh your mind and body, Luba. And then we will talk again, no?'

She explained how taking a break from performing would make my absence felt even more, increasing the demand for my unique services, increasing the price. She suggested that together, she and I could arrange it so that my appearances would become even more exclusive, rare even. That I would only perform at times and in places of my own choosing from here onwards. Madame Denoux begged me to consider this possibility once I had completed my sabbatical. Would I?

I reluctantly agreed.

After the previous night, I wasn't sure that I would ever dance again, but I also knew that I would never get any satisfaction from anything else. I had come to enjoy the travel, the lack of earthly ties. I would find a way to recover from this and I would find it soon. I had nothing else in life.

Maybe even one day I would come across Chey. Somewhere exotic, somewhere new. Both outlaws, adventurers.

I had answered his letter. My words had been feeble and tentative, but I had tried, in my own way, to forgive him for what he was or might turn out to be. I'd left the door open. Confessed to the pain that being parted from him had caused in my soul. But the letter had, after passing from post to post, been returned. He was no longer living in Gansevoort Street and had left no forwarding address.

Right now, my future was a blank space. I could do whatever I wanted to do.

Today, I decided I would visit Amsterdam's museums. I'd never had the opportunity to do so before. My hotel room on Leidseplein was available for two more nights and had been paid for in advance. Tomorrow I might call on a travel agent and exchange my return ticket to New Orleans for a flight to somewhere else. Maybe the Caribbean again. But Barbados or Jamaica this time. Become an explorer. Meet people. Have adventures.

I was hungry. I washed my face and teeth, dressed. A simple spring cotton dress with discreet polka dots reaching to just below my knees, which left my shoulders bare.

Found a thin cashmere jumper in my luggage and put on flat ballet shoes and strolled out.

There were stalls by the Central train station selling chips with mayonnaise, which I had sampled on the day I arrived. That's where I would go, then I'd catch a cab for the Rijksmuseum to look at the Rembrandt collections, just like any other tourist. My heart already felt lighter at the prospect of a swathe of empty days ahead. Maybe I could rediscover myself. Find peace.

By the time I reached the ticket counter, there was only an hour left before closing time. I would have to rush. Or then again not, as I could return the following day and take my time. I smiled. It felt like a luxury.

I was in the West Wing contemplating *The Night Watch* when I heard an amused voice over my shoulder.

'Has anyone ever told you that you are as beautiful clothed as you are naked?'

I turned round.

The face was familiar from countless photos I had come across in newspapers and magazines. An English rock star who called himself Viggo Franck. I'd never actually heard his music. His band, the Holy Criminals, had a reputation for excess and mostly played arena tours, I knew.

In the flesh, he was shorter than I expected, although his thin frame provided him with a form of illusory height. Up front, his long, untidy hair was a cuckoo's nest of artful tangles that hadn't seen a comb since the Middle Ages. His spindly legs were encased in the tightest pair of jeans I had ever come across, as if sprayed on, fraying at the bottom edges where his heavy black leather boots took over, showing half an inch of pale ankle. Had I been wearing heels, I would have towered half a head above him.

His dark eyes glittered with mischief and his smile was disarming, almost a little boy's, questioning, gazing at me with both undiluted appetite and genuine curiosity, as if I was a rare specimen in a zoo or a shop window.

I calmly withstood his attention, my eyes unavoidably checking out the significant, and obvious, bump inside his jeans which the uncanny tightness of the material only served to emphasise.

He followed the path of my eyes and his smile turned into a knowing grin.

'You have an advantage over me,' I remarked.

His face lit up.

'Love your accent, girl . . .'

I raised my eyebrows.

'Are you really Russian?' he continued.

'From the Ukraine, actually,' I pointed out.

'Wonderful,' Viggo stated.

The previous night was the only time I had ever performed in Amsterdam, whether just as a dancer or as part of a sex duo, so it made sense that Viggo Franck would have seen me there.

Seeing me pensive, Viggo continued, 'Yesterday night I was a spectator. I had an invitation.'

'I see.'

'I've seen a few live sex shows here and there, Hamburg, the old 42nd Street joints in New York when I was still a callow youth, Tijuana, here, but yours was beautiful. You turned it into a thing of grace. Truly. I'd been warned that you were unique, they were right. It was worth it at any price,' he said.

'I'm flattered,' I said. 'However, it was a bad night to catch me. I can do better when my heart is in it.'

Out of the corner of my eye I caught the fixed gaze of the little girl in the yellow dress as she stood in the light in Rembrandt's painting.

'If that's the case,' Viggo Franck said, 'I must arrange to attend your next performance and see you at your best.'

'There might not be further shows,' I pointed out. 'I have no plans for future performances.'

His mouth opened slightly in a gesture of disappointment, like a child being denied an indulgence.

'I find that sad,' he remarked.

'All good things must come to an end.'

'It wasn't just the sex, you know,' Viggo Franck went on. 'It was a combination of everything, the way you danced, the elegance and the eroticism, the music, you made it into an unforgettable experience. And I know a few things about stagecraft . . . A thing of beauty, truly.'

There was an announcement on the Tannoy that the museum would be closing in fifteen minutes and we had to make our way to the exits.

I was about to retrace my steps through the labyrinth of the Rijksmuseum's long corridors and galleries with the English rock star trailing in my wake, tightening my grip on the canvas bag hanging from my bare shoulder, when I heard him cry out, 'Wait!'

'Yes?'

'Join me for a coffee?' he asked.

I had no other plans. And his company would save me from the terror of my own, alone in the hotel room with nothing but my thoughts. I accepted.

Night was falling. There seemed to be no bars or coffee

houses in the immediate vicinity of the museum so we ambled south, exchanging indifferent small talk until a few blocks away we reached yet another canal that was bordered with a variety of cafes and restaurants. As we selected one and stepped inside, I noticed how Viggo's unkempt appearance attracted attention from the passers-by, mostly women of all ages.

I remembered he was known as a ferocious ladies' man, although to me right now, he was amusing and harmless, eager like a puppy. I knew I had that effect on men, but that was from the vantage point of my presence on stage, when I was highlighted by the spotlight and the artifice of the situation, not necessarily when I was the same old Luba, wearing a simple polka-dot cotton dress and flat shoes, and no make-up, the one I saw in the mirror every day. The girl Chey once knew.

'Can I ask you just one thing?' I said as I sat down and ordered a double espresso from the young waitress who couldn't stop staring at Viggo as he installed himself in the facing seat and asked her for a glass of white wine. Not once had she even looked at me, rapt as she was by the rock singer's appearance in the cafe.

'Of course,' he assented.

'Don't bombard me with questions about how I became a sex performer, okay? I'm a dancer. The rest just sort of happened, I suppose. But it's not something I wish to talk about. Not now.'

His lip curled in disappointment, as if I had just torpedoed the whole thrust of his conversation. Then a sparkle appeared in the corner of his eye and he livened up.

'Then tell me about the tattoo – the gun?' he asked.

'It's a long story,' I replied.

'Then give me the abridged version. I'm an impatient man,' he said.

'It was a whim, a spur-of-the-moment thing.'

'Is that all?'

'Because of a man. Someone I knew. He owned a gun and something happened . . .'

'He shot at you?' The words rushed out.

'No. I shot his television screen.'

'Wow,' Viggo said.

Remembering that day, I smiled. In retrospect, it now felt madly amusing. It wasn't at the time.

'I couldn't keep my eyes off it while you were dancing,' Viggo Franck said.

'Just the gun?' I asked mischievously.

'Not quite,' he confessed, licking his lips, retrieving the taste of his wine. 'There was a lot more to see, and I have perfect vision.'

His eyes locked with mine. This man who had seen me fucked by another.

I remained silent.

'You're the sort of girl I'd like to write a song about, babe,' he said, altogether serious again.

Ever since Chey's letter and the unwitting revelation of what he saw in me and thought of me, I had often tried to imagine how others pictured me. The fact that I was so often on display and couldn't fathom how the vision of the spectators accorded with the diffuse vision I had of myself. In a way, I wanted to be the heroine in my own story, the shining star in my own life.

'You're sort of mysterious, aloof but terribly real,' Viggo continued.

'Real, because you've seen me naked, having sex, you mean?'

'Not just that . . . Can I call you Luba?'

'It's my name.'

The mention of song-writing about women brought a memory floating to the surface of my mind.

A few weeks ago, as I'd crossed the Atlantic on an overnight flight that brought me to Europe and the two gigs I'd signed up for first in Cannes and then the recent one in Amsterdam, I'd read a book I'd picked up at the bookstore on the concourse of O'Hare airport in Chicago. It was by an English novelist, titled *Yellow*, and told the turbulent story of a young foreign woman in Paris in the 1950s who fell in and out of relationships in the Latin Quarter amongst a crowd of jazz musicians and expatriates. Somehow I had identified strongly with her and the novel had affected me in a curious fashion. I convinced myself that the character was based on a real person, someone I could feel was real and tangible and that I almost knew. I had never heard of its author before – it was a first novel and he was listed as an academic in London. What was it about Brits that they wanted to be inspired by imperfect women, that they were attracted by the flaws in our characters, the damage?

'Maybe I will. Write that song,' Viggo concluded, emptying his glass.

'You're welcome. Just keep my name out of it,' I said.

He paused, contemplating me in a dreamy way. He was an interesting man, there was no doubt about it, but his reputation preceded him and I knew deep down that he was not a man for all seasons. He was the kind of guy the old Luba might have amused herself with just for a night or two. I hadn't stayed with any of the men I'd slept with after Chey for more than a single night – apart from Lucian. After the sex, they had bored me. Sometimes I sighed with ennui even as we made love. Viggo felt as if he was maybe worth a week. But inside I felt nothing but empty. I couldn't face the silence of my own mind, but I did not feel ready for company.

The truth is that I didn't know what I wanted.

He looked at me with hunger.

'Listen,' he said. 'And please don't be offended. I know what you do, or have done if you've decided to stop, but would you ever consider . . . performing . . . just for me? Your price,' he said, lowering his eyes, as if shameful that he was proposing money.

I sighed. I knew the question had been inevitable. At least he was tentative and not full of himself in the knowledge that he was rich enough to acquire anything.

'You say "perform",' I noted. 'Did you mean just dance, or have sex with you?'

'Beggars can't be choosers. Whatever you would grant me.'

I pondered.

Perhaps someone so warm and honest in his nature might be just the thing to ease me back into things. With him I would be secure, for a time, and I would not be alone. I felt myself with Viggo Franck. Perhaps I could dance for him. And if I could dance for him, then I could learn to dance for others again.

Even though Chey had a hold on my soul and he was never far from my mind, I knew that if I wallowed in the dire pain of his absence it would torment me for ever. I needed my peace of mind back. It wasn't a question of being faithful to someone who had abandoned me; that was a silly notion. It would be a way to keep a grip on my emotional sanity.

I waved to the young Dutch waitress who had been observing us from the bar's counter with both curiosity and envy and ordered another coffee. Viggo did not want another glass of wine.

I finally answered his question.

'I will not have sex with you, Viggo Franck. I do not have sex with men for money. Then again, I might dance for you at a time and a place of my choice. Not today, maybe not even tomorrow, but I might . . .'

'How? When?'

'Anyway, why should you spend money on me? I'm confident that half the women in the world would rush to your bed at a moment's notice and never even contemplate payment, no? But it would be nice to become your friend and dance for you, Viggo Franck.'

Viggo beamed, like a little boy who's just been granted his most heartfelt wish.

'The gun tattoo was a whim,' I explained. 'I suppose I'm a creature of whims, of impulses, that Russian soul, you know . . . It's just what I am.'

'So?'

It now felt like a game. I could feel some of my old spark returning. I wanted to play with Viggo Franck. But my sort of game. And I could sense he was the sort of man who would enjoy sharing these sorts of games.

'As I said, it's not a question of money, but if you bring me just one thing, I will dance for you. In private.'

'What?'

In my own way, I didn't want to make it easy for him. I

wanted to present him with a challenge. To test him. To check if my theories regarding his character were true. I looked outside the cafe. It was now night. All the stores in the city would be closed. I felt uncommonly warm inside, despite my bared shoulders and the thin cotton of my dress.

I provided Viggo Franck with the name of my hotel on Leidseplein and told him that at eight the next morning I would be sitting in the breakfast room, and if he was there with a gift of a piece of amber, not only would I consent to sharing my breakfast with him, but I would also, later, dance for him privately.

His eyes opened wide.

'Fuck!' he exclaimed.

I tut-tutted.

'Excuse my language,' he said with an amused smile. 'That's just a hell of a challenge in little more than twelve hours.'

'I know,' I said. 'I wouldn't want to come cheap or make it easy, would I?'

He furtively glanced at his watch, and realised what time it already was, and it dawned on him too that all the main Amsterdam stores would now be closed.

He slowly rose from his chair, straightened the creases creeping up his tight jeans, blew me a kiss and assured me he would be there for breakfast.

'Don't be late,' I reminded him.

As he walked out of the cafe, both my eyes and the waitress's were fixed on his tiny bum, sheathed as it was by the narrow, skin-tight jeans. I didn't think I'd ever seen such a small posterior on a woman, let alone a man.

That night I slept peacefully, with a smile on my face.

No dreams or nightmares.

*

Whether he spent the night crisscrossing Amsterdam in search of the amber piece or set his people to the task, I don't know. Or even if the sought-after gift was actually found in the city, or couriered overnight from somewhere in the whole wide world where jewellers' or antique stores were still open.

I walked down to the hotel's breakfast room and he was sitting there at the table I'd booked.

He was wearing the same clothes as the previous day and had clearly not shaved since.

I was wearing a see-through white silk blouse, highly aware that my breasts were fully visible through it, and a long white skirt that brushed against my ankles. I felt invincible.

He rose, rushed to my side of the small round table, pulled out my chair and prompted me to sit down.

On my plate sat a crimson velvet box, circled by thin black ribbons. It could have held an engagement ring, or a watch. But it didn't.

It was a beautiful piece of amber.

He looked up at me with a gaze of deep satisfaction.

'Can I have this dance, Miss Luba?'

8

Dancing Across the Whole Wide World

Viggo and I quickly came to an arrangement. I had consented to a private dance for him, but I was not ready to perform just yet. Not now and certainly not here in Amsterdam.

He suggested London, where he lived, describing to me the underground swimming-pool grotto he had at his mansion there. It sounded wonderfully decadent to me and appealed to my imagination; the first thing that sprang to mind was that I could be a mermaid, and I was already thinking what I might wear and what music would be right for the performance.

As he spoke, he looked like a wide-eyed little boy describing his toys. I agreed, although I reminded him, 'No funny business. I will just be dancing, so I don't want you to get any ideas, okay?' He nodded. I was fearful at the thought, but a little voice inside my head was also whispering that I would eventually have sex with Viggo. I refused to spend my life alone, dreaming of a man I could not have, and who clearly didn't want me any longer. For surely, Chey would have found me, fought for me – at least let me know where in the world he was – if he truly loved me. And anyway, even though I had become tired of the live sex shows, I had not lost my adventurous spirit, and it would be too much of a temptation not to taste a man half the women in the world were fantasising about. But I would take my time and make him clear it was my decision and not his.

We flew to London that afternoon.

Throughout the journey, Viggo was gallant, attentive and witty and his eyes never strayed from me.

His Buick was waiting for us in the short-term car park at Heathrow. He drove into the city like a man possessed, eager to show off his house – or perhaps eager to show me off to his friends.

It was situated in a leafy area just minutes from Hampstead Heath and the immense mansion was a garden of delights as he eagerly walked me through its features like a male Alice in a rock 'n' roll wonderland. The first thing I noticed was how much Viggo was attached to objects – the place was a treasure trove of sculptures, paintings and prints, and even rare first editions that seemed too fragile to handle, let alone read. First he showed me to the guest room that would be mine as long as I wanted to stay there, he informed me. It was a vast bedroom, with its walls alternately painted black and white and dotted with small prints that I guessed were all originals, mostly impressionists and many of the sea in every shade of blue and green under the sun, pointillist, discreet, hypnotic. I felt certain Debussy had seen many of these images before he wrote 'La Mer' and had found inspiration in their palette. There was also an en-suite bathroom, with a deliriously gothic bathtub, all metal claws and twisted limbs, and a modern shower cubicle with sleek glass and shining metal.

I only had the clothes I had taken to Amsterdam, which I dispersed through the immensity of the deep glass-fronted sliding-doored closet. If I stayed here longer, I would have to retrieve some of the wardrobe I kept back in New Orleans, as well as buy myself some new outfits in London.

Viggo returned to fetch me a couple of hours later and guided me down a circular staircase to the underground areas of the mansion. And there it was: his grotto, the emerald shimmers of the pool's water as its zigzagging stream bisected the low-ceilinged subterranean cavern, like the breath of an invisible sea god. Here again, on every side of the pool were pieces of art, mostly modern, large and small, bizarre and incongruous.

'It's enchanting,' I said. 'But even this girl can't dance on water.'

'Look,' Viggo said, and pointed to the far end of the room where the waters of the pool emerged like a cascade from an artfully constructed hill of small, shiny rocks.

My stage. A large, rectangular black stone slab. Like a sacrificial altar.

When I saw the pool and the platform, I knew that this dance for Viggo would be the healing balm that I needed to restore my equilibrium. Here, where the water would wash over me like a baptism, cleansing my body of sins - both known and unknown. It would be ritualistic. Pagan. I would be the priest presiding over my own ceremony. I would peel away all the layers, tear off the skin, and I would return to the old Luba in one swift, sharp shock.

I danced for him the following evening. A dance of undulating desire, of pale flesh and shocking pink, a private offering like the first one I had long ago performed for Chey.

I was wanton and raw, more than I had ever been, as I ensured that Viggo Franck would want me like he had never wanted a woman before, my body, my intimacy, but this time the power would be all mine. As the music circled me and my slow, deliberate movements to its rhythm, I could see on his face, his eyes transfixed by my earthly presence, how much he yearned to possess me, add me to his collection. But I danced on, smiling inside. This would be my new domain, the underground lair of Viggo's mermaid. When the music stopped, we were both holding our breath, facing each other, electrified.

There was only one thing to do: I burst out laughing and jumped naked into the cool water, to douse the fire.

As I swum to the side and exited the pool, Viggo was waiting for me, holding out a large white towel.

'Even mermaids need to dry themselves,' he said, smiling broadly.

'Oh no, they don't,' I said. 'They have lackeys to do the task.'

'I've never been called a lackey before,' Viggo said, and approached me, wrapping me up in the fluffy material as it absorbed the water still dripping from my shoulders and across my skin. As I didn't object, he began to rub the material against me, first my back, then my hair and then, impudently, my arse. 'But I think I could definitely enjoy being one,' he concluded.

We ate together later in his large, modern kitchen. The food had been supplied by a famous restaurateur. It was exquisite. Viggo was funny, bombarding me with anecdotes and striking stories about the excesses of the rock 'n' roll lifestyle, teaching me how to slurp oysters and to taste vintage wine properly. Behind the rock-star monster was a good man. Only bad men knew how to play my chords, but perhaps that was a good thing for the moment. I could relax and reinvent myself with Viggo.

He was a connoisseur of beauty, he told me, and he wanted me to stay. I would have the run of the house, could even help him out when necessary with the dreary minutiae of everyday life that his managers and agents were not involved in. A personal assistant, a companion, a muse. The rest was up to me. If I wished to dance again, he would welcome it but there would be no obligation to do so again on my part.

I was now an associate Holy Criminal. I was even put on the payroll, no doubt as a tax deduction as I saw the eyes of his accountant light up when I was introduced to him to arrange the formalities. And I was not even required to dance onstage with the band.

I spent most of the following two days in the pool area, naked, sprawling, wet, in a state of blissful innocence. Viggo would join me in the room, sharing small talk while watching me with undisguised avidity. I suggested he join me in the water, which he did, but only after I observed the arduous operation during which he had to slide out of his eternally skin-tight jeans while trying to retain a modicum of dignity.

He had a lovely cock. Thin, straight, long.

He dived into the pool. I sauntered towards his point of entry and playfully held his head down under the water when he tried to break through, keeping his eyes and his mouth level with my smooth cunt.

I let go and he burst through, spitting water, feigning anger. I just laughed again. His cock, I could feel, was already rock hard, brushing against my thigh. My feet stiffened and I prepared to push him away, but to my surprise the touch of his penis against my leg gave me a thrill and I realised that Viggo had genuinely grown on me.

This would not be a relationship like the one that I'd had with Lucian, which had felt more like a business arrangement. No, I would make love to Viggo Franck and enjoy it.

That night, I walked to his room on the top floor and joined him in his outrageously large bed. It was not a bed in which you should sleep alone. I hadn't been with a man since my last dance in Amsterdam, and all the recurring thoughts of Chey were forming a knot of pain in my heart. A pain that I wanted rid of, even if it hurt to have it removed, like a rotten tooth. I wanted to rid myself of the memory of bad fucks I'd had since Chey, and it might have been a cliché but the only way I could think to do it was to fuck the pain away. The sexy musician with all his kindness and his contradictions and his tight trousers was just what the doctor ordered.

'Well hello, darling,' he said when I crawled across the covers to lay down beside him. 'Couldn't resist me after all, eh?'

Coming from any other man his easy confidence might have seemed like arrogance, but Viggo was so humorous that even his boasts seemed self-deprecating and endeared me to him more.

I laughed, and leaned forward and kissed him.

It was all the invitation that he needed.

He was as confident in his lovemaking as he seemed, on the surface at least, in every other part of his life. His mouth was soft and he kissed languorously, as though we had all the time in the world and he intended to make use of all of it.

I propped myself up on my shoulder so that I could run my hand over his body, but he pushed me back down on the bed again.

'First, my turn,' he said playfully. 'I think Luba the dancer needs to have a turn at staying still for a while. Or do you need me to make you stay there?'

'And how do you propose to do that?'

'Close your eyes,' he said, 'and I'll show you.'

I followed his instruction, but within a few moments I heard the squeak of his bedside drawer rolling open and curiosity got the better of me. My lids fluttered open and I sneaked a look at him.

'Tut-tut,' he chided. 'I see I'm going to have to take care of that too.'

I snapped my eyes shut again.

'Better,' he said, obviously watching me. 'But I think I'd like to make sure you stay that way.'

His tone was light and playful. Viggo clearly planned to demonstrate what I imagined was a vast repertoire of bedroom skills and I was only too happy to let him.

'Have you been blindfolded before?' he asked.

'Never.' I'd done a lot of things with Chey, but surprisingly not this.

I realised that I was holding my breath in eager anticipation. My mind was active and usually when I was in bed with someone new I spent at least some of the time glancing at my surroundings and thinking about one thing or another. What to do next, or whether I liked or disliked my bed partner's taste in furniture. But lying on my back in Viggo's bed with my eyes closed, my senses were partially cut off and I was tuned in to his every sound, his every move. He hadn't restrained me, but I lay still to humour him and now I was utterly aware of the sensation in every part of my body.

'Hmm. I think you like that idea,' he added. I couldn't

see him but was certain that I could feel his gaze locked on me and watching each infinitesimal response as my muscles clenched and unclenched, patiently waiting for his touch.

When the silk scarves touched my skin I gasped. They were cool and deliciously soft, and with my eyes closed and totally unaware of what he was trailing along my legs and torso, and then over my breasts, I felt as though I was being brushed by the lapping of an isolated wave.

'Do you like that?' he asked, softly.

'Oh yes,' I said.

I was unaccustomed to talking during sex and I had already made up my mind not to beg for it, if that was what he was aiming for, but by the time he had run the fabric over my now stiff nipples and then down across my pussy and over my thighs and down my legs, I was ready to do anything that Viggo Franck asked of me.

He wrapped the silky material around each of my ankles and my wrists and tied the ends to the head and foot of the bed so that I could move just enough to reduce any discomfort but was trapped in a starfish-like position and entirely subject to his every whim. Then he lifted my head gently and secured another piece of cloth around my eyes so that I couldn't see even if I wanted to.

The drawer creaked open again.

By now I could feel my clit swelling and my pussy becoming embarrassingly wet. I wanted to plead with him to just abandon the foreplay and fuck me there and then, but I forced myself not to. No matter how aroused I was, I had my pride, and I didn't want Viggo to think that he was some kind of sex god with the ability to make me swoon with the lightest caress.

The cover on the bed shifted slightly as Viggo laid down whatever he had taken out of his drawer of tricks.

One by one he teased me with sensations until my nerve endings had been worked into such a state that the slightest touch made me writhe and buck, desperate to feel more.

First, soft, tickling strokes over my inner thighs, my swollen and damp pussy and then around my nipples in soft, delicate circles. He was brushing me with a feather, I think. Then, the sweeping of something warm and velveteen, like a fur glove. Then something sharp but not painfully so, like the blade of a blunt knife that he traced firmly over the most sensitive parts of me as I moaned and strained on the restraints, not to escape but out of an intense desire to feel more.

'Please,' I said at last, 'fuck me.'

'Not yet,' he whispered into my ear, following his words with the caress of his tongue and the flow of his breath hot against my skin.

He trailed his tongue all the way across my neck and then down to my chest, taking each of my nipples into this mouth and sucking on them and biting them until they were painfully hard, and I murmured in the agony of arousal mixed with frustration. He licked down my torso and then around the border of my pussy just a torturous inch from my clit. I bucked against the ties, pulling until the headboard thumped in an attempt to get closer to his mouth, but he had tied me expertly and my struggling was in vain.

When he finally lowered his mouth and licked with firm strokes I came hard in seconds, straining at the silk scarves until I thought I might break the bed as the heat of my orgasm sent my body into spasms.

'Oh God, stop,' I begged, as my pussy became so sensitive that each touch was painful instead of pleasurable.

He removed the blindfold from my eyes and each of the ties from my wrists and ankles and I lay still in a state of bliss enjoying the post-orgasmic glow until I had relaxed and was ready to go again.

'Christ, you really do have some stamina, and not just for dancing,' he said, as I reached for his cock.

He was still hard, but after the intensity of my orgasm I was close to spent and I didn't think I could take him in my mouth even if I wanted to. He chuckled and rolled on top of me, not caring that I couldn't reciprocate the favour. Gently he slid inside me, brushing against my still sensitive lips and eliciting from me a low moan of pleasure. He began to thrust, slowly at first, and I felt complete, at home and basking in a type of affection that I hadn't experienced for such a long time. Not since Chey.

Viggo wasn't the type of man that I could see myself falling for, but he was definitely someone that I could enjoy being with immensely and perhaps for quite a long time.

After we'd fucked, and he offered me a cigarette, which I turned down, I rolled over to his side of the bed across the bruised sheets and tangled covers and said, 'I'm not going to fall in love with you. I just like you. Is that enough?'

He looked me in the eyes and once again I saw the young man he had once been, before the wild, long hair, the airs and stances, the public image and the tight trousers.

'Sure, Luba. Yeah, we can just be mates . . . with the odd benefit thrown in for good measure,' he added with a cheeky smile.

There was no need to draw up a contract. We would be friends, lovers when it suited us. We could both see others if we wished. For now, that was good enough for me. And for Viggo.

It was all agreed.

He pulled the sheet away from me and peered with fascination yet again at my strategically situated tattoo.

'Jeezus,' he said. 'Call me a perv, but that gun sure makes me hard.'

'Fuck me then . . .'

And he did. And it felt good, having sex with a friend. Not for money, not for art, but because your soul and your heart dictated it with all the energy of despair.

The sex itself was fine, it was reasonably athletic, neither rough nor smooth. Viggo was a talented lover, although at times I did feel as if he was going through the motions, mentally ticking off all the pages of the 'how to' manual in an effort to satisfy me, please me. I knew that I was going through the motions at times too. And I began to worry again that something inside me had been lost, and perhaps I would never get it back. There was nothing wrong being made love to this way, far from it, but it lacked adventure. Maybe it was that the past eighteen months or so, doing it professionally, so to speak, had blunted my appetite or my needs. In fact, I began to realise that Viggo's enthusiasm waned once the wooing – the chase – was over. That was the part of the sex game he clearly enjoyed most. He also liked to use toys, in order to diversify his menu, a practice I had not previously experienced and which failed to arouse me as much as I thought it would. I couldn't help but worry that something was wrong with me, though intellectually I knew that the problem was more likely Viggo doing the wrong thing or the two of us simply being unsuited to one another. But I was determined to change my life and gradually get my mojo back again, so a lack of fire presented me with no problem. Being with Viggo satisfied my basic sexual needs and provided the space that I needed to rediscover myself again.

For a singer and songwriter, it seemed Viggo hadn't much imagination. That's what I found most unexpected. But for now, he was the cure to my problems and I was happy to enjoy his company for what it was as much as he enjoyed mine.

Soon after I moved into Viggo's place, I arranged for Madame Denoux to ship my belongings to London. I could afford a whole set of new clothes, but there were outfits and garments that I was attached to, so it made sense not to leave them behind in my attempt to begin this strange new life I had inveigled myself into.

Viggo was an easy person to be with. Like me he was, in spite of appearances and reputation, something of a loner and enjoyed his moments of silence and isolation, even if the second he was in a crowd he came alive again and was invariably the soul of the party. The house was big enough so that we could spend hours not seeing each other, though I occupied most of my time either reading in my room or lazing around the emerald pool and, of course, exploring London.

It was a city that had everything, as if all of the strands of my past life were coming together in one place: the greyness of Donetsk, the beauty of St Petersburg, the energy of New York and the sexual radiance of New Orleans. Of course, I had been here before. There was the time when I met Florence and enjoyed an evening of wonderful sexual intoxication, which I often remembered with a sigh of yearning. But living here now with no schedule to follow, things to do, places to go, assignments to complete, made exploring the city a totally different experience altogether. A new place I could enjoy at leisure, absorb through every pore of my skin.

I loved the way I could melt into the crowds of Camden Town and become just a wave in a mighty ocean of colour, movement and smells, before taking just a few steps to the side and finding myself down by the locks of the canal, and the only living thing around for hundreds of metres, as the dirty waters of Regent's Canal, lapped against the underside of the bridges and carried the silent stream of barges along. And then just a few more minutes walk in another direction, I could find myself in the labyrinths and greenery of Hampstead Heath, by ponds and clearings, undergrowth and isolated bandstands that, in my wild dreams, had hosted a variety of previous excesses under cover of darkness or by the pale light of dawn.

The teeming markets of Borough where you could taste samples on almost every stall from cheeses to dips, and truffle oils and a million variety of breads, and of the East End where the fragrant whiff of curry blended with a gazillion notes, spices, beer, life, sweat.

Truly a city with a thousand faces.

For the first time, I felt as if I could spend a lifetime here and always be surprised.

Viggo was in between tours and hoping to record a new album soon. He was usually busy writing new songs or rehearsing with his band in a studio on Goldhawk Road. He had also been given a contract by his record company which allowed him to sign up promising new bands that he could chaperone and even produce. His latest discovery was a trio of English and American musicians who called themselves Groucho Nights and he had agreed they could open for the Holy Criminals the following night at a one-off gig he was playing for charity at the Brixton Academy.

'You must come along, babe,' Viggo insisted.

'To be your arm candy?' I queried.

'Nah. You'll just be you.

'The one and only.'

'I'm allowed to come dressed, am I?'

'Naturally. We don't want to start a riot, do we?'

It was the first time I'd been out with Viggo in the public eye. Of course, we had been to restaurants and walked together outside since I'd come to London, but never to events where there would be interested onlookers or press and photographers, so I was a bit anxious about the trip to the concert venue where I would, inevitably, be seen as his latest conquest, his current consort.

What would I say if people asked me what I did, who I was?

I had deliberately dressed down for the occasion, avoiding any music world connotation. I'd opted for a short denim skirt and a white embroidered Victorian-style cotton blouse with ivory buttons. And ballet shoes so I didn't tower over Viggo, even with his four-inch Cuban heels.

'Say you're just a close friend, or if you prefer, say that you're my assistant now,' Viggo suggested. 'Sometimes there's no harm in just telling the truth.'

We crossed the Thames at Parliament Bridge on our way to what Viggo referred to as the wilderness of south London. He'd once joked that there were actually two separate Londons: North and South. And that many of its inhabitants never ventured onto the opposite bank of the river from where they lived unless it was a matter of life and death, or, more prosaically, work. He was a north Londoner through and through. On both sides of the bridge the lights of London were shining bright, between the shadows of far buildings and nearer landmarks. The London Eye turned at the pace of a snail, its capsules brightly lit moths travelling across the dark horizon, and the geometrical buildings of the South Bank complex stood like mastodons on the river's bank.

Soon, the landscape changed and a succession of dreary roads and intersections flew by as the gleaming black sedan he was driving roared along unending straight roads until we reached the narrower streets of Brixton.

I could see the crowds milling outside the Academy, queues snaking their way down the block and a bottleneck of traffic ahead of us.

'This is it, babe,' Viggo remarked as he edged towards the kerb and briefly drove on to the pavement. 'Rock 'n' roll.'

He opened his door and indicated I should get out too, leaving his keys in the ignition as a long-haired young guy in regulation skinny jeans and black Holy Criminals T-shirt shook hands with him, took his seat, and drove it away.

'Who was that?' I asked Viggo.

'One of the roadies. Part of my road crew. He'll be parking the car somewhere. It's a nightmare to find a space down here.' Various individuals were peeling off the crowd outside the Academy's doors when they noticed us. Half of them were holding cameras and began snapping at us. The flash bulbs blinded me.

'Just ignore them, babe,' Viggo said, holding my hand.

'Who's the new squeeze, Viggo?' someone shouted, but Viggo paid no attention and in an instant we were beyond the club's doors and the security people had closed them securely behind us. The Academy would not be opening to the public for another half-hour.

A couple of young girls rushed up to us, asking Viggo for his autograph. He complied with a leering smile. I wondered how they had got in early, and memories of what I'd been up to back in Donetsk against the red-brick wall flashed through my mind.

He asked one of the attendants for the direction to the Green Room and we were shown to the right corridor.

As the door opened to a throng of people I'd never seen before, I wondered whether the photos of me entering the building would make newspapers tomorrow or later.

And would Chey ever catch sight of any of them?

Chaos unfolded around me. The room was abuzz with activity and the hustle and bustle of people rushing and pushing, carrying equipment and shouting about sound-checks and security and last-minute photographs. Just a few minutes of it and my head was throbbing.

Viggo's attention was sucked away as quickly as if he'd been catapulted into another universe. This was his element and I could feel his energy and excitement starting to build as he began to swagger like a cockerel in front of his band and crew. The little boy was gone, and the rock star had taken his place. I found the change bemusing.

I slipped out of the door again at an opportune moment and made my way to an unused dressing room at the end of the corridor. The security guard posted in the hall soon coughed up the key with a little sweet-talking. The room was cramped and smelled of stale cigarettes, but it provided a safe haven where I could perch on the single rickety stool and read a book for an hour or two in peace and quiet.

Some rock 'n' roll gal I was. I imagined what the headlines might say, and how they might compare to the reality of me shut in an empty dressing room with a worn copy of *Harp in the South*.

I was so engrossed in the book that I missed the opening act that Viggo was sponsoring entirely. I crept down the corridor to the stage wings to watch him when he came on. Two women had tucked themselves up behind the stage curtains and were whispering and smiling to each other, obviously making their assessment of the band members. One of them had long, vivid red curls and was dressed like I was in a short denim skirt, tights and a white blouse.

Something about the way she moved seemed familiar. I paused a moment to watch them and then scampered through another set of corridors to the other side of the stage where I would be alone. I was in no mood to explain who I was to any of Viggo's devout female fans.

It was the first time I had heard or seen Viggo sing. All of his rehearsals took place at his studio on Goldhawk Road and having been so fearful of being photographed with him, I had never gone along.

His voice was rough and seductive, but I had heard better singers in the dressing rooms at The Grand where Blanca had made a point of hiring girls who could croon as well as shimmy – a dancer singing 'Makin' Whoopee!' whilst writhing on top of the piano always went down well with the punters. It was Viggo's charisma and his evident sex appeal that had made him successful. That and no doubt some quiet genius in his PR team who had orchestrated his appearance in the tabloids and cemented his status as a ladies man par excellence.

Watching him on stage made me lonesome for the days when I had had my turn in the spotlight. I recognised that look on Viggo's face, remembered the hedonistic thrill I had always felt exposing myself to an unknown audience. It wasn't the nudity so much as the invitation to strangers into the furthermost reaches of my soul, allowing people that I couldn't even see to watch me perform, that was most dear to my heart.

I was ready to make a beeline for home the moment Viggo finished his last encore to ensure that I would miss the storm of fanatical fans and journalists ready and waiting to snap our picture together or ask for autographs.

By the time I made it back to the Green Room, he had already been swallowed up by the crowd, so instead I pleaded with the long-haired roadie with the keys to the sedan to drive me home. I decided then and there that one day soon I would finally learn to drive, and no longer prove such an easy hostage to fortune.

I didn't notice Viggo's missed call and voicemail until I arrived back at the mansion in Belsize Park.

'Hey, babe,' he crooned. 'I'm having a few people back. Will you dance for us?'

I froze for a moment, considering the idea. I had not danced for a proper audience since the night in Amsterdam. A spark had lit in my belly and was slowly unfurling into a burning flame. The prospect excited me, and the twinge of fear beneath it all that something might go wrong spurred me to action. I was not afraid, I told myself. I would wrestle out any hint of trepidation and trample it into nothing with my dancing feet.

By the time they arrived I was in position and beginning to get cramp. I had chosen to perform in the vast harem-like room on the second floor of the mansion. It was like another world compared to the bare and stark entrance floor. This room was decorated with thick carpets, chandeliers and gothic furniture and of course the fountain in the middle that I had chosen as my platform. I felt so peaceful in the presence of water. The fountain didn't give me a lot of room to move, but it would be a short set, and rather than demonstrate my athleticism I planned a piece where I would seem like a statue slowing coming to life in the water. It would be set to Debussy's 'La Mer', my usual introduction piece.

The opening notes, which had always soothed me, now made my heart pump a little faster. Images flashed into my head. The crack of the ringmaster's whip. The inhuman expressions on the procession of animals. The heady smell of tropical flowers. The brush of ferns against my skin. The grip of a stranger's fingers on my arm. Hot breath on my face.

It was too late to back out now. I could hear voices moving up the stairs. A blend of accents: Antipodean, American, English, the Scandinavian lilt of Dagur the Icelandic drummer and of course Viggo's blend of transatlantic worldliness. My unknown audience had arrived and Viggo had been true to his word. It would be a small one.

I closed my eyes and stood perfectly still, settling my mind with sheer force of will, ignoring the horrors that threatened to creep up like poisonous vines and strangle all of the life out of me. I focused on my first memories of the melody. When I had been on the beach with Chey and he had played his iPod and I had danced for him and only for him, letting the impressionistic, almost crystal-like shards of sound sweep through my body like a tide, my movements following the rhythm as naturally as one wave follows another.

That night I danced softly. I moved as gently as shallow water in the most protected bay. I was dancing for me, dancing for Chey.

When I opened my eyes, I saw her: the redhead who had been backstage watching Viggo's show. And I remembered where I had seen her before. I had watched her dance on New Year's Day at The Place in New Orleans and, likewise, the night before she had watched me perform.

She was staring at my pussy. Then her gaze focused on my tattoo and her pupils widened in recognition.

I met her eyes and smiled.

Viggo was an efficient stage master and without my having to tell him he flipped the lights when the music came to an end, theatrically plunging the room into darkness and allowing me a few moments to escape through the back door without having to ruin my act by clambering down ungracefully from my platform and finding the exit in front of the audience.

I changed quickly into a long black chiffon dress, not bothering with either knickers or a bra. I was eager to return to the party and learn more about the red-haired girl and the man that she had been with that night, and besides which they had all just seen me naked anyway. Though my show was over, I also felt that I had a certain appearance to maintain for my audience. Presenting myself to them in a T-shirt and jeans would have taken some of the magic away from the image of *Luba* that they had now formed.

The girl was speaking to one of the musicians from

Viggo's intro act that I hadn't met yet. Her expression was forlorn, and I hung back by the doorframe to eavesdrop before entering to introduce myself.

It seemed that she had lost her violin.

Then I recalled the unusual piece of music that she had elected to dance to. Vivaldi's *Four Seasons*. The image on the old record that sat gathering dust in the rehearsal room in St Petersburg sprang into my mind.

'You should play with us more often, Sum,' said the curly-haired young man who she sat next to and who was barely looking at her at all, so focused was he on a short-haired blonde girl who sat across the room making eyes at Dagur.

Slowly but surely, the cogs slipped into place in my mind. Sum . . . Summer. The amateur dancer was Summer Zahova, the sexy violinist who I vaguely recalled had made a splash in the US after posing nude for a concert flier. One of the rich men at a gig I had danced had invited me to one of her concerts after he had watched my Debussy set and expressed his surprise that a woman would strip to classical music instead of some predictable pop song. I reminded him of Summer Zahova, he had said.

Then she said *Luba*, rolling the sound in her mouth as men tended to do when they wanted to sleep with me. Clearly my dance had stuck in her mind all this time, as hers had in mine.

'There's always *Luba*.'

Curly-head looked up at her in surprise.

'How did you know her name?' he asked.

Her face was flushed and she was stuttering a feeble attempt to cover up the real nature of our previous meeting.

I stepped into the room and to her aid.

'We met briefly in New York,' I said. 'I attended one of her concerts.'

Along with relief, another expression flooded across Summer's face. It was not just her voice that betrayed her. I watched with amusement as she tried to avert her eyes from my nipples, which were no doubt visible through the thin fabric of my dress and she squirmed into the sofa as my skin brushed against hers.

She was clearly not much accustomed to hiding her emotions, though everyone else in the room seemed entirely oblivious to both her discomfort and her arousal.

This game would be much easier to play than I had expected.

I lifted a lock of her red hair and whispered directly into her ear, brushing my lips ever so slightly against her lobe as I did so.

'I want to hear the story, about how you ended up in a place like that. And the man you were with.'

'Dominik?' she replied.

Yes. That was his name, I recalled, as another stream of memories from that night at The Place came back to my mind.

It wasn't until later, when I left all of the love birds to it and returned to my room to crawl into bed, that I realised why the name Dominik made me feel as though a word was stuck on the tip of my tongue. Another memory was brewing inside somewhere, just waiting to bob to the surface.

Dominik was the name of the British author who had written *Yellow*, the book about the red-haired Paris traveller that I had so enjoyed. I smiled inside. Surely it must be too much of a coincidence? But there it was on the cover.

Dominik Conrad. I flicked through the pages again and then put the book down and fell straight to sleep. If I knew Viggo, Summer would still be here in the morning, and probably the morning after that.

There would be plenty of time for investigation later.

The following day I slept in for hours, revelling in having a bed to myself to stretch out in. Then I slipped on my bathing suit and padded down the long, winding wooden staircase and into the basement where I planned to spend the afternoon floating in the cool water.

It would only be a matter of time before the violinist came looking for me, as I knew that she was still in search of her violin. Eric, the road manager who had been in charge of the equipment, had seen neither hide nor hair of it. I'd called him under Viggo's instruction and he had been impatient and bordering on rude.

I was drip-drying on the rocks when she appeared. It took her a few moments to notice me as her eyes darted all over the room, blinking to adjust to the low light and the strange decor. Our eyes locked briefly but she didn't say anything, just headed straight for the cabinet where Viggo stored an array of old instruments pegged to the wall like insects trapped under glass.

She stretched out her arm and stroked her fingers across the case. She was mesmerised by his collection of violins but the disappointment that hers was not among them was obvious in the hunch of her shoulders, as if she'd had all the breath knocked out of her.

'He won't mind, you know, if you want to borrow something. Will you play for me?'

As soon as I asked her to play, all of her hesitation seemed to dissolve and she reached eagerly into the cabinet, caressing the instruments until she found one that suited her. It was out of tune and badly in need of repair, but the look that filled her face as she played was hypnotic. It was no wonder that Viggo had wanted to add her to his collection.

She was a striking woman anyway, but as soon as she picked up a violin she fairly radiated. She closed her eyes and her lips parted ever so slightly, highlighting the sensuous curve of her mouth.

I moved closer, entranced by her melody and the way that she had responded so readily to my request. Had a virtual stranger asked me to dance for them, I would have bridled at the idea, but she was as eager to please as a puppy and I could not help but imagine the possibilities that her innate pliability brought to mind.

When she finished her tune and removed the violin from her chin, I kissed her.

Her response was so eager that I nearly laughed.

I took her by the hand and led her up the stairs to Viggo's bedroom. He probably wouldn't have minded if I had taken his new pet away for an hour or two to my own bed but seeing as they had only had one night together, it seemed churlish of me to steal her so soon.

The sound of water running and Viggo singing softly reached my ears. He was in the shower but had left the bathroom door open.

'Come on,' I said, approaching the door to the en suite. 'Let's wish him good morning.'

Introducing Summer to our sex life proved to be no chore. If anything, life as part of a threesome suited me to a tee. I had begun to find Viggo's lovemaking less adventurous, and

Summer added a little extra spice. She had the highest libido of any woman that I had ever known, but with it an eagerness to please that was almost intoxicating.

When we were together, I amused myself by holding her head onto Viggo's cock and watching the strange way that her wetness increased the more I ordered her around, and I could not help thinking of Dominik, the man who had made her dance.

Summer seemed happy enough, but I felt instinctively that Viggo and I were both too mild for her. I was content enough to pull her hair or rake my fingernails down her back, but that was all the violence that I was comfortable dishing out and Viggo was a softie through and through beneath his outward bravado. Sometimes after our love-making bouts I caught her looking pensive and melancholic, as if she was missing something. Perhaps she was missing him, her man, as I still missed Chey.

The sex we had was actually pretty torrid, but somehow I always felt as if I was a spectator and taking my cues from unknown observers as we thrashed together wildly in Viggo's vast bed (and a variety of other places as all three of us were partial to sudden improvisation . . .), limbs akimbo like a three-headed spider caught in a net, never quite a single beast but an amalgam of lusts, desires and athleticism. Summer revelled in being at the centre of our scene, a die-hard exhibitionist who relished the gaze we cast on her, both as Viggo fucked her or as she went down on me and abandoned herself to pleasure. And the twinkle in her eye as we both serviced his beautiful cock was a joy to behold, her tongue brushing against mine, our lips melding as we took him in turns. But it always felt like something of a game, an entertainment that was heartless and lacking in tenderness. But so much fun . . .

Still, our three-way relationship also gave me more time to myself. More time to read, more time to swim, more time to explore the long, green stretches of Hampstead Heath. And Summer's presence gave the press something new to latch onto, so I worried less about my picture appearing in the paper. That was her problem now, not mine.

Summer never spoke about Dominik. Nor did she ask me exactly how I had ended up travelling from a stage in New Orleans to Viggo's bedroom in Belsize Park. It was as if there was some unspoken agreement between us to ignore the past. Perhaps she thought I might be ashamed of my history as a stripper. Viggo was by far the chattiest of the three of us.

She was soon roped into touring with Groucho Nights, the band who had opened for Viggo and the Holy Criminals at the Academy, and then I barely saw her at all, as all of her days and nights were crammed with rehearsals.

So when I saw that dark head of hair and recognised the profile of his face lit up by the stage light just a row in front of me at their opening show at the Cigale concert hall in Paris, I was unsure whether Summer even knew that he was in the audience.

I was still not even certain that Dominik the dance master was also Dominik the author, but my suspicions were confirmed when he was accosted in the dressing room by a couple of young local journalists who wanted to know what a serious writer was doing backstage with Viggo Franck. Research for his next novel?

Dominik was clearly embarrassed by the attention and brushed them off. He hid himself in the corner, looking distinctly uncomfortable and nursing a bottle of mineral water. I approached him later and handed him my phone number with a seductive smile. He didn't call, but then having seen the way he watched his flame-haired violinist as she dominated the stage, I never really expected him to.

Weeks past, most of them spent alone in the big house as Summer was touring and Viggo was busy with his various musical commitments, which only occasionally required my presence.

I had oceans of free time to waste and I spent much of it thinking of Chey, wondering where he was now, whether he was okay. But it wasn't just Chey who consumed my thoughts. I couldn't help my mind wandering to the mysterious dark-haired writer, Dominik, and the passion I had seen shining clearly in his eyes.

'Are you still on your extended vacation, Luba?' Madame Denoux asked me. It was mid-afternoon in London, and the colours of spring were returning to the nearby Heath. It must have been early in the morning in New Orleans, which hinted that this was not just a courtesy call. Madame Denoux seldom left her bed until midday unless she had a very good reason to do so. I briefly imagined I could smell the magnolias and hear the flow of the Mississippi down the phone line.

I was sitting outside a Jewish patisserie on Golders Green Road savouring lemon tea and a plate of small cakes, just like the ones I remembered from my childhood in the Ukraine. I'd jogged all the way here from Belsize Park, up Haverstock Hill and Hampstead High Street, puffing my way up all the small hills and dips. Even though I was no longer dancing regularly, I tried to maintain my physical fitness. My vanity was stronger than my passionate distaste of formal exercise.

The leisurely downhill pause here was my reward. I was reading Dominik's book for the second time. Now that I had come across him, my fascination was growing, as was my interest in his relationship with Summer. I was now totally convinced that the character of Elena in his book was based on her. There were too many similarities, not only in the way he repeatedly described Elena, and not just her features, but also her body in the most intimate of ways. It felt a bit like a detective tale meticulously separating the fiction from the reality. He'd been extremely clever crafting his story, but now that I'd come to know her, and to a lesser extent him, I had no doubts.

'It's no longer a vacation, Madame Denoux. It's fast becoming a way of life.'

'Good for you, young lady . . .' She paused. 'So, totally happy, then?'

In truth, I'd long come to the conclusion that I wasn't the sort of person who knows what happiness is. There was always something missing. A man. A place. An unfocused emotion. Something.

'At peace,' I finally said.

'Good,' Madame Denoux said. 'It's just that we've had a wonderful offer for your Tango piece from a very wealthy benefactor' – she never used the word 'client' – 'and although he knows from the current edition of the catalogue that you are no longer available, he is very insistent.'

The Tango had always been my favourite set. There was something primal about it and about the music I would dance to, and the nameless partner I had performed it with had so reminded me of Chey.

An unexpected wave of nostalgia hit me, bringing back to me the first time I'd tried the dance and my initial excitement about the whole affair. Like a fire rushing through my insides. Putting Viggo and all the others, men and women, since that day into a poor perspective.

Yet I still wasn't sure if I could go through with it, after I'd vowed never to do that type of dance again.

'Are you still there?' Madame Denoux asked me.

'Yes,' I stuttered, returning to reality.

'The pay involved is unheard of. You could afford another few years off with it, you know.'

'It's never just been a question of money,' I reminded her.

'I realise that. You are an artist, Luba. It's just a terrible pity that—'

I cut her short. She knew how to play me like a violin. I wouldn't be talked into it so easily, I swore to myself. I would think it through and make my decision carefully, although there was a part of my soul that now yearned to be on a stage again and hear the audience gasp as I moved, and feel the river of lust washing down my veins, kindling that terrible fire I feared had now been extinguished.

'I'm not saying yes. I'll think about it.'

'That's just great,' she replied. 'You have my number. In your own time, let me know. No pressure . . .'

'My usual partner?' I queried.

'Absolutely. That will be a cast-iron guarantee.'

'Out of curiosity, you know, what would be the location?'

I didn't particularly want to perform in Amsterdam again, or in London now that I lived here. It would have to be somewhere else.

'It's a small port called Sitges, just half an hour south of Barcelona, in Spain.'

'Okay,' I said and hung up the phone before she could push me further.

I swept up the last crumbs of the cake with my fingers and put Dominik's book back into my small running backpack.

The walk downhill was always faster than the uphill jog. Viggo's mansion was empty, an eerie silence travelling through the many rooms. I went to mine and took a long, cleansing shower. Swaddled in a fluffy bathrobe, I collapsed on the bed and returned to the book. Although I knew what happened in the final chapters, I felt as if I was rediscovering the story and characters from a new perspective altogether.

Once I turned the final page I went online. I wanted to find out if Dominik had published any other books. He hadn't. Neither did he have a website of his own, but I discovered quickly that there was a page for the book, and him, on his publishers' site. It featured no further information about Dominik or another novel, but my eye was quickly caught by a schedule of promotional appearances, most of which had already taken place – bookshop signings, festivals, readings. The final one listed was the one that caused me to smile. Call it fate or coincidence, but he was due to visit Barcelona for something called Sant Jordi in a few days' time.

Madame Denoux quickly picked up the phone.

'That was fast,' she remarked. I could picture the smile of delight spreading across her face, as if she knew what I was going to say.

'I'll do it,' I said. And I gave her the date. It was either then or I wouldn't get involved.

'Nothing is impossible, my dear. I'll have the arrangements made within a few hours. I hope you're in shape.'

'More than ever.'

My heart was running faster. I had the old Luba back again. And if I was honest with myself, I was unsure whether it was because of the prospect of seeing the enigmatic Dominik or being fucked in public by Tango again.

9

Dancing on the Heath

Sant Jordi turned out to be my idea of heaven.

Almost.

The Ramblas north of Plaza Catalunya were lined on each side with stall after stall displaying books and flowers. I breathed in deeply, savouring the very particular scent of roses and pages. A hotchpotch of Mediterranean life floated on the soft breeze as passers-by of all ages, couples old and young, paraded through the busy avenues boarded with trees. Everywhere I looked women were carrying deep-red flowers close to their chests to protect the petals from the pushes and shoves of the teeming crowds. Seen from a distance, the whole city appeared to be bleeding in unison, bright spots of colour blooming against their hearts like gun-shot wounds, as if Barcelona had been taken down by Cupid's arrow.

If it weren't for the sheer number of people that filled the thoroughfare and the tourists who walked slowly enough to drive a person to distraction then it would have been a perfect day. But I'd soon had enough of standing and queuing in the hot sun, listening to the various writers' fans drone on or watching the ruder types barge to the front, thumb through books and throw them disdainfully back down on the pile right in front of the author whose face inevitably fell until the next smiling devotee appeared.

Writers must either have terribly brittle egos or develop thick skins quickly. At least a dance was temporary and imperfections in form or errors in timing faded quickly from the viewer's mind. I was grateful that my artistic infelicities were not immortalised in print for evermore.

I finally spotted Dominik, but the queue for his stand was long and moving even more slowly than some of the others.

It seemed that I was not the only woman who had related to his heroine and become curious about the man who created her. Lingering at a neighbouring stall I took a few moments to observe him chatting with one of the many female readers who waited for him. She was slim with long dark hair piled high on her head and tendrils hanging loose that gave her a gypsy-like appearance, particularly in combination with her sandals and thin, loose cotton dress. When she bent down to invite him to sign the title page of the book that she had just purchased, I noted that her dress was terribly low cut and her full bosoms threatened to tumble out in front of him. Dominik was clearly aware of her display and he smiled at her with a strained expression on his face and averted his eyes at the earliest possible opportunity.

Evidently he was a man who preferred subtleties.

He would be around for some hours yet, I knew, as I'd noticed his name on several of the lists of authors visiting other stalls later in the day. But even if I managed to steal more than a few minutes of his time, he would quickly be obliged to return to the fray and satisfy the demands of his eager audience, at the service of his publishers and the many local bookstores involved in the event. And having come all this way and agreed to perform Tango again primarily for the sake of an opportunity to learn more about a man who fascinated me, I was not going to blow my hand with a few ill-chosen moments amongst a herd of other women eager for his attention.

I was hot, sticky and casually dressed in a pair of cotton shorts, flat shoes and a loose blouse. I turned and ambled back down the street towards Plaza Catalunya and stopped to sit and sip an espresso beneath an umbrella on one of the metal chairs at Café Zurich by the square. I was much more comfortable sitting rather than standing in crowds, watching the people go by and amusing myself by wondering what secrets they hid beneath their respectable public veneers. A young woman in a yellow shift dress and matching kitten heels, a red rose tucked into her blonde hair, was rushing back to her overprotective parents as if she was late back after a lovers' tryst – probably with an unsuitable but terribly good-looking young man who worked in a mail room, I decided, or perhaps with a charming but married company director at her place of employment, or maybe even with the company director's charming wife. She ran a finger firmly around her lips as she hurried past me, brushing off the stray smears of lipstick that had spread over her mouth during frantic goodbye kisses.

In traditional Network style, my hotel was both plush and discrete, tucked amongst the stone buildings and wrought-iron verandas that peppered the winding streets of the Gothic Quarter. It might be the last time that I would be put up in such sumptuous surroundings by an employer, so I took every advantage, pouring salted pistachios from the mini bar into a china bowl and taking a large sip of chilled champagne directly from the miniature bottle, coughing as it frothed into my mouth.

I peeled off my clothes slowly and stood under the

showerhead for an age, deliberately making use of every single one of the cosmetic products provided until I was drenched in lather and every fleck of dust gathered during my day's exertions had run down my body and into the drain.

Two hours later I was relaxed and ready to strut my stuff, sheathed in a red Roland Mouret dress that I knew clung gently to my shape but also covered my flesh from my neck to my calves so could not be considered distasteful even by the most modest of men. It was the colour of roses, my nod to Sant Jordi.

The heat of the day had faded and the early-evening light had fallen like a balm over the hustle and bustle of the Ramblas. Many of the stallholders were packing up for the day, no doubt on their way to enjoy further festivities that would continue to burn brightly until another sunset turned into night.

For a moment I feared that I had left it too late and had missed him as I had passed stall after stall and still saw no sign, but then I spotted him huddled amongst a gaggle of assorted writers and a few of the most patient and enthusiastic readers who had made it to the end of the day and all the way down the queue of stalls.

He was as handsome as ever, though dressed all in black with no hint to fashion or the Catalan heat. His arms had turned a pinkish copper from a full day sitting unprotected in the Spanish sun and I imagined that when he removed his shirt he would be faced with heavy tan lines marking his English skin.

'You wouldn't begrudge a friend a signature, no?' I asked, boldly holding my worn copy of his book aloft through the small throng of people hanging around the stall table to catch his attention. I had been careful to bring it along to Barcelona with me.

I laughed aloud at his response when he recognised me. 'A friend or a stalker?' he replied.

A fleeting expression of fright in his eyes suggested that he wasn't entirely joking, though he readily agreed to accompany me for a drink. It seemed to me that Monsieur Dominik liked to orchestrate every aspect of courtship, not just the occasional nude public dance. He did not take well to women hitting on him. I remained unaware of the particular circumstances that had drawn Dominik and Summer together, but I would bet my night's wages that he had made the first move.

To a private dancer was his inscription. If I had caught him off guard he had quickly regained his footing.

I was surprised when Dominik asked if he could some-how purchase a ticket to watch me dance later that evening after I'd explained the purpose of my trip to Barcelona. I told him that it was a private party and tickets were not on sale, but that I would be happy for him to come as my own personal guest.

He flirted politely with me over dinner at the tapas bar we'd stumbled across just off the Passeig de Gracia and expressed an unusual interest in my life and relationship with Viggo – quietly doing research for his latest book, I suspected – but I did not believe that he was angling to get into my bed. I guessed he was still besotted with Summer; or maybe I just wasn't his type. I shrugged inwardly and slotted him into the category that I kept aside for male friends and acquaintances who were unlikely to become my bedfellows. It made a nice change from being pawed at and propositioned all the time, and if my ego was a little stung then I would soon recover. Before long I would be naked and vulnerable in the arms of Tango and I was more than a little pleased to have someone that I knew and trusted in the audience. Dominik's presence would help settle my nerves and as a performer I was entitled to bring a guest along whenever I chose, so procuring his entrance would be no problem.

I did, however, warn him to acquire more formal attire for the occasion as he told me he hadn't travelled to Spain with much in the way of clothing.

The chauffeur collected Dominik and I at 10 p.m. sharp and whisked us away in the spacious comfort of a luxury limousine. We barely spoke as we drove along the winding coastline that led to an opulent yacht at the end of the Sitges marina in Aguadolc. A bright full moon shone across the water to our left and I spent the duration of the journey concentrating on the peaceful shimmer of the still ocean in an effort to calm my nerves.

Dominik sat comfortably in the silence, and I was relieved that he was not the sort of person who felt obliged to release a stream of inane and perpetual chatter to fill a gap in conversation.

The hostess for the evening, a middle-aged Network matriarch clad in a dark-green velvet evening gown with a white lace collar and a pair of heavy gold tear-shaped earrings, spotted me as soon as I arrived and I was ushered away from the guest area and into a makeshift dressing room in the lower level of the yacht, leaving Dominik to his own devices. He had bought an Armani tuxedo at one of the exclusive stores off the Passeig de Gracia, but still looked out of place, apparently unaccustomed to the sheer scale of the unabashed and often tasteless wealth that surrounded us.

'La Mer' complemented the setting perfectly and my limbs moved indolently to the rising beat of the music without any accompanying feelings of disgust or shame at the thought of dancing with a total stranger that night in Amsterdam. My bad memories had faded and tonight Debussy was just Debussy.

When Tango stepped into the spotlight, any remaining tension in my posture relaxed and I slid happily into his arms, relieved to see him again and delighted that the pleasure I had first taken in his body and the delicacy and grace of his skilful movements had returned to me.

Tango had always been my favourite dance partner. He was the most handsome and the better dancer of the three of my companions, and he was the one that I felt the most warmth towards. He always greeted me with a smile and a wink before putting on a show of domination that matched the routine I had devised and seemed to fool the audience, but that I knew was as theatrical for him as it was for me. Unlike the man that I had danced with in Amsterdam, Tango seemed genuinely to care for me, as much as it was possible for two people to care for each other in such limited circumstances.

With Dominik in the audience, I was even more eager to put on a good show. As I imagined his eyes on my body and the arousal that he might feel at the spectacle of my nudity and the athletic public coupling that we were about to present, I felt myself tingle with anticipation.

When Tango took my hand and pulled me against him, it felt like the first time that we had danced together, thrilling and dangerously erotic. In response, my nipples hardened like beacons and wetness gathered between my thighs, ready for his penetration.

He inserted himself inside me and I was barely able to control my body enough to continue the routine, so desperately did I want to just pull this tanned and muscular man on top of me and simply fuck him on the hard wooden floor of the yacht, audience be damned. But living with Viggo had taught me that restraint can sometimes be as pleasurable as fulfilment, and besides, I was a professional and here to put on a class act, not an animalistic and pornographic display full of heat and passion, even if that was what I desired at the time.

Tango squeezed my hand gently in farewell as the music came to a finale and I tiptoed backstage, masked by the sudden cut of the stage light. In the dressing room, I took a few deep breaths and resolved to calm myself down and present a professional front to Dominik. I was not inclined to explain to him the history of my dancing or the feelings that appearing on stage aroused in me, and I had by then decided that I did not want to take him to my bed or pursue him any longer.

Dominik was apparently shocked and awed by the performance.

'That was beautiful,' he said as the chauffeur returned us to our respective hotels.

'It was also well paid,' I replied, even though the money bored me now. I was no longer impressed by the dripping wealth that was always on display at these events and neither did I care if I possessed it or not. I just wanted to dance.

Dominik kept on asking me question after question about Viggo's art and music collections until I began to wonder if he'd turned into some sort of amateur sleuth. Or perhaps he had got wind of the disappearance of Summer's prized violin, which had gone missing the night of Viggo's charity performance at the Brixton Academy. Did he suspect that Viggo was in some way responsible for it? More likely he was seeking details of real people to hang his latest novel onto. He had told me over dinner that he was writing the story of an instrument and its passage from one owner to the next. A fascinating idea and one that required much ruminating on the subject of collectors. I wondered whether it had occurred to Dominik that he was one of them, a voyeur like any other, wandering the world in search of characters, motives and emotions to snare like butterflies in the net of a lepidopterist and pin down onto a page.

The Belsize Park mansion was empty when I returned. Summer was still touring. A postcard from Berlin was waiting in the mail box addressed to Viggo and I. She would be home soon, following concerts in cities across Scandinavia – Copenhagen, Oslo and Helsinki – with the tour then ending in Sarajevo and Ljubljana. At this rate, Summer would turn into more of an international wanderer than I.

Viggo was on his way to join her and Groucho Nights for a special one-off appearance in Stockholm. I had declined the opportunity to go with him. Somehow, even though Finland was geographically nearer, it was too close to Russia for comfort. I knew the feeling was irrational. When I thought of Russia, I thought of St Petersburg and Donetsk and my friend Zosia from the dormitories in the School of Art and Dance, and her sunken face, the thin features of her child and her garden of skeleton trees. It was not a place that I ever wanted to set foot in again.

Time passed as it always did, but not without the

inevitable waves of loneliness that were part and parcel of having virtually nothing to do. Without my dancing, any other form of employment or my two lovers to keep me company, my life took on a certain aimless quality and it was only by immersing myself in the imaginary worlds contained within the books that I found on Viggo's endless shelves that I was kept from going stir crazy. On one particularly uneventful day I amused myself by attending a cookery class near Oxford Circus, where I irritated the chef by imperiously suggesting that he was far too heavy handed with his macaroons.

When Summer eventually returned a few weeks later I greeted her with all the enthusiasm of a young lover, but after the initial passion of our reunion she became withdrawn and spent little time at home. She never mentioned Dominik and I did not inform her that we had run into each other in the Catalan capital, seeing little point in causing her pain if thoughts of him touched a nerve.

Viggo and I were still lovers but our feelings for each other had long since lost their fire and I felt little for him besides a playful friendship. Still, we seemed to draw comfort from each other's bodies as I woke most mornings tangled up in his arms with Summer a short length away from us curled up alone at the edge of the bed.

Since her return from the Groucho Nights tour she lived in a permanent state of distraction and had lost her usual joie de vivre for our group lovemaking sessions. Summer had always been the spark that lit our triad's fire and, without the vision of her pliant body pressed against Viggo's and the temptation to pull her into one position or another using her mane of fiery hair as a set of reins, I spent more time pleasuring myself alone in the shower or the guest room where I had slept when I first moved in. I always thought of Chey when I masturbated, reliving our time together and imagining the athletic and sometimes perverse sex sessions that I wished we could have.

The motivation for Summer's strange behaviour became clear when I awoke late and bleary-eyed one morning after an evening spent with her and Viggo at a private preview for a photography exhibition on the South Bank close to the hotel where I had bedded my first woman, Florence. Summer and Viggo had gone home early while I stayed for the afterparty, drinking champagne until the wee hours. I'd crawled into the bed we shared blissfully unaware of Summer's absence and totally ignorant of the events that had unfolded without me.

When I padded down to the steps to the breakfast bar I found Summer radiantly happy and half naked, her slim waist encompassed by one of Dominik's arms. His hand strayed only occasionally down to the cleft in her arse and the bare flesh of her thighs, every now and again slipping between her legs and caressing her mound, while Viggo looked on, grinning like a child in a candy store, and Summer blushed a dozen different shades of red despite the fact that Viggo had seen her naked a hundred times and more and touched her in those same places. None of them were yet aware that I was watching from the stairway.

Dominik was like a different person when he was with her, I observed. Gone was the melancholy man that I had met in Barcelona and in his place was a confident and powerful man whose self-assurance seemed unquestionable. She nestled her head against his shoulder tenderly, apparently inviting him to exert his playful brand of dominion over her. In his presence she lost that hard edge she so often assumed, the veneer of coolness that I had only otherwise seen dissolve when she was playing the violin or having particularly vigorous sex. They were made for each other.

And Viggo seemed pleased by the whole affair.

'Morning,' I announced, tightening my satin bathrobe and cruising down the last few steps as though I had only just awoken and as if finding the three of them in various states of undress in the kitchen was not unexpected in the slightest.

They looked up in unison, each wearing an expression that drifted halfway between happiness and embarrassment.

'Morning, Queen of the Night,' said Viggo. 'How is our ethereal mermaid today? Did you leave any ladies at the party unsullied?'

'Only the dull ones.' I grinned back at him. Actually I had spent the night engaged in only the most mild of flirtations with a pair of girls clad in matching bright satin dresses, but I saw no harm in perpetuating Viggo's idea that I broke hearts wherever I went. He seemed to take some kind of perverse satisfaction from the thought that every man and woman in the world would happily worship at my feet given half a chance. It was a fantasy that cemented my status as the jewel in his crown of beautiful things.

'And how were your respective evenings?' I asked collectively.

There was a long silence while I wondered whether Viggo, Dominik and Summer had spent the night engaged in a new threesome combination that excluded me. Viggo had previously hinted at the occasional past dalliance with a male lover in his never-ending quest to savour every experience under the sun. I was unsure of Dominik's persuasion but did not doubt for a second that Summer would have relished an opportunity to be sandwiched between the two men.

But as it transpired, the nocturnal activities of my three companions were of a quite different nature altogether. I listened as Viggo explained that between the three of them they had managed to track down Summer's lost Bailly violin and Dominik had apparently risked life and limb to retrieve it.

'So, who was it who had the instrument?' I asked, perplexed.

'We won't bore you with the details,' Dominik replied smoothly. 'It's rather complicated and not nearly as exciting as Viggo makes out.'

'But it gave you some good material for your next novel, I hope?'

'In a manner of speaking. I don't like to stray too close to real life.'

Summer snickered. Dominik smacked her playfully on the backside.

'Shall we leave these two lovebirds to it?' Viggo asked, offering to treat me to breakfast at a nearby cafe on Hampstead High Street.

Summer and Dominik were gone by the time we returned, and within two weeks she had collected her few belongings and left the Belsize Park mansion for good in favour of Dominik's more modest house further up the hill in Hampstead proper. In between shifting boxes and sorting through our joint wardrobe, there were many promises of keeping in touch and seeing each other for dinner and walks on the Heath and so on, but in reality I knew she was happy with Dominik and ready to close the book on this particular chapter of her life.

*

One day, some weeks after Summer had left our lives – and our bed – I took Viggo up on his invitation to join him in his studio on Goldhawk Road where he was recording some new songs with the Holy Criminals. Summer had inspired him to create an album with a more classical bent, and he had been auditioning young classical musicians from the nearby School of Music to fulfil his penchant for sponsoring the many hopefuls who didn't have much of a chance at a record contract without a foot in the door.

I was quickly checked off the security list and pointed down the corridor to the recording studio to find that I had picked the one day in weeks that Viggo was not actually present.

'He's in a meeting with some record company folk,' announced a tall blonde girl with a cello leaning between her spread legs when I asked if anyone had seen him.

'But you're very welcome to stay and watch us,' she added with a flirtatious smile and a bold wink.

With that kind of welcome, it seemed rude to decline, so I settled myself into one of the leather beanbags that rested on the studio floor and watched her play.

She didn't lose herself in the music in quite the way that Summer had, but it was still a delight to observe the sharp angle of her wrist as she coaxed note after note from the strings and the way that she clenched the instrument so firmly between her open thighs.

'I'm Lauralynn,' she purred, extending her hand in a gesture of greeting when she had finished her set. For a moment I wasn't sure whether she intended for me to meet her hand with my own, or to bend down and kiss it. 'Fancy a drink?'

I accepted her invitation, and we shared a bottle of wine and a plate of bread and olives at the Anglesea Arms on Wingate Road near the studio but soon grew tired of the loud guffawing from nearby tables filled with Sloaney types and Yummy Mummies.

When she excused herself to go to the ladies' I could not help but admire the way that the fabric of her black jeans clung to her arse, which I was sure she was swaying for my benefit. She wore her denims as tight as Viggo did, but she managed to get out of them a great deal more gracefully as I discovered when I took her back to Viggo's bed that night.

Lauralynn was an enthusiastic and generous lover and a good conversationalist. She was familiar with New York and interested in my life there, my dancing and the other places that I had visited. Before I knew it I had told her my story from beginning to end, leaving out only the more intimate details of my relationship with Chey which I relished as if they were precious nuggets, like his gifts made of amber that I always kept nearby.

There was something inherently dangerous and sexy about Lauralynn, her confidence, her unflinching stare, the cruel twist of her mouth when she brought me slowly, excruciatingly to climax. I thought she could have moon-lighted as an assassin when she wasn't playing cello. We all have our secrets. The thought of her dressed as a Hollywood-style contract killer, sheathed head to toe in a skin-tight femme-fatale-style catsuit had interrupted my memories of Chey and I turned onto my side to face her, moved my hand to her sex, hot and wet once more, before gently trailing my fingers up to the silver rings that pierced both of her nipples ensuring that they remained permanently erect.

We were stretched out in Viggo's bed rather than the

guest room because his was by far the largest, and when I had explained our unusual relationship to her, Lauralynn had laughed loudly and throatily and suggested that we surprise him by wrapping ourselves up in his covers like a present. Making love in his bed without him added a clandestine thrill to the proceedings, even though I knew for certain that Viggo did not care a jot who I brought home or where I bedded them.

As it turned out, Viggo stayed out all night with his record company execs and by the time he was home again Lauralynn had gone with a loose promise to call me sometime. She called sooner than either of us expected.

'Luba?'

'Yes?' I replied. She had only been gone for a couple of hours so I presumed that she must have left something behind. It was too early even for the most keen of suitors to call back for the sake of romance.

'I have a bit of a favour to ask you.'

'Go on . . .'

When Lauralynn explained that she was required to leave her accommodation as she had just discovered that her writer-companion's long-lost love was moving back into his house in Hampstead and I realised that she was also a friend of Summer and Dominik's, the situation seemed too serendipitous to ignore. Besides, Viggo was so often away and I was tired of knocking around the vast mansion alone most of the time.

She was back with all of her things packed into boxes later that afternoon.

Lauralynn settled in as if she had never lived anywhere else and within just a few months life reverted into a gentle, if unexciting, routine. Viggo was now spending most of his days, and often nights, in the recording studio across town where work on the new album continued in earnest. Somehow I couldn't get excited about the project. Lauralynn was more enthusiastic about the whole thing, helping on some of the backing tracks, playing her cello or orchestrating string parts. They were both musicians, after all, and their affinity kept on growing.

I'd so quickly become a third wheel.

In bed, as much as I appreciated Lauralynn's vigour and imagination, we had quickly established we had too many similarities and that there wasn't much of a submissive bone in me. It went against my nature. When Viggo joined us, however, she was soon unpeeling secret layers of his sexuality like an onion skin, much to his and my surprise.

It made me happy, but wasn't any help.

I had a bad case of the blues and began to question what I now wanted out of life, conscious of all the mistakes I had made so far. Viggo seemed genuinely fond of Lauralynn; they had discovered they had so much in common, the music, the quietly perverse playfulness. Summer had found Dominik again and I imagined them in his house, just a mile or so up the hill, fucking away like rabbits in perfect bliss and harmony. And there I was: a dancer who no longer danced.

A voice inside me was telling me it was time to turn a new leaf, but I had no direction to follow, no idea as to what I should, or could, do next. All I did know was that there were so many things I did *not* wish to do. Ever again.

I'd become lazy, always the last to rise, deliberately keeping my eyes closed and feigning sleep when either Viggo or Lauralynn slipped out of bed, secretly treasuring the fact that the covers were now all mine and I could spread my limbs in all directions and doze on for a few more hours while they went about their affairs, or had sex in the nearby bathroom as I pretended to still be out for the count. More often than not, it was Viggo who was the loudest.

Only when the front door slammed shut and I knew I was alone in the mansion would I open my eyes properly and face the day, tiptoeing to the kitchen and having a glass of milk or a bite to eat, alongside the strong coffee Lauralynn always left behind. And the day would slowly pass by: a leisurely swim in Viggo's underground creek, hours spent on one of the ample sofas in the games room reading. I generously availed myself of Viggo's impressive first-edition collection and read and read. Always novels. If he knew my ungloved paws were handling the rare titles, no doubt he would have been annoyed, but books are there to be read, aren't they? I'd found half a dozen CDs of Russian folklore melodies and dances in Viggo's treasure-trove music collection and I would listen to them again and again, wallowing in Slavic melancholy until my own heart was singing along, humming the tunes, whispering the words and savouring their comfort.

On days like this, by mid afternoon I would feel the need for fresh air and would often slip on an old tracksuit I had inherited from Lauralynn and take a brisk walk down past the Royal Free Hospital and the parade of shops by the train station.

By this time of day, the approaches to the Heath were busy with nannies and prams and small pre-school children noisily running around and feeding the ducks while their distracted overseers gossiped in a variety of foreign languages. Joggers of all age would puff their way through the narrow paths that led to the more private grounds of the Heath, past the ponds and the open-air swimming area that held no appeal for me, its waters no doubt as cold as a Ukrainian stream and unappetisingly murky. I would usually take a sudden turn to the left and enter a whole other world.

It was eerie how within the space of a few yards walking around this part of the Heath you could almost leave civilisation behind and find yourself in what felt like an immemorial wood, desolate and empty, undisturbed by the ages. Here were places to meditate, to feel at one with nature, although there was also a slight buzz in the pit of my stomach when I travelled through these more remote areas that was definitely sexual, as if there was a supernatural call to suddenly cast my clothes aside and run naked along the sparse vegetation, felled tree-trunks and dirt tracks, to open my legs wide and offer myself to the Great God Pan. It was irrational, I knew, and of course I never did so, but I felt certain that others had followed these tracks and experienced the same feeling as me. The real world felt a million miles away and even the sounds of twittering birds had been cut off. I could lose myself amongst these meandering paths and often did so but, today, I felt drawn elsewhere.

I trampled through the canopy of trees and made my way to the small hill where an old, wrought-iron bandstand stood. It had become one of my favourite places to go and I was always surprised that so few people came here. Emerging from the sheltered penumbra of the woods into the sudden brightness of the clearing was like landing on another planet. Bathed in sudden light, the glorious green of the grass was like an unspoiled canvas. A couple were sitting in the grass at the far end of the naturally created arena, enjoying the late-autumn sun, but the bandstand was empty and I made my way towards it. The day before, I'd began reading a battered paperback copy of Scott Fitzgerald's *The Crack Up* that I'd found in a jumble sale at the Hampstead Community Hall – I wouldn't have dared take any of Viggo's rare editions out of the house. Now I sat on the stone steps and opened the book at the page where I'd stopped reading when Viggo and Lauralynn had joined me in the bedroom the previous night, intent on including me in their sexual whims. I had only forty pages to go and a couple of hours before the light faded, I reckoned.

'That's one I've never read. Is it a novel or one of his short-story collections?' a voice said behind me.

I froze, the words on the page blurring in front of my eyes. That voice. I turned and lifted my eyes in the direction of the speaker.

The sun was in my eyes so all I could see at first was a silhouette. A powerful wave of relief, fear, anger and apprehension washed over me like an unleashed tsunami of feelings.

Chey.

I tried to control my nerves. Keep my cool.

It was a moment I'd visualised happening for months. Dreamed about, fantasised about, but never thought it would ever come true. Not like this, not here. In these circumstances.

'How did you find me here?' I cried out, probably too loud. 'How . . . ? Have you been following me?'

'I have,' he confessed. His eyes clouded as he looked down at me.

The relief that he was here, that he was alive and well, subsided and anger surged through my veins. 'You bastard.'

Chey stayed silent.

'Since when? How long have you known where I was and haven't come to find me?' I continued.

'I've been tracking you since you left Viggo Franck's house,' he said.

'And how long have you known that I was in London?'

'There was a photograph in a magazine – you and him at some function, I think. That's how I knew where you were. I know you've started a new life, you're happy, but I had to come.'

He looked the same as ever, handsome in his own feral way, although there was a tiredness about him, his posture uncertain. He wore a pair of dark-blue jeans, a tight white T-shirt, and a brown leather jacket hung over his shoulder. His boots were scuffed.

My composure was slowly returning as I simmered down.

As I refused to stand up, he sat himself down at my side and took the book out of my hands, setting it down on the stone step.

'Talk to me,' he said.

'Shouldn't you be the one to do the talking?' I answered back.

The couple in the grass from earlier had now gone and we were the only ones in the clearing. A final cloud obscured the sun as the shades of the day grew darker.

'The moment I found out where you were, I had no choice,' Chey said.

'Didn't you?'

'So you've abandoned dancing, have you?' He changed the subject.

'Dancing abandoned me,' I told him.

I looked into his eyes and was overcome by his soulfulness.

My resentment was shrinking by the second. But my mind was awash with questions. His disappearances, the gun, the gifts, Lev, it was all too much. I needed answers.

'Why?' I asked him.

He opened his mouth and I moved my fingers to his lips to momentarily silence him.

'The truth, Chey. I just want the truth. Please tell me no lies.'

The all too brief contact with the hard softness of those lips electrified me, memories of the way he kissed and held me once upon a time rushing back to the surface like past scars I had clumsily managed to conceal but whose imprint had marked my DNA.

Sensing my reaction, he brought a hand to my cheek, brushed away a stray strand of hair.

'It's a long story . . .' he began.

'I have all the time in the world.'

He was a rare amber dealer, he informed me, and it was not just a front. It was a small business he had inherited from his grandfather and the uncommon diversity of the resin and its use as jewellery or even as medicine or as an ingredient in perfumes had seduced him when he was still a teenager. When we were briefly together, he had once lectured me about the history of amber, its properties and its colourful history, but this time the story he related was another one.

For geological reasons, much of the best amber originated in the Baltic States and was a significant export. One day, his warehouse had been raided by the authorities who had inside information that a particular shipment he had brought in had been used to smuggle a sizeable quantity of heroin from Kaliningrad, where the Russian mafia was particularly active. The crates in which the amber stones he had legitimately acquired and even packed himself at source had, it appeared, been manipulated before the shipment had taken place and replaced by double-bottomed wooden crates in which thousands of heroin sachets had been hidden and then covered by the actual amber.

Under interrogation, Chey had been unable to prove his innocence. He had arranged not just the original packing but also the paperwork, which did present some irregularities as he had been somewhat elastic about the actual quantities he was importing in order to avoid a surfeit of duties on arrival. Naturally, this didn't make his case any easier. Whether the FDA agents supervising the case believed him or not, he was in a spot.

He was made the proverbial offer that he couldn't refuse and agreed to work with the Federal agents and continue his imports of amber and inveigle himself into the organisation that he was now aware was mafia-connected. He would work as an unofficial double agent.

This had been going on for several years when he had met me and was the reason for his frequent absences, his often dubious acquaintances and manners and the fact he kept the gun in his apartment, if only as a precaution should his role be uncovered. He'd had to live two separate lives and there was no way he could have revealed this to me without putting me in danger.

'So why now?' I asked him.

'Things went wrong,' he admitted. An operation had ended badly and to keep himself afloat he'd had to betray

not just his criminal acolytes but also the Federal authorities, as a result of which he'd had to flee New York and was
now on the run. He didn't know what to do or where to go.
He had been in hiding in a cabin by a lake in Illinois that
he had told no one else about when he had come across the
newspaper cutting with the photo of Viggo and me. He had
a set of false documents which he would now be able to use
again and had come to London. That was it.

My initial thought was that we were now one of a pair,
both with our false passports and identities.

And I believed him. I'd always wanted to believe him, but
he hadn't had the courage to tell me the truth before.

I took his hand in mine and squeezed it tight. I wanted to
kiss him so badly, yet something was still holding me back.

But the warmth of his skin against mine already lit me up
inside. As if being hand in hand was a promise of more to
come.

'So what are you planning to do now?'

'I have no idea.'

He looked at me with reverence, as if I was wearing the
finest material and the slightest sudden movement would
tear or crumple it, rather than the old tracksuit bottoms and
T-shirt I had slipped on for my walk to the Heath.

It felt like our first time all over again. And this time, it
would all be done right, with the benefit of experience and
the joy of our reunion making up for the decidedly less than
idyllic surroundings.

His bank accounts had been frozen by the authorities and
with no means of accessing any money at all besides what he
carried in his pockets, he was staying in a downmarket bed
and breakfast near King's Cross. It saddened me to see him

living in this place as I recalled the sleek, clean elegance of his Gansevoort Street apartment. But when I had suggested we could go to the room I occupied in Viggo's mansion and explained that we were unlikely to be interrupted there, Chey said it would make him feel uncomfortable.

So we had made our way, giddy with anticipation, up the winding stairs of the building, stopping occasionally when Chey pushed me against the wall to steal a kiss, or slip a hand down past the elastic of my trousers, working a finger along the line of my panties and sending a shiver of pleasure coursing through me.

When we finally reached his room he tossed his leather jacket on a chair and sat on the bed watching me, his arousal plain to see even through his jeans. He held his breath as I pulled my clothes off and unhooked my bra, letting my panties pool at my feet before kicking them away. No music, no slow swaying or grinding. I'd spent years taking my clothes off for men for money and for me there was nothing sexy, let alone romantic, about a strip tease.

'You don't know how many times I've imagined seeing you like this again,' he said. His voice was soft, almost as if he was speaking to himself. I came towards him and he brought his hand to my face and stroked the line of my jaw gently. I turned and pressed my lips against his knuckles, inhaling the faint fragrance of his skin as I did so. His scent was ineffable but familiar and deeply comforting.

For the next few hours, neither of us said more than a few dozen words. There were already so many words unsaid between us that silence felt more appropriate.

I was bare. The room was bare, just a small cupboard, a bedside table, a bed with a dark-blue chenille bedspread, and a small rucksack in a corner that probably held all his present earthly belongings.

Chey's eyes and fingers were drawn to the gun tattoo near my cunt. It was the first time he had seen it.

He stroked it tenderly, but he didn't ask me any questions about its provenance. And when he took his eyes off the Sieg Sauer flower, as I had come to think of it, he went down on his knees and kissed it with his soft mouth. His lips were warm. His tongue slid across the tattoo just an inch from my opening and I wanted to moan and beg him to move closer. But I didn't. I did not wish to interrupt the tender magic of the moment because of the rise of my lust. My need.

I knew that he must be able to smell me, my arousal, my wetness. I distractedly passed a few fingers through his thick hair. Unhurried, casual but deliberate, a signal to let him know that all was well and we no longer had to rush things.

We didn't. He didn't.

Chey's examination was intense and thorough. I stood stock still in the shadow of his gaze as he reacquainted himself with my pussy, applying all the fervour of an explorer who has discovered an unchartered land. There had never been a more attentive audience, not even in The Place.

I revelled in his scrutiny.

I spread my legs apart knowing that this was the view that he had always loved most, this intimate vision of me.

His fingers separated my folds delicately. His tongue slid along the length of my slit. The pad of his thumb grazed my nub as delicately as the brush of a rose petal.

With every new sensation the fire of my ardour grew, coiling from deep inside me and snaking its way up my spine and into my brain until the two blended and I was aware of nothing but the exquisite feelings that Chey was so expertly orchestrating, as if he had spent the years we had been apart doing nothing but memorising all the ways that he had pleased me when we had been together.

He rose to his full height and we kissed again, his lips sea-wet with the salt-tart tang of me, his tongue seeking solace in the harbour of my mouth.

I ran my hands under his T-shirt, tugged at his buttons with tremulous fingers, pushed it up to reveal his perfectly muscled torso, keened with all the frustration of unsated desire.

He slipped the T-shirt over his head and, undoing his belt, dropped his jeans to the floor. Slipping his boxer shorts down, he finally released his growing erection and it was now his turn to present himself naked to me; his powerful shoulders, the darker targets of his hard nipples in the sculpted landscape of his chest, the long, solid legs and the straight line of his powerful cock. He was as hard as he would ever be now, his erection rising from the curly jungle of his pubic hair, his heavy balls hanging low.

I looked him in the eye, seeking his approval.

He nodded and I dropped to my knees, took hold of his cock and brought it to my mouth.

His smell was natural, heady, real. I wanted to taste him, to experience the primal reality of what he was.

Somehow he grew even harder against the pliant softness of my tongue. I took him as far into my throat as I could manage, wanting him to fill every part of my being until the melancholy of his absence had been completely extinguished.

I sucked him like a woman possessed, as if catching up

for the days, the nights, the weeks I had missed, as if the way to his heart journeyed through the beat of his cock. Sensing the madness of my appetite, Chey slowed down his own movements inside my mouth, patting my head as if to say we had all the time in the world. Right there and then I felt unleashed, wanting him to come and flood my mouth with his juices, to drown me. But he was right, there was no hurry.

I had to savour every moment of our first lovemaking in ages. Make it last. I loosened the grip of my lips on his shaft.

Finally, as we both reached a nirvana state of exhaustion, he said, 'I want to come inside you', and my heart exploded. My avid mouth let go of his cock and I allowed him to lay me out on the bed, to widen the angle of my legs and, like a carefully rehearsed ritual, to lower himself between my thighs.

As he penetrated me, I quickly reached that mental beach where the whole world disappears from sight, and I existed only as an extension of my nerve endings and I could think of nothing else than the union of our bodies, and how every part of my life had been leading to this moment, my vagina pulsating against the hardness of his cock and orchestrating the rise of our mutual pleasure. We were one, as we once had been. Made for each other. Every piece of our souls and our bodies fitting together like a jigsaw. This was no longer a dance of opposites, it was Chey and Luba, together, joined again in the most intimate way.

He began to move against me, his rhythm picking up pace as I matched him, thrust for thrust, feeling every inch of him as he pushed further and further inside me.

It was good.

It was fucking more than good.

It was what I was born for.

And when I came, I screamed. My lovemaking had never been particularly noisy, but the howl that rose over the industrial rooftops of King's Cross that evening was like the sound of my rebirth, an affirmation of life.

In response to the sheer strength of my arousal, Chey jerked hard moments after I did, crying out my name as his hot come flooded my pussy.

Damn the neighbours, I thought, as we simultaneously lost control. I thrashed wildly in his embrace, feeling the weight of Chey's hard body anchoring me, pressing against me, adhering to me.

I was cunt.

I was Chey's.

We stayed in his room that whole night and the whole morning that followed. Only water from the tap sustained us.

We fucked, we made love and then we fucked again. We were raw, we were mad, we were happy, we had a reason to live.

And even though the future was patiently waiting for us around the corner, it could wait.

For now.

10

Dancing with Death

The first thing I wanted to do was get Chey out of that King's Cross bed and breakfast. Not only was the place unfit for purpose, but I found it demeaning for him to be staying there. He argued that its anonymity was best suited to his situation, but I quickly managed to convince him that moving in with me into Viggo's mansion was the natural solution. Even though the building's security was minimal, the fact that Viggo was in the public eye was a form of reassurance, as whoever was trying to locate him would not think of the Belsize Park house as a natural hiding place. The place was roomy enough and both Viggo and Lauralynn were now spending such long hours in the studio that his presence there would neither displease them nor prove an inconvenience. I explained the loose nature of the relationship that had somehow evolved there with my two sometimes lovers and friends and he took it in his stride, a faint smile lighting up his face, as if amused by my propensity for left-field behaviour.

He agreed to my plan.

We waited until evening and he settled his meagre bill in cash. He thought it would be dangerous to use his credit cards and had enough money to last a few months, he told me. The US Federal authorities had cut him loose after his identity as a mole with the Russians had been uncovered, and his role in the whole affair had been expunged from any public records. Not only would they not prove of assistance, but Chey had a suspicion that some of the officers involved had links to the Russians and had actually given his identity away. He could expect nothing from their quarter.

Viggo and Lauralynn were wonderfully understanding when I introduced Chey to them. I had mentioned him in passing once or twice and they had noted the melancholy that took hold of me whenever I thought of Chey, and they appeared to be genuinely happy for me. It had been obvious to them during the course of the previous weeks that our triad of sorts was coming apart and the bond between the two of them was becoming stronger despite Lauralynn's professed preference for women, but they liked me enough to welcome the fact that my new lover was also my old lover. Even gentle perverts have a soft streak.

The arrangement worked. A month passed during which we all settled into our new roles and shared the large house while maintaining our respective privacy. Chey and Viggo actually became good mates when Viggo discovered that Chey was a treasure trove of information and knowledge about rock music, something I had never known. Many an early evening was spent with the two of them selfishly sitting chortling in a corner, filling their iPods with new playlists they were coming up with, while Lauralynn and I cooked or gossiped. For the first time in ages, I didn't even open the pages of a book for four weeks in succession. I had other things to do at night, rediscovering Chey and learning to fully relax in the clutch of his embraces and live for the moment, as he orchestrated every emotion in my body and heart to repeated climaxes I never even knew I had in me. Now there was no shadow in our relationship, we could see how well we fitted together, not just bodies but minds. Even the silences we often shared, after our lovemaking or at odd moments during the day, were filled to the brim with significance and intensity.

We were lying in bed, sated from our earlier exertions, his hand delicately washing like a wave over my exposed rump, his touch light like a feather, as we both awaited the seductive and replenishing embrace of sleep when his mobile phone buzzed. It was the first time it had rung since he had joined me in Viggo's house.

We both glanced at the bedside table, surprised by the insistent sound.

'Do many people know your number?' I asked Chey.

His face darkened. 'No. Very few.'

He gingerly picked up the phone and brought it to his ear.

The muffled rumour of a voice reached me as Chey nodded a few times and hummed and hawed. Then the conversation ended abruptly, with him just saying 'Thanks' to his distant interlocutor.

He turned to face me.

'It was Lev,' he said.

'Lev?'

'We worked together, straddling the good side and the bad side, so to speak. He's okay, if often a real pain in the arse,' he explained. 'He's still involved. Somehow his cover wasn't blown, although it must have been a close thing. It seems they know I'm in London.'

'Damn . . .'

'Just the city; not where I am.'

I was afraid. It felt like a circle was closing in, threatening our happiness.

It made sense that we couldn't remain in Viggo's house indefinitely. It had always been a temporary solution while we stepped back and gathered our thoughts. In any case, being cooped inside it was becoming increasingly frustrating for Chey, with just a few short walks along the more unpopulated paths of the Heath in the early hours of the morning possible to alleviate his voluntary imprisonment.

Not only did he have to escape to somewhere faraway where no one would know him or of him, but he also had to convince his pursuers that he was no longer harmful to them. Sadly, these were not the kind people you could negotiate with or have reasoned conversation with to clear the muddied waters. They were dangerous men.

I only knew one thing: wherever he went, I would be going with him. I was determined that nothing would sunder us apart any longer.

'You'll need a different identity, a whole set of new papers,' I said. 'And that's just to begin with.'

'Not only is that expensive and difficult, but you need the right contacts to set it up properly. You'd require complete professionals, not a back-alley store with would-be inexperienced forgers. And all the guys or organisations I once knew on that side of the law are not the sort of folk I could now run to begging for a favour. They would just give me up,' he reasoned.

However, as distasteful as it might prove, I could see the glimmer of a solution.

I fetched my handbag and pulled out my current German passport and the identity card that I had been using and handed them over to Chey.

He gave them a long look and then asked, 'These are yours? You have false papers?'

I nodded.

'Do they look authentic enough?'

He held them up to the light and studiously peered at them.

'They look very good, although I'm of course not an expert. But yes, they seem real,' he admitted.

'I can get more,' I said.

'How?'

'From the same people.'

'How much would it cost?'

'Just our pride,' I said.

And I revealed to him how I had been provided with the false set of papers by the Network and the work I had undertaken for them.

Chey knew that since our first time together I had been with other men. He had met Viggo, of course, but had quickly realised that the rock singer had been more of a fuck buddy to me, where emotions had not been involved and, anyway, he had taken a liking to the guy and had not been jealous that I had been to bed with him. He must have guessed there would have been others, anonymous pick-ups and solaces for loneliness here and there, but I had never told him the story of the dancers and what we did for rich customers.

'If I agree to one final performance, I am confident they will provide me with a new set of papers for you to use,' I said.

He bowed his head.

'And you think that is the only way?' he whispered, already aware of the likely answer.

'Yes.'

He took me into his arms and hugged me close.

'Okay,' he said, 'but let me be the dancer, let me be your partner this time. You can train me beforehand, teach me.'

We kissed.

'The client much admired your set on the boat in Sitges,' I was told by Madame Denoux. 'He's been wishing to book you for a repeat performance ever since. You're lucky.'

'I'm pleased.' Actually it was more relief that I felt. I'd feared that in the many months since I had voluntarily dropped off the Network's radar and catalogue, I might have been forgotten and replaced by new dancers.

'And when he heard that you proposed a farewell performance on New Year's Eve, your swansong so to speak, he was absolutely delighted that he would be in a position to make it happen.'

'And he agrees to all my terms?' I asked.

'Yes. Cash at the door, albeit without our commission and the cost of the papers you desire duly deducted, naturally. Your choice of dance and partner, although the client, who is Russian as you no doubt guessed, one of your compatriots—'

'Not necessarily, I'm from the Ukraine.'

'Oh.' I could sense her frowning at the other end of the line back in her New Orleans house.

People always thought we were all the same. Although I'd grown up speaking both Russian and Ukrainian, because of my mixed parentage, they were two distinct languages, and our cultural heritages were very different. But over the years I had grown tired of correcting the people in the West who made that common mistake.

'Well, he's the client so who cares about the nationality,

eh? He's paying and paying well. He's been told the set will be something truly special.'

'Oh yes,' I confirmed hastily, although at this stage I had no idea what Chey and I would be dancing. All three of the scenarios I used to perform with my erstwhile professional partners were fairly elaborate and the fruit of considerable prior training and I didn't think I could teach Chey all the steps let alone the particular subtleties of the required movements in time. 'And someone from the Network will meet me on arrival with the documents we ordered?'

'They will. Why do you require the papers right there and then? We could FedEx them to you in London . . .'

'I have my reasons,' I said.

'Then of course the client has also agreed to the date you specified – New Year's Eve, although it is at very short notice, Luba. Your terms did make the negotiations rather awkward. Fortunately, he has a residence in Dublin so, as requested, it will all take place in the British Isles.'

That was something Chey and I had insisted on, to avoid facing too many airports and officials with his current documents.

I'd never been to Dublin. Neither had Chey. But we'd achieved our first goal of obtaining a new set of documents for him. Mine had not aroused any suspicion during a few years of globetrotting, so I felt safe to use them again.

The only problem was the second half of the plan. Where to run to and how to disappear and escape the clutches of Chey's pursuers?

We had a week left to come up with a miracle. And we were clutching at straws.

'I think we have to rely on the kindness of strangers,'

Chey said. 'We need outside help. This isn't something we can manage alone.'

'Who?' I asked. I briefly thought of Dominik, thinking as I did so of how attracted I'd been to him in the absence of Chey and the way I had shamelessly approached him in Barcelona. He was a writer, maybe he could come up with something, but then I quickly remembered the strongly autobiographical nature of his book. Another creative man who didn't entirely rely on his imagination . . . Just like Viggo.

Chey just sighed in response.

I heard the mansion's front door slam and Viggo and Lauralynn entered the large lounge where we often gathered for drinks together in the evening. They had just spent a whole afternoon finalising overdubs in the studio. After we greeted them, Lauralynn quickly excused herself and went up to her room, exhausted by the repetitive recording process.

Viggo poured himself a glass of bourbon and settled into his usual leather couch. He also looked tired and nothing like the rock god of stage and paparazzi pictures.

'So what's up, lovebirds?' he asked.

I looked at Chey, silently seeking his approval to tell Viggo the sorry state of our affairs. So far, all he knew was that Chey was in some sort of trouble but we had not revealed its specific nature and he hadn't asked. In fact, he'd seemed rather chuffed at the idea of hosting a fugitive of sorts, but likely assumed it was creditors Chey was hiding from, and not dangerous mafia-connected drug-runners.

'We're up shit creek, Viggo,' Chey said.

Viggo raised a querulous eyebrow.

'Tell me more, mate.'

Viggo listened attentively to Chey's story, occasionally nodding sympathetically and refilling his glass, drinking the bourbon straight, with no ice.

'Wow,' he finally said when Chey concluded his tale.

'Wow indeed,' I mimicked, ever so slightly annoyed by his wide-eyed response and the look of amusement spread across his features.

'So, if I understand things correctly, you have the means to leave the country for parts unknown, but without some sort of subterfuge to prevent them from continuing to track you down again, it's worth fuck all?'

'That's certainly one way of putting it.'

Viggo chortled.

'What you need is . . . magic, guys.'

'Magic?'

'Yep. Magic.'

'I don't get it,' I said. Chey remained silent, glancing dubiously at Viggo's smirking face.

Viggo crossed his legs, set his empty glass down and began manically gesticulating.

'We have to make you disappear. Easy as that!'

'How would you propose to do that?' Chey and I asked in unison.

'Stagecraft, my friends. Stagecraft. Now that's something I know something about. Did I ever tell you how I loved Alice Cooper when I was a teenager? All his theatrical tricks, the artifice . . .'

'Viggo, can you speak English?' Chey asked.

Viggo triumphantly rose from the couch.

'Mate, leave it to me. Let me think it over, sleep on it, talk it over with Lauralynn maybe, but I already think it's a brilliant idea, I really do, and tomorrow morning, hey presto, I will provide you with your means to escape.'

I was nonplussed, thinking he had maybe drunk too much bourbon but then realised I had never seen Viggo drunk. Despite his slim frame, he had the constitution of a horse.

As he left the room, he winked mischievously at me.

Viggo's mood was just as jovial and as irritating the next morning.

I watched in silence for as long as I could stand it as he capered around the kitchen wearing just his underpants and a smile. Bacon hissed in a griddle pan and he worked the waffle machine with the efficiency of an assembly-line robot until the pile of battercakes formed a tower, Pisa-like, that threatened to tumble onto the tiled floor at any moment. Pans of all shapes and sizes covered the counter top, balanced precariously wherever he had lobbed them in his search for the griddle, and were sprinkled liberally with spilled flour and sugar.

He paused in his mad culinary dance for just long enough to pour a coffee from the filter machine and slide it in front of me as carefully as one might offer a sacrifice to an angry god.

'So,' I said slowly, only mildly appeased by the appearance of the hot brew, 'are you going to share this fine plan of yours any time soon?'

'Patience, my dear,' he replied, waving a spatula in the air with a theatrical flourish. 'We must at least wait for the others to arrive.'

The others? My heart sank. How many people had Viggo confided in?

Chey was still in the shower where I had left him. The fear of going on the run again had made him even more appreciative of his creature comforts and he had begun bathing with the sort of languid thoroughness that I saved for the pool in the basement. And with little else to occupy his time, he spent hours each day working out in Viggo's elaborate and rarely used home gym. Bar a little of his initial cockiness, he was almost back to the Chey that I had known in New York.

There was a knock at the door.

'Hello, my darlings,' Viggo cried as he shooed the new-comers into the house, still holding his spatula aloft like a baton.

Dominik and Summer had arrived, and were looking just as mystified as I felt. Dominik observed Viggo's state of undress and raised an eyebrow. Summer did not seem even to notice.

She had her violin case tucked under one arm as she always did. Her red hair tumbled loose around her shoulders and a fuzz of tiny wisps stood out from her scalp like a halo, as if she had been walking in a stiff wind or was sorely in need of a new brand of conditioner. I knew from my brief interaction with Dominik that he seemed to prefer his women natural, without artifice, and I had watched the change in Summer since their return to coupledom with amusement. These days, I rarely saw her wearing lipstick.

Lauralynn was the next to appear. She was almost as scantily clad as Viggo, wearing just a buttoned-up men's shirt that barely covered her arse.

'Is it laundry day for you two?' Dominik asked drily as Lauralynn raced over to give him an exuberant kiss on the cheek.

'An early morning treat,' she replied. 'I know how you like a woman in men's clothing.'

Dominik snorted. Even after all this time I still found his relationship with Summer fascinating. She was not the least bit puzzled to see her friend flirting with her boyfriend, and I was sure that Lauralynn would never dare tease Chey in my presence in quite the same way.

Lauralynn took over in the kitchen and sent Viggo upstairs to put on some clothes.

'Do you have any idea what this is about, Lu?' Summer asked, pouring her and Dominik a coffee and then slipping onto the barstool next to me. I caught a faint whiff of her perfume, musky and sweet.

'He hasn't told you yet, then?'

'Not a word. He called before the sun was up and invited us over for breakfast. Brunch is so much more sociable,' she sighed. Summer was almost as fond of her lie-ins as I was, perhaps a characteristic that we'd both developed over years of irregular employment.

Dominik stood behind her and began running his hands through her hair. No wonder it was such a mess, if that was how she combed it these days. She leaned back against him and purred.

Viggo appeared moments later, dressed this time, though frankly I didn't think that his jeans and ripped old T-shirt were much of an improvement. Chey trailed mutely a few steps behind him. His expression was forlorn, hopeless, and made me all the more determined to find a solution.

'Right, kids,' Viggo announced, rubbing his hands together. He was clearly enjoying this, and if his plan wasn't any good, I resolved to toss my now cold cup of coffee over his head to wipe the smile from his face. 'Have you seen *Romeo and Juliet*?'

'The Baz Luhrmann version?' asked Summer.

'That's not really the point, my dear. Allow me to explain.'

He looked over at Chey and I, as if asking for permission to elaborate.

'For God's sake,' I hissed, 'get on with it. Please.'

Viggo grinned.

'You're going to fake your own deaths. And we're going to help.'

Lauralynn looked as pleased as Viggo. They were both bonkers. Summer and Dominik now looked even more perplexed.

'Did we miss something?' Dominik asked.

'Our friends here are on the run, mate. Probably safer if you don't know all the details. Just in case, you know. If it all goes tits up and we're interrogated, it's best if you don't have anything to tell them.'

'Right,' Dominik replied.

'Luba has created the perfect opportunity for a diversion,' Viggo continued. 'One last dance. In Dublin. There isn't a lie that can't be told on the stage, if you do it right. Particularly if a naked woman is involved. Or two.' He cast a questioning glance over at Summer, who shrugged as if to say that on-stage nudity was too trivial a matter to even be remarked upon. 'We're leaving at the end of the week,' Viggo continued. 'Are you in?'

'This sounds nuts, but for you, Viggo, how could we refuse?' said Summer.

'Wonderful. Because I'll be needing your violin again.'

I noticed her arm imperceptibly tighten around the case of her precious Bailly, but she did not protest.

The conversation then turned to the matter of breakfast, and nothing else was said on the matter. If Viggo gave the others more details separately about the parts that we would each play, he didn't share that fact with Chey and me.

'We don't have any other choice, sweetheart. We have to trust him,' Chey said to me as I vented my frustration and anxieties once we were out of earshot.

He was right, but that didn't make me any happier about the situation. Our lives, as well as our deaths, were now in Viggo's hands and there was absolutely nothing that we could do about it.

A few days later, we were on our way to Dublin.

The Network had booked us into a sprawling, palatial room in the Gresham Hotel, at the top end of O'Connell Street. Summer had arranged to be in the same hotel but had organised it separately, while Dominik was staying in a smaller bed and breakfast near Trinity College on the other side of the river. Chey and I had brought little luggage, as we knew we wouldn't be checking out. All we would have would be the clothes on our backs and the single suitcase we had hidden away in a left-luggage locker at the Heuston train station shortly after we had arrived in the Irish capital.

Dominik had gone ahead of us. He had deliberately made his own way to Dublin and, apart from a brief telephone conversation with Summer to touch base and verify everything was on schedule, had neither been in contact nor been seen with us since we had arrived. Vouched for by Viggo who had once been an appreciated customer of the Network, he was going to be a legitimate member of the audience, hopefully beyond all suspicion. Back in London before our departure, Summer had jokingly remarked that they'd had to go out and purchase a dinner jacket for him, especially for the occasion.

We had no idea where Viggo and Lauralynn were lurking, but assumed they were already in town and in position. Viggo had still not explained all the details of his plan to us as he wished to retain an element of surprise. My only reservation was that with his enthusiasm for matters theatrical and his warped sense of humour, whatever he had planned might prove somewhat over the top and unconvincing. We were in his hands now, however, and it was too late to turn back.

I wanted us to take a cab to the designated venue, but both Chey and Summer were nervous and suggested we walk the short distance from the Gresham to Temple Bar on the other side of the Liffey, if only to clear our heads.

The New Year's Eve celebrations were in full flight, with inebriated groups of youngsters cruising up and down O'Connell Street, swaying in all directions. Temple Bar and its myriad restaurants and bars were draining the crowds and we followed in their wake as midnight approached. I glanced over at Chey and Summer as they walked by my side. Both looked preoccupied and I realised, with a minor shock of recognition, that of all the people making their way towards the heart of the festivities, we were probably the only ones with glum faces. Not only were we not here to celebrate the turn of the year, but we had all been careful not to drink before our planned performance for fear of messing up Viggo's utterly crazy plan.

The closer we got to the hall, the more I convinced myself that this would be a total fiasco. And not only would we be left totally humiliated and with egg on our face, but Chey could end up dead, for neither of us had any doubt that the oligarch who had booked us for tonight must have some sort of underground connections and that Chey's name and face would have been circulated in their midst.

The building was halfway down Temple Bar, with a buzzing restaurant on the ground floor which people were queuing up for, in the hope of cancellations for the final service of the year. To the left of the restaurant's main entrance was another closed door, with a sign indicating a set of functions rooms. The whole top floor had been booked for a private function. That meant us.

I rang the bell and the door promptly opened.

The security man who greeted us and checked us off against his list was built like a ton of bricks and fitted uneasily inside his badly cut tuxedo. His shaven head reflected the light from a single bulb that illuminated the narrow entrance and a deep corridor that led to a set of wooden stairs. Although he remained silent and nodded us on, I knew the man must be Russian. Our guest had his own full-time protection and didn't rely on local talent from the looks of it.

As we passed him and walked to the stairs I could feel his stare in my back. Or maybe he was fascinated by Summer's fiery mane of curling red hair. We Russian blondes were a common sort but redheads were more of a rarity.

I'd noticed our names were on a separate page of his checklist. Just us three. The entertainment.

As we took our first steps up the stairs, we heard another buzz at the door and I turned my head to see the security giant ushering in a middle-aged couple in ostentatious evening attire and tick them off the list. Guests.

On the third and final floor we were greeted by a young Irish woman with jet black hair, dressed in Confederate-style crinolines. The outfit was incongruous, but suited her pale complexion and green eyes.

'I'm your hostess for tonight. Welcome,' she said.

'We're the artists,' Summer pointed out.

'Oh, I know that, Miss Zahova. It's an honour to have you performing for us tonight. I'm a great fan of yours, by the way. I was so terribly excited when I heard from Oleg that you would be . . . involved.' The young woman looked over at Chey and me. 'It's an incredible bonus to have you playing for your friends. So unexpected.'

Summer forced herself to smile.

'Where can we change and . . . prepare?' she asked the Irish hostess. I wondered briefly if this girl was on the oligarch's permanent staff or had just been recruited as a greeter for the evening. Did she know the exact nature of the performance we had agreed to undertake?

'This way.' She led us to a large empty room in which piles of dining tables and chairs had been pushed into one corner. At the centre of the room a large mirror and a trestle table had been set up for us.

'It's not ideal,' the woman pointed out. 'But it was awkward to find a venue of the right size at such short notice.'

'It'll be fine,' I said.

'Good,' she said. 'I'll let you prepare. I'll be back in a while with your envelopes, as arranged. You come on at fifteen minutes past the hour, yes?'

I breathed a sigh of relief as she departed, her impossibly high heels clicking against the parquet floor of the function room that was now to serve as our changing room.

We all looked at each other.

The costumes that Chey and I would initially be wearing were simple and functional. For me, a white silk semi-opaque camisole that reached all the way down to my ankles. I would dance barefoot. For Chey we had come up with a pair of black, sharply creased, toreador trousers and a loose white shirt with billowing sleeves which he had at first objected to, but we didn't come up with any better alternative and he had conceded defeat.

Summer slipped out of her jeans. She had been wearing them commando and the fire of her pubic bush was now on full display. I glanced at Chey as he noticed. Despite the tense nature of the situation, I could sense his calm appreciation of her wild beauty. I had encountered her in New Orleans, had tasted her exuberant nudity there, and I knew how she revelled in this form of exhibitionism, but this would be the first time I would actually see her perform in the nude, as she had agreed to do to accompany our curious dance. It was something Viggo had suggested. The perfect diversion, he had called it. Somehow I wasn't surprised that Dominik had consented to this. I couldn't help but be fascinated by the undercurrents and erotic quirks of their relationship.

Now fully naked, Summer stood proudly, a triumphant look on her face. She leaned over and took her violin from its battered case.

I held my breath in awe.

Right then the young Irish woman returned, not even batting an eyelid at the spectacle of Summer naked with her instrument in one hand.

She handed us a series of thick jiffy bags and envelopes, which we had to bureaucratically sign for.

'Your fees as agreed,' she said, giving both me and Summer different envelopes. Summer had negotiated to be paid separately.

Then she passed over the larger brown jiffy bag to me. It was securely sealed. 'From your employers,' she added.

Chey's new documents – a passport and an identity card, even though we still didn't know what name he would now have to pass himself off as. And would we ever have the opportunity to use these documents?

Chey nervously glanced at his watch as I passed our envelopes over to Summer, who locked them inside her violin case with her own, as we had agreed beforehand.

The sounds of fireworks and drunken cries reached us from outside as the New Year arrived in full swing.

We had just a few minutes to kill before our dance of death. Chey ordered us each a shot of tequila from the bar to steady our nerves before we went on stage. I gulped mine down, coughing as the bitter liquid burned my throat. He had forgotten to bring lemon and salt, and there was no time to go back for it. Thus fortified, the three of us waited, dressed and undressed for the next episode in Viggo's preposterous scenario to unfold.

My heart stilled as the music began.

Life as I knew it might be about to change irrevocably, but for the next ten minutes my heart and my feet would be engaged in the one activity that I enjoyed most. Dancing. With Chey.

At least, if I were to die tonight, I would die in the arms of the man that I loved.

Teaching Chey to dance in less than a week had been no minor feat, but we had managed it. We'd pushed all the equipment in Viggo's gym against the walls and had the run of the place, complete with wall-to-wall mirrors and beautifully smooth wooden flooring. It was a much nicer studio than any I had ever danced in as a youngster, a fact that I reminded Chey of regularly.

Fortunately, he proved a quick learner, perhaps in part because of his years of martial arts training. The routine that I had devised included no fighting manoeuvres, but Chey's easy athletic grace, balance and sense of discipline meant that he was far better than most beginners.

The moment we made our appearance at the centre of the strong spotlight on the temporary wooden stage that had been erected for the evening, I caught a tremor of whispers travelling across the audience, many of them strongly Russian-accented. I knew this initial reaction was not just due to me; I was still clothed, although revealingly so. No, Chey's face was the trigger. Photographs of him must have been circulating for some time across the far-flung reaches of the Russian mafia, and a handful of guys in the audience either had recognised him instantly or were presently busy surfing the web on their phones to verify whether he was indeed the wanted man.

We had no choice but to ignore them and begin our performance. The die was now cast. It helped too that we were dancing together. We were so familiar with each other's bodies that when we danced we virtually melded into one. I responded to Chey without thought or hesitation, as naturally as I breathed in after I breathed out. When he applied the lightest pressure to my spine to direct my movement I floated along with him as though we had been practising together for years rather than days.

The notes emanating from Summer's instrument were

long and mournful. She had elected to play a violin version of 'Gloomy Sunday', the sombre Hungarian song that had supposedly been a soundtrack to countless suicides. I'd always found it a little dreary, but Viggo had been enthusiastic about the idea on the grounds that our audience might find our 'deaths' occurring at the end of it a predictably amusing and not terribly smart piece of stagecraft and therefore hesitate in their seats before rushing forward to help or to call the police, presuming the whole thing a subterfuge and wanting to appear clever by acknowledging the trick rather than appearing the one fool in the crowd who fell for it.

We stepped in time to the music. It was a slow dance, a sad dance, a lovers' dance. We were entwined with one another, coiled together like two strands of a single rope. I played the part of the pitiable little woman, deep in the throes of lament. He was the strong man who carried my gracefully limp form, twisting and turning across the stage so that all could view my depression. Such an act was not difficult to fake, with the dismal tune reverberating through the auditorium like a funeral dirge and the fear that lurked deep within that some flaw in Viggo's plan would reveal itself at any moment and Chey would be wrenched away from me and imprisoned or, worse, killed.

Beyond the sound of the music an eerie silence had fallen over the audience. Perhaps the adrenalin had made my hearing more acute, or maybe it was the added theatrical effect of Summer's soulful melody playing live rather than the digital recordings I normally used, but the usual whisper of shock or creak of a chair as an onlooker leaned forward to achieve a better view were mysteriously absent from tonight's proceedings. I could not even hear the sound of a breath being drawn.

Every one of my senses was in overdrive.

Viggo had practically thumped me with the urgency of appearing normal, of behaving exactly as I would in any other performance. He knew that the oligarch who had booked us had seen me perform before in Sitges, albeit with a different dance partner. I was hoping that Chey's appearance instead would not ring any unwelcome signals. It took every ounce of effort to relax my limbs and maintain eye contact with Chey as I usually would instead of scanning the audience for signs of trouble.

Summer drew her bow across the strings, producing a sound that was so pensive and beautiful that I could not help the tears that welled up and flowed gently down my cheeks. My emotions were getting the better of me as my fear about the latter part of evening grew. She had a spotlight trained on her also and every now and again when we spun in her direction I caught a glimpse of her standing with her instrument raised to her chin, her breasts and cunt on proud display. She was barefoot like I was, and looked as solid as an oak tree, implacable and rigid, as if there was no force in the world that could sway her. The imperious woman who played for this audience was a world away from the blushing girl that I had watched dancing in New Orleans.

Chey turned me away from him, my cue to slip out of my dress and reveal my nudity. This too had been Viggo's emphatic suggestion. The sight of my naked body would distract the audience, if the sight of Summer's hadn't caused them to forget Chey altogether already. He also felt that naked I would appear more vulnerable and therefore less likely to be involved in the deceit.

Honey traps were the oldest trick in the book, I reckoned, but according to Viggo, men have terribly short memories, particularly when confronted by the body of a naked woman.

Desire, he said, did much to overwhelm the senses, including overwhelming common sense altogether.

Removing Chey's clothes had proven a trickier point. I refused to allow him to wear any kind of cheap Velcro ensemble that would make him seem no better than a stripper at a hen night. He could not merely half undo his toreador trousers and then continue to dance with them pooled around his feet. But we could not devise any way for him to step out of a pair of trousers and a buttoned shirt without appearing a fool.

And so I was left alone for a moment under the burning glow of the spotlight, whirling rhythmically as Chey stripped under cover of darkness, off to one side of the improvised stage. This was my opportunity to ensure that every eye in the audience was upon me and that Chey was forgotten and so I danced like I had never danced before, twisting my limbs into every darkly erotic position that I had been able to dream up.

Viggo, I was certain, must have planted members of his trusted stage crew into position which would explain why the lighting was unusually dull for a few moments, enabling me to see past the penumbra of the beam that surrounded me and into the auditorium.

Beyond the first few rows, I could barely make out any features on the blurred crowd but I was certain that I could see movement. Huddled forms drawing together to whisper to one another. The electronic displays of mobile phones lighting up to make calls. The faint, quick steps of someone running in a corridor. The hostess rushing to and fro, her stilettos tapping a staccato rhythm on the stone flooring.

The Russians had discovered our plot. I was sure of it. Every faint sound or rustle of movement cut into me like a whip. I had begun to feel a little strange, as if my limbs wouldn't move when I asked them to and water was flooding into my brain. The effects of shock, I thought, or adrenalin; and I forced myself to keep moving as the room tilted sideways. A scream rushed through my throat and threatened to burst from my mouth, but I swallowed it back and continued to shimmy as though my life depended on it, because tonight it did, and Chey's life too.

Chey stepped back into the stage light, which had now been turned up a notch and lit us as brightly as the beam from a desert sun. He was utterly bare and beautiful. His abdomen muscles ran down in a V shape to meet his pelvis. His cock was hard and pointed up towards my sex like an arrow. His bush of pubic hair was untrimmed, black and lustrous, framing his penis in savage style. In that moment I forgot what it was that we were there for and I fell to my knees as if to worship him, wrapping my lips reverently around his organ as a nun might take communion.

This was not part of the programme. I had broken from Viggo's tightly choreographed and rigorously detailed scheme to satisfy my own desire, because I had wanted nothing more than to feel the silky skin of his cock against the wet pillow of my tongue.

Chey crouched down and clasped my chin. He pressed his lips against mine.

I did not even notice when he lifted the gun to my forehead and fired.

'I'm sorry, Luba. It had to be this way,' he whispered tenderly, his voice quiet and meant only for me.

Summer screamed.

My world went black.

I slumped against the floor, barely aware of the babble of sound around me and the heavy *phut* of another shot. A loud *thump*! Another scream. A man's voice from the crowd shouting; 'I'm a doctor, I'm a doctor.' I realised it was Dominik's voice. Heels clattering. The voice of the hostess coming to me as if through a tunnel, 'Luba, Luba, Luba.' Then, 'She's dead. Oh my God, she's really dead.'

A stranger's hand wrapped around my throat.

'I can't feel a pulse,' someone said.

'There's so much blood.'

No trapdoor had opened in the stage floor below us as I had been half-expecting. Viggo's men were not assembled to whisk us away.

And where was Chey?

'This one's a goner.'

'Shot himself straight in the head.'

'And her too.'

Voices in Russian babbled in garbled voices. Their words floated around me like hummingbirds, quiet, quick, impossible to catch. I reached up an arm to snatch at them but my limbs would not move.

Lubov Shevshenko, Luba Shevshenko, my love, my life, my private dancer.

There was a sound like wind rushing in my ears and a barrage of thoughts and images, so no matter how I tried to concentrate on my surroundings in case we needed to flee, I could not decipher what was reality and what was dream.

Sirens rushed towards us with alarms like magpies screeching. The noise came to me as if I was standing at the mouth of a cave and listening to echoes. More heels clacking, enough pairs to shoe an army.

And then I was being lifted and carried away into the night.

The next sound I heard was laughter.

'Christ, I think even *she* thinks she's dead!'

My eyes fluttered open.

I blinked.

Lauralynn was staring straight down at me, an enormous grin on her face. She looked as unglamorous as I had ever seen her, with her hair pulled back into a loose ponytail and the rest of her encased in a baggy yellow high-visibility jacket and a pair of thick dark-green trousers. I craned my neck for a better look. Even her shoes were ugly thick-soled black clompers. Besides when she was getting in and out of the shower, it was the first time I had ever seen her outside of her trademark stiletto heels. She wasn't even wearing a scrap of make-up and her eyes looked tired and wan.

'Thank God for that,' she said when I lifted my head. 'I was beginning to think I was actually going to have to use this.'

She was holding a defibrillator.

'Where am I? Where's Chey?'

Memories of the evening had turned into a scrambled mess in my mind and I couldn't piece any of it together.

'Calm down, Lulu, he's right here. He should be awake in a minute or two.'

I pushed myself up into a sitting position and shrieked when I saw Chey's face covered with blood. Lauralynn was carefully wiping it off with a wet cloth.

'Don't worry, it's fake. Fake gun, fake bullets, fake blood.' She spoke as though she was explaining something to a very slow child.

My head thumped and everything was spinning, as though I'd just gotten off a merry-go-round. I had a vague feeling that something important had just happened and I'd slept through it, but if I just thought hard enough, it might come back to me.

'Here,' said Viggo, leaning over from the front seat. 'This might help.' He passed me a bottle of water.

'What happened?' I asked. 'Where are we?'

We were lying on stretchers in the back of an ambulance. The windows were small and high up so I could not make out our surroundings, but we were driving through the night and the street outside was quiet, the New Year's festivities audible but some distance away.

'You went straight down the K-hole,' Lauralynn said, chuckling to herself.

'What?'

When I tried to speak, my mouth refused to form the words, as if a wall had been erected between my brain and my body functions.

'We didn't trust either of you to play dead well enough,' Viggo added. 'So we knocked you out. Spiked your tequila with ketamine. Just enough to get you to lie still for a while. We had to tell Chey, to check you didn't have a heart condition or anything . . . I didn't want to be responsible for actually killing you.'

'Can you move?' Lauralynn interrupted. 'As educational as this is, we need to get you two out of Dublin.'

She passed me a rucksack and with a great effort of concentration I was able to pull on the pair of cheap, stone-washed jeans and the oversized Metallica T-shirt inside it. A pair of Converse trainers, a baseball cap and a puffer jacket finished the look. I tucked my hair under a cap and down the back of my T-shirt and wrapped a heavy green scarf around my neck, the sort that tourists buy in tacky souvenir shops.

'You've never been more beautiful,' Viggo said, glancing at me quickly as he crawled across to check on Chey.

He looked like a matchstick draped in a tent, in his paramedic's costume that was loose cut and about three sizes to big for him.

'Those baggy trousers suit you,' I replied. 'You should try wearing them on stage. The women will go wild.'

He snorted.

'Shut it, or next time you get yourself in a fix I'll let the Russians kill you.'

'Shit,' I said, as it all rushed back. 'Where are the Russians? Are we safe here?'

'Sure,' Viggo replied, his lopsided smile growing wider by the minute. 'We created a little diversion and they forgot about you and your man here quicker than you can say Picasso.'

'He never learns, this one.' Lauralynn sighed. 'He's got some of his boys out raiding the oligarch's mansion. Millions of pounds' worth of stuff in there, apparently.'

'You know me better than that. It's not the money, honey, it's the art. And all of it wasted on a thug like that anyway. I'm not stealing, I'm liberating. Taking it to a better place.'

'You have very loose morals, my dear. No wonder I love you so much.' Lauralynn leaned forward and kissed him on the lips.

Chey began to stir.

'Luba?' he whispered. His lips were barely moving, as if he had been cast in marble and was slowly coming to life.

'I'm here.' I moved towards him, taking his hand and holding it to my face.

'This is very sweet,' Lauralynn announced, 'but we really need to get you two out of here.'

She unscrewed the cap from the bottle of water that she was holding and threw it over Chey's face.

'Fuck!' he gasped like a fish stuck out of water and sucking for air.

'Sorry about that.' Lauralynn threw him another rucksack. 'You'll have to get dressed while we're moving.'

She climbed over into the driver's seat and started the engine.

'Stay down,' she hissed behind her as I lifted my head to peer out of the windows. Instead of drifting quietly down side streets, Lauralynn threw on the siren and raced through the centre of town.

'We're less obvious this way,' Viggo said, noticing the look of fright that spread across my face. 'An ambulance crawling slowly through dark streets is memorable. One racing through a busy city on New Year's Eve when Dublin is full of sirens is not even worth a second glance.'

New Year's Eve. I wasn't even sure if we'd missed the countdown.

I stared at Chey, drinking in every last molecule of him in

case we should ever be parted again. He was struggling with his buttons, his co-ordination still suffering from the effects of the drug. Viggo had packed him a pair of jeans, a loose cotton shirt and a ribbed wool jumper with a casual jacket to go overtop, a woollen hat and scarf. We looked entirely unremarkable, like any two poor backpackers visiting Dublin to ring in the New Year.

'Where are Summer and Dominik?' I asked, as the night's activities slowly pieced together in my mind.

'Both safe, and on their way home,' he replied. 'We messed up all the CCTV cameras too so none of it's been caught on film. They'll find a tape to match our adventures but it's all faked. And this isn't a real ambulance. Just a panel van with a perfect paint job.' Viggo slapped his thigh in self-congratulation and chortled. He'd pulled the whole gig off with aplomb and had obviously enjoyed himself.

'Dominik sure made a hot doctor,' Lauralynn called from the front seat. 'He has a career on *House* waiting for him if the writing doesn't work out. And at least we've given him plenty to write about.'

'Not that anyone would ever believe it,' I replied, staring wondrously at Chey and thinking of the bizarre history that we had shared together. 'Truth is so much stranger than fiction.'

The clock at the front of the van read 01:55 as we pulled into the station. The next train was fifteen minutes later.

'Well, lovebirds, this is it,' Viggo announced. 'Don't stay in touch. Looks like we're in the clear for now but you'll need to lay low for a while.'

'Viggo . . .' I reached out and squeezed his hand to thank him. The words that I was trying to express were lodged in my throat and all I could manage was a weak smile.

'And this is for you.'

He passed me an envelope brimming with banknotes, together with the brown jiffy envelope that Summer had trusted to him with our fee for the evening and, most importantly, the false papers that we had picked up earlier.

'I can't accept this,' I said to him, pointing at the additional cash. 'You've done too much already.'

'Nonsense,' he said, 'call it a bonus. Your commission on my newly acquired pieces of artwork. As far as I'm concerned, your little episode was the perfect diversion for the art heist of the century. You should look at some of the stuff we snaffled. It's going straight to the vault. And there's not a thing your Russian friends can do about it because they stole it all in the first place.'

'Viggo, don't be foolish. They'll come for you,' I pleaded. 'These men do not take lightly to humiliation.'

'They might do if they had the faintest idea that I was involved. But as far as anyone knows, I'm playing another last-minute live charity gig at an underground bar in Brighton. Look,' he said, showing me his mobile phone with a web link to a live camera. 'I gave a Viggo impersonator the gig of a lifetime, and a massive payout, of course. Ain't he doing a grand job?'

On the tiny screen, a reed-like man with a mop of teased-out hair and long legs encased in Viggo's trademark skinny jeans was gyrating and miming his heart out as the audience screamed the house down, entirely unaware that their hero was not even in the country, let alone in the building.

'I might employ him more often,' he added. 'Just imagine; I'd never need to work again.'

'Three, two, one!' screamed a group of drunken lads who

were trying and failing to navigate from one side of the street to another without tumbling over.

The clock struck one, another year had now begun.

Chey pulled me into a tight embrace and locked his mouth to mine. I could have happily spent the next three hundred and sixty-five days engaged in that kiss.

'Get a room!' Lauralynn yelled, checking that we had all of our belongings packed up and our disguises were in order. 'And get out. You have a train to catch.'

We waved the pair of them away for the last time and stood together on the platform, hand in hand.

The lights on the board advertising the next train promised that we would be waiting for five more minutes.

Silence surrounded us like a fog, and I could not think of a single word that felt important enough to break it.

'After a night like that,' Chey said, eventually, 'I can't help but wonder what will happen next.'

'Whatever comes,' I replied, 'it's no matter to me. So long as I have you.'

He bent his head to mine, and kissed me again.

Epilogue

One Last Dance

The heavy vault door swung shut behind Viggo with a slow hiss.

He smiled in satisfaction, thinking of the prizes that he had added to his collection and imagining the expressions on the faces of the Russian nouveaux riches when they realised that their precious investments had been lifted from under their noses. If the thick necks and dim-witted responses of their security team were anything to go by then they might not even notice at all. As soon as Luba had told him which Russian oligarch they would be performing for, who also had a residence in Dublin, he'd realised it happened to be a well-known fellow collector who'd all too often gazumped him when certain sought-after pieces of stolen art came to market. The opportunity had been an invaluable one and he had seized it.

No doubt about it, the mission had proven a success in every respect. It was a damn shame really that he would never be able to reveal to anyone the precise details of his accomplishment. Of course, the others knew snatches of what he had arranged. They had to be informed so they could play their parts. But he hadn't revealed the entirety of his scheme to a single soul, so that it could never be used against him, or any of his friends. Viggo sighed. The secrecy was necessary but also a source of regret. His life would make a wonderful film, he thought, if only he could tell anyone about it.

He imagined himself playing the lead role to a crowd of appreciative onlookers as he made his way up the wood-panelled staircase to the upstairs bedroom where Lauralynn awaited.

'You've been a very naughty boy, haven't you?' she said as he entered the room.

'Yes, Mistress,' he replied, dropping to his knees and prostrating himself at her stilettoed feet.

'And what happens to naughty boys?' she asked.

'They are punished, Mistress.'

She had spent the past hour closeted in the bathroom, dolling herself up for evening. He had only managed to catch a glimpse of her form before he fell to the floor and now, with his eyes locked onto her shoes, he would have no further opportunity to admire her until she allowed him to. It had been long enough, however, for him to memorise the precise way that her latex catsuit clung to each curve, the particular cut of the long blonde hair that framed her face like a curtain, the rich red of her lips and the regal twist of her smile.

Viggo loved these moments. He'd never been a religious man, but he'd spent his life worshipping beauty in its every manifestation, and here it was embodied in front of him in the form of Lauralynn. And better still, for the next hour or day or lifetime or however long it was that she allowed him to, he could bow down in awe and adulation and receive benediction from a goddess.

Why anyone would choose to visit a priest when women like Lauralynn existed in the world, he truly had no idea.

'Get up.'

Her voice was cold and uncaring.

Viggo scrambled to his feet.

'Don't look at me.'

He kept his eyes lowered, watching the point of her boots as she paced up and down the room.

This was his favourite part. Wondering what she would do next. What new perversities she had dreamed up. Viggo had always had a vivid imagination and a theatrical bent from the time he had been a child, but even his flights of fancy and inventiveness were nothing compared with Lauralynn's. She was a creative genius when it came to matters of sexuality, he thought proudly.

Sometimes she had him dress up in the most profoundly ridiculous costumes. In memory of Luba she had him don a leotard and a tutu and pirouette around the house like a ballerina. *My private dancer*, she had called him. On another occasion she had saddled him up like a pony and he had carried her from room to room. Once she'd had a friend over for dinner and he had spent the evening on all fours with their plates resting on his back as if he were a makeshift dining-room table while they giggled and gossiped as if he didn't exist. For a week she had clipped an electro-bracelet around his balls and zapped him with a low-voltage shock via a remote control each time she had fancied watching him jump. He'd taken her out to dinner at Nobu and they'd both smiled when a paparazzi had taken their picture and an article had appeared in a tabloid magazine the following day advertising the ladykiller's latest squeeze but without any mention of the anal plug that she had forced him to wear almost all evening long.

No one was aware of what Lauralynn and Viggo's relationship truly entailed. Chey and Luba had been in the

guest bedroom sleeping soundly or fucking loudly and blissfully ignorant of the fact that Viggo was bent over a stool in
the bathroom while Lauralynn walloped the hell out of him
with the palm of her hand and called him names and made
him her sex toy, and he loved every minute of it.

Dagur, the Holy Criminals drummer, had raised a curious eyebrow when he'd come over for a jam session once
and nearly sat down on the leather riding crop that Lauralynn had left out in the living room by mistake, but he
hadn't said a word about it.

He'd taken great delight in wearing a latex G-string
beneath his jeans one day to a meeting with a group of
record company executives and spent the hour grinning to
himself as he imagined what the staid old fools would think
of him if they only knew what secrets lay beneath his bad
boy exterior.

As far as Viggo was concerned, the menu of perverse
delights that Lauralynn had served up when she came into
his life were just another part of rock 'n' roll.

He waited patiently to discover what manner of delicious
cruelty she had in store for him today.

Finally the tap-tap of her heels striding back and forth on
his shining wooden floors came to a halt in front of him.

She reached out her arm and lifted his chin so that his
gaze met hers.

'Kiss me,' she said.

'Yes, Mistress,' Viggo replied, grinning from ear to ear.

The small boat we boarded in Galway was just the initial
stage of our journey south. It took us as far as the French
coast where we transferred to a larger vessel that was headed
to Australia by way of Singapore. We didn't even set foot

on French soil and were then carried in a small fishing craft to the main vessel just a few miles offshore, with the Brittany coastline a straight line through the mass of grey clouds floating across the waves.

By the time the ship reached Singapore, it felt like an eternity had already come and gone. Isolated from the rest of the world, with just the vast expanse of the sea and its blurred ever-receding horizon as constant companions, we both began to feel safe for the first time in ages. It wasn't a journey for which tickets could be acquired and our presence on the vessel was semi-illegal so, to avoid advertising our presence on-board to the majority of the unknowing crew, we had to remain in our narrow, claustrophobic cabin during daylight. In the evenings we made our way to the captain's cabin where we dined with him and two of his subalterns.

The captain was a gruff Dutchman whose pink skin had been scoured by the elements. He was a man of few words. The two officers who joined us were both Asian and didn't appear to speak much English. But the food we were served was hot and nourishing, thick frugal soups and cuts of cold meat and, of course, fish in all sizes and shapes. I'd always preferred white fish, the taste of which paradoxically wasn't 'fishy'. Herring, sardines and mackerel were definitely out. The captain enjoyed his 'fishy' tasting fish, however, so I often had to resort to dipping large chunks of bread into my soup to give it more consistency and appease an appetite that the sea air had done little to moderate.

At night, when few of the crew ventured on deck, we would often spend a few hours gazing at the moon, the gazillions of stars now revealed to us in all their glory and the immensity of the sea, swaddled in whatever warm clothing we could find in our sparse luggage. The utter silence of the night was awesome as it enveloped us in its heavy cloak, with the chuff-chuff of the boat's engines just a background punctuation. It was like being on another planet, a world of water, a world where only we belonged.

Shortly after he had picked us up, the captain had suggested I continue to keep my long blonde hair concealed inside my baseball cap so as not to inadvertently provoke members of the crew who were unaccustomed to having a woman on board. I'd tried to do so, but my unruly locks would keep spilling out so Chey suggested we cut it.

My initial reaction was one of horror.

As a child, it had taken forever for me to grow my hair, and when I'd finally managed to get it long enough it had been an occasion for pride and triumph. After my parents' death, when I was taken in by my aunt, one of her first diktats was to have my hair cut considerably shorter to make my upkeep easier. I had protested in vain, but had no choice in the matter. I was in mourning for months. Since leaving my aunt's house, I had always worn it long, even if the teachers at the ballet school complained of the time and effort it took to keep it under control when the corps de ballet all had to appear with matching chignons.

But the captain and Chey were right. We were carving ourselves new identities, and our future safety might depend on this.

And so, one night in the cabin, Chey tenderly cut my hair until I looked like a page boy. It was disconcerting and I felt terribly self-conscious every time I looked at myself in the mirror, but then I began to like it. Without the untamed tangle of pale locks, my features seemed more pronounced, my cheekbones sharper, my eyes wider. A more 'gamine' version of the woman I had always been.

'What do you think?' I asked Chey once he had completed the task.

'You look beautiful,' he said. 'And, after all, it's still you, isn't it? Just another side of you. You'll get used to it and, when we get to our destination and settle down somewhere, you can always grow it out again, can't you?'

'I suppose so . . .' I replied, gazing at the new Luba in the small, stained mirror above the cabin's sink.

The following evening, as I was undressing with my back to Chey and about to slip into the old tracksuit I wore to bed on the ship, I realised that the regular sound of Chey brushing his teeth behind me had ceased. I turned round.

He was sitting on the edge of the bed just looking at me, pensive, dreamy.

'What is it?' I asked him. He was still holding his toothbrush in one hand, but had wiped his mouth with a towel now held in the other.

'With that short hair you now have, your silhouette, naked from the back I was thinking you looked a little like a boy,' he said.

'Do you?'

'Hmm . . .'

I had a ballet dancer's shape. Long but strong legs, narrow hips and a round perfect circle arse and wide shoulders, a body trained and moulded by years of training and practice.

'You like it?'

'Absolutely.'

'I didn't know you were into boys . . .'

'I could gladly make an exception.'

'You wonderful pervert.'

I shook my backside in a parody of all the bad strippers I had come across in my previous journeys.

'Oh yes, I could most certainly fuck that,' Chey remarked.

His arm shot forward and the flat of his hand firmly slapped against my arse. He had meant it to be playful, but the cabin was so small that his proximity and the impact proved stronger than he'd wished and it stung.

I winced.

'Ouch . . .'

Chey smiled. 'That's what happens to bad boys when they misbehave. They get spanked.'

I turned up my nose in a pretend sulk.

'Oh, come here. Let me kiss it better.'

I was barely a step away and backed up to him. My buttock, probably now with the faint red imprint of his hand well in evidence across my natural pallor, on a level with his lips.

'Yes, kiss me. Better.'

His lips were like a balm, soft as velvet and full of warmth.

He kissed my arse cheek with total reverence, like a penitent kneeling for forgiveness or confession. We were frozen in time, like statues, despite the lack of heating in the cabin, me naked and Chey just wearing a grey T-shirt.

After an eternity, his lips detached themselves from my skin and his hands gripped both of my cheeks and spread me open. Next, his tongue was inside me.

Licking.

Exploring.

Digging.

Lubricating me.

Teasing me.

The moment the tip of his tongue breached my rosebud, the buzz inside me rose to another level and I was electrified. Wanting him wildly.

My sense of arousal was racing through my veins and travelling across my body at the speed of light or even faster, tiptoeing its way onto the wet tip of his intrusive tongue until he could feel its tremor of excitement.

On and on Chey went, playing with my lust until I felt like screaming for him to just take hold of me, however roughly he had to, and unreservedly do to me what he wanted. What I wanted.

Every nerve ending in my body now seemed to have assembled at the apex of my arsehole and I felt as though my legs might give way if he didn't fuck me now.

'Inside me, please,' I begged.

'Like a boy?'

'Like a boy,' I sighed, abdicating the notion that I had any control over my senses any longer.

Chey rose and entered me, bending me over the bed as he did so.

The initial discomfort rapidly vanished and he fitted into me as he always did. Chey was my dam, my lock. I pressed against him and relaxed, letting him carry me away on the totality of his ardour.

It was another sort of dance altogether.

Now that I was also his sailor.

A boat horn sounded in the distance on the high seas. In another two or three days, the captain had informed us over dinner that evening, we would be reaching port and the end of our long journey.

*

Summer tucked her precious Bailly gently back into its case.

Oh what stories the instrument could tell, if it had a voice, she thought. In a way the violin did have a voice, if only through melody.

She often thought of Luba and Chey and that night in Dublin when she had helped them to run away together. A tear came to her eye when she remembered the moment that she had noticed Luba's heart rising imperceptibly in her chest and realised that the whole thing had been a terribly clever trick. They'd played their parts so well that for a brief, awful moment she had thought that Chey had actually killed Luba and then turned the gun on himself.

Summer had never been much of a romantic, and she felt reassured by her delight in the handsome couple's happiness. She'd even agreed to take dancing lessons, to Dominik's surprise. His gladness amused her. She would have jumped at any opportunity to have him lead her, and if that was in a waltz at the local community hall rather than on the end of a leash at a fetish club, well, each was as good as the other in its own way as far as she was concerned.

The familiar sound of furious tapping reached her ears as she eased open the study door. She watched in silence for a few moments, gauging the mood of her lover as he thumped the keyboard, caught in the white heat of creative fever.

He'd been like this since they'd returned from Dublin, desperately transmitting all the thoughts, emotions and images that he had absorbed onto the virtual page. He seemed to be living in fear that if he didn't type quickly enough all the best stuff would vanish back into whatever wormhole it had popped out of in the first place and he would be left with nothing but a vague feeling that he'd nearly caught a good idea by the heels.

It was a lonely existence, playing the muse – long stretches of waiting for the other to emerge from a cocoon-like state of daydream and return to the land of the living. Harder still was dealing with the seemingly insurmountable stretches of writer's block, when Dominik forgot all of the good chapters that had gone before and stared dismally out of the window, complaining that each new word was like wringing blood out of a stone.

She had been just as bad, she knew – probably worse – a few months ago when she'd been working non-stop on her New Zealand-inspired album, spending night after night in the studio and moaning that getting each note exactly right was agony and so much harder than she had expected because of all the memories of home that had come flooding back and drowned her bow instead of energising it.

But these long islands of time where they inhabited their own worlds entirely gave them each a chance to be solitary, and that made the coming together again even better.

Hours later, night had fallen across the Heath and Summer had returned from her evening jog and was standing under the shower head and luxuriating in the hot running water that pooled over her body and soothed her aching limbs. She didn't hear Dominik leap up the stairs two at a time and pull open the bathroom door. She remained lost in the fabric of a waking dream until he slid naked into the shower cubicle with her and dropped to his knees, burying his face in the refuge between her legs.

Taken by surprise, Summer moaned, and tangled her hands in his thick hair, holding his head in place, enjoying the rising sensation that was slowly saturating her, and the building excitement burning through her sex with each forceful lick.

She had once worried that he might drown like this, and she would be responsible, but she consoled herself with the memory of the time she'd confessed her fear to Dominik and he had laughed and told her he could think of no better way to die.

He rose to his feet when he could no longer stand the ache in his knees and the water running into his eyes, and spun her around so he could rest the hardness of his erection against the cleft of her arse. Dominik took a moment to watch it sitting there, marvelling at the vision of her firm cheeks and the jut of her backbone and the inward curve of her waist and the way that she so easily relaxed and allowed him to move her about as he wished to with no thought to comfort or practicality. He leaned forward and turned the water off, cupping her wet breasts in his hand and squeezing her nipples before leading her into the bedroom.

Still damp, she knelt on the bed on all fours and stretched lazily, bending her spine like a cat and pushing her buttocks towards her heels and into the air, presenting herself to him. Dominik pushed her legs apart gently and observed the expectant pinkness of her vagina as her labia unfurled like the petals of a flower blooming.

It was the singular beauty of these images that made the pornographer's heart inside him skip a beat. Dominik had never been the sort of man who read lads' mags or watched X-rated film clips in all their predictably airbrushed tedium. He far preferred the purity of real life and the way that Summer so openly and intimately displayed herself to him.

He stretched out his hand and ran his fingers against her

slit, testing her wetness. She sighed with all the pleasure of familiarity and pressed herself against his palm.

Dominik leaned forward to whisper in her ear.

'Kiss me,' he said, tilting her face with his free hand and pressing his mouth to hers.

The first thing that I noticed when we landed in Darwin was the heat. We'd arrived in the middle of the wet season, having first made port in Sydney and then travelled the remainder of our journey to Australia's Northern Territory by plane.

I had expected a sky as bright and blue as a computer screen and empty of so much as a single cloud, with red mountains lining the horizon like the postcard pictures that dotted the racks of newsagents through the airport. Instead, when the terminal doors opened, we were trapped between a plain as flat as any I had ever seen and the heavens as grey as an elephant's skin and seeming to drop lower and lower to the earth with us squeezed in the middle like a sandwich.

The air felt heavy and cloying, pregnant, as if the atmosphere might burst and suffocate us or tighten around my neck at any moment and leave me strangled. We were here now though, and I made up my mind to make the best of it. Chey had selected Darwin after careful research, feeling that the Russians, should they not have swallowed the saga of our deaths hook, line and sinker, would expect us to choose a major city with a large population that we could lose ourselves in, and probably somewhere in the US or Europe. In the top end of Australia we would stand out like sore thumbs and therefore no one would bother to look for us here.

It was a quiet time of year as many of the city's

inhabitants had left for more moderate climes and the tourists would not begin to arrive in their droves until the dry season began in April or May, so we were able to take our pick of the empty apartments available using our cash as a deposit.

Chey still had money left, and I had built up a fair sum during my dancing years. Having always been in fear of the law and also eager to evade the taxman, I had ensured that the Network always paid me in cash directly after each event. I'd been keeping my profits the old-fashioned way, sealed in envelopes under the mattress in Viggo's guest bedroom, and in combination with Viggo's gift we had enough money to keep us going for a few years.

We rented a small apartment in Nightcliff. It wasn't much. We didn't want to attract attention to ourselves, and in any case I'd grown weary of the trappings of wealth. Thinking of the sumptuous hotel rooms and the beautiful gowns that had been part and parcel of my employ with the Network left me feeling a little ill. So I was happy beyond measure with our little flat with its tiny veranda that overlooked the ocean, a view that would have cost a million in California, but was taken for granted by Darwinians. Like them, I grew used to seeing the sea from nearly every direction, to the noisy air-conditioning unit and thick protective screens on all the doors that kept out not just the flies but all manner of brightly coloured lizards with ruffs on their necks that puffed out like Dracula's collar when they were angry or frightened.

At ten past four each day for weeks the heavens opened, dousing the city in a flood of rain. Big, heavy droplets, the sort that soaked you to the bone in two seconds flat if you got caught in it and left behind a feeling of relief, cleanliness and the sweet smell of the eucalyptus trees, a little like the scent of damp fresh wood shavings. I began to love Darwin, even in the wet season. It was so different from anywhere that I had lived before and with all its weird animals and crazy weather conditions it had a vibe about it that was so vital, so alive.

We spent the rest of February and most of March making love indoors with the air con blasting at full pelt, only venturing out to walk along the beachfront after the sun sank casting a stream of pink, orange and violet ribbons into the sky in its wake. Chey laughed at the care I took to remain a few paces back from the waves that slapped lightly at the shore, always convinced that salt-water crocs were lurking beneath, ready and waiting to snap me up and swallow me whole at the slightest provocation. I might have been paranoid, but my fear was not unfounded. The local paper was full of stories about the latest croc sightings and tourists getting themselves into trouble.

After a few weeks of leisure time we began to get bored, and Chey rented a small shop in the Smith Street Mall where he sold precious stones and jewellery to the tourists. It was too dangerous yet for him to make enquiries about the import of amber, but we covered costs and made a small profit selling South Sea pearls and Australian opals.

Chey, who had always been a natural salesman and had cut his teeth in similar circumstances when he was still a teenager, manned the shop most days and I helped out by managing the stock and accounts, and when I decided that I needed more variety I took a jewellery-making course and began to work on minor repairs and stringing a few necklaces and earrings together. The work was precise and detailed and it appealed to my natural sense of order and minimalist aesthetic. I made sure that nothing with even an iota of tackiness was allowed through the doors and before long we had developed a reputation for taste and quality that set us above the neighbouring stores that flogged joke tea towels, fridge magnets and novelty soaps along with their silver and gold.

I bought a bicycle and for a few days cycled the half-hour journey from Nightcliff to Smith Street, but after having the wits scared out of me when a lightning storm descended without warning, I asked Chey to teach me to drive and we purchased a second-hand Mazda, painted as bright blue as the sky in the dry season and I subjected the city to my frequent stalling and engine revving before I finally got the hang of it.

In May, when the rain disappeared, the clouds cleared and the touch of the breeze on my skin was like the lightest velvet, we set up a stall at the Mindil market two nights a week. I wore brightly coloured flowing cotton dresses and sandals and chatted to the endless variety of folk who stopped to watch me carefully beading a necklace or quickly piecing a pair of earrings together to match a customer's request.

Darwin was a strange place, full of people who were running from something or had never quite managed to leave. There was a quotient of military people who inhabited the local army barracks, a bevvy of scientists and doctors who were attracted by the ever-changing meteorological conditions and the tropical diseases, a stream of Irish and English backpackers who landed by the busload, staffed the local bars and partied until October and left when the rain came, and then the hippies who stayed all year round attracted by the hot weather and the slow pace of life and the sweetness of the mangoes that I consumed in such great quantities I was left with a rash on my hands from the sap.

Amongst this hotchpotch of life Chey and I fitted in as easily as two peas into a pod. For the first time in my life I made friends, and felt as though I had a purpose besides dancing.

A year passed and wc did not hear so much as a peep from anyone from our chequered past. I still danced, but only in the living room, or on the porch in the cool of the evening, like a pagan welcoming in the night under the glow of the enormous tropical sun.

There was still an evening left until the New Year and Edward and Clarissa were sitting at a table at the beach cafe, sipping cocktails and enjoying the relaxed atmosphere at the boat club. They had no particular plans for the evening. Their world cruise had been ongoing for three months and the following week they were returning to the US.

As they reminisced about the good times and the bad times, they agreed they had led a full life already, and whatever happened to them next would just be a bonus, more butter on the bread.

There had been wild parties, epiphanies and a joyous breaking of taboos, once they had gracefully grown into middle-age and had begun to ignore the opinion or judgement of family and conservative-leaning offspring, and they had lived for themselves and no longer had to adhere to the conventional strictures of society.

This had meant a prolonged involvement in the world of BDSM and they had witnessed its dark side and its dyonisiac aspects, and had wholeheartedly enjoyed both.

How could one truly appreciate life if you hadn't tasted its extremes? They had no regrets.

They had reached the plateau in a couple's relationship where silences had become as important and significant as words and they wallowed in the peace of their happiness. The waitress brought them another round of brightly coloured cocktails.

The terrace with its ring of palm trees and thick white sun umbrellas looked over the vivid blue of the ocean, almost deserted but for a handful of windsurfers riding the modest waves.

'It's really peaceful, isn't it?' Edward remarked.

'That it is,' Clarissa agreed.

'I was thinking,' Edward continued, 'rather than seek out a fancier restaurant back in town to spend the festivities, why don't we just stay here? There's a lot of seafood on the menu, I see, and it won't be as crowded . . .'

'Such a pleasure to be so casual,' Clarissa added.

'We've certainly dressed up enough for a few lifetimes, haven't we?'

She nodded, her eyes clouding over as so many parties and past ceremonies came rising up from her memories.

'Let's do it, then.'

They went back to sipping their drinks with not a care in the world.

When the sun began to disappear below the marine horizon and the light slowly faded, Edward perused the menu.

'What do you think? Coffin Bay oysters to start with?' he suggested.

'I'd love that,' Clarissa replied dreamily.

'Nothing but the best for you, my dear.'

He took hold of the wine list. The young waitress from earlier had finished her shift and had been replaced on the terrace by an older waiter with a Greek accent and a mellifluous manner.

Edward made his choice and ordered.

Life was good.

Their coffees had just been brought to their table and the empty plates from the meal whisked away, when the beach restaurant's sound system was switched on and strains of soothing music began to lullaby the customers spread across the two dozen or so tables.

'It's a waltz, Ed,' Clarissa said. 'Maybe we should dance.' She pointed at the improvised dance floor made of bamboo matting that extended all the way into the sand.

'Maybe later, when it's actually New Year?' Edward said. 'Let me digest a bit before that. A concession to our advancing years?'

Clarissa smiled, noticing a couple rising from a nearby table and making their way to the dance floor. They were younger, holding hands all the way. Both tall and athletic and casually dressed, she in a simple and modest white cotton dress that fell to just below her knees and flat ballet shoes while her partner wore denim jeans and a white shirt. The woman was blonde, her hair cut short, and there was definitely something Eastern European about her face, Clarissa reckoned. She walked, and then danced with grace and composure. Her partner was also quite distinctive in his looks, although she was unable to pinpoint his background. Both displayed wonderful golden tans, as if they now spent their whole days lazing on the beach. The young woman's nails were painted emerald green and the only jewellery she wore was a pair of elaborate amber earrings.

They came together on the improvised dance floor, their eyes never leaving each other, and both Clarissa and Edward felt a gentle thrill buzzing through their hearts as they watched the young couple glide across the floor like birds in flight. Both had the same thought and winked at each other. The two dancers reminded them of their own youth.

It was a pleasure to just watch them and note how oblivious they were to their surroundings, each bathing wholeheartedly in the other's glow.

There was an elegance about the young woman's movements, surely the result of ballet training at some stage in her past. Her long legs solidly carried her gentle frame along as her partner's hands held imperceptibly to her waist, guiding her movements along, leading invisibly but firmly.

Clarissa realised she had seen the young woman once before, although her hair had been much longer then. She gazed at her again and it confirmed her intuition. It had been in Paris when their son had played in the brass section for the group that Viggo Franck was sponsoring. Yes, she had been in the post-gig dressing room. It was definitely her. She racked her brains to remember whether the young woman was one of those present who had then followed them to the riotous and somewhat debauched evening that had ensued at Les Chandelles. Clarissa concluded that if she had there had not been any interaction between her or either Ed and Clarissa. And recalled, with a sigh of relief, how their conservative son had also declined to join the throng. The man she was dancing with had certainly not been present on that faraway evening.

'Are you thinking the same thing as I am?' Edward whispered to her as the young couple untangled as the slow Tennessee waltz faded to an end and was replaced on the sound system by a jollier, faster melody.

'I am,' Clarissa said.

'It feels like a world ago, doesn't it?' Edward told her.

Clarissa nodded.

'For a brief moment, I had the idea we could invite them over to join us for a drink.'

'You're right, Ed. Let's just leave them alone. We're just old rakes; we've done our part a hundred times over. Surely they can find their own path in life without our interference.'

Midnight was approaching. Other couples were now treading the dance floor.

'The next slow dance is yours,' Edward informed Clarissa. 'Even if we have to wait for the New Year.'

'Do you think there'll be fireworks?' she asked him.

'There are always fireworks at the stroke of midnight,' Edward said, settling his arm around her.

At the other table, the young couple had returned to their seats and were kissing.

Just a stone's throw away, sitting on a high stool at the bar, another young woman sat. She was small, with jet-black hair cut in gothic style with a razor-sharp fringe line. She was alone and had been so all evening, one step removed from all the celebrations. She watched with such sadness in her eyes, Clarissa thought, as Luba and Chey kissed. And for a minute, Clarissa thought she was crying, but then realised that below her left eye, she had a minuscule teardrop tattoo.

The lonely girl with the unusual tattoo was watching as the kissing couple rose again, hand in hand, oblivious to everyone but each other, and made their way to the sand for one last dance.

Acknowledgements

As the Eighty Days series continues, the authors have had to call on the patience and generosity of many people whose involvement was invaluable. First and foremost, our respective partners who – although they cannot be named here as we seek to retain our mysterious anonymity – have had to keep on enduring our neglect during the long writing hours and have done so with equanimity and good humour. Sarah Such at Sarah Such Literary Agency, our editors Jon Wood and Jemima Forrester, Rosemarie Buckman at the Buckman Agency, and all their colleagues have been instrumental in the success of the series and cannot be thanked enough.

One half of Vina would also like to thank Scarlett French of www.scarlettfrencherotica.com whose leather-bound books and reading of *Shoe Shine at Liverpool Street Station* sparked an interest in both erotica and riding boots that is likely to last a lifetime. Finally, she would like to thank her employer for her unending support, and Verde & Co. who have unwittingly fuelled a number of the adventures contained within the Eighty Days series with the provision of a cosy spot to sit and type, the occasional chocolate, and an endless procession of the best flat whites in London.

And finally Vina Jackson must also acknowledge the hospitality of the Groucho Club where every title was planned, conceived, broken down and reassembled prior to the actual writing – without any neighbouring members even batting an eyelid as, for hours on end, we debated who should bed who and other delicate technicalities.

Want to know more about Vina Jackson and Eighty Days?

Connect with Vina on Facebook/Vina Jackson, or follow her on Twitter @VinaJackson1.

If you enjoyed **Eighty Days Amber**
look out for . . .

Eighty Days White

the sexy new novel in Vina Jackson's pulse-racing
series.

Available January 2013

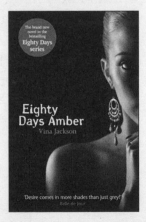